CRY
FOR
MERCY

CRY FOR MERCY

KAREN LONG

bookouture

Published by Bookouture in 2020

An imprint of Storyfire Ltd.
Carmelite House
50 Victoria Embankment
London EC4Y 0DZ

www.bookouture.com

ISBN: 978-1-80019-260-7
eBook ISBN: 978-1-80019-259-1

for Tom, Maddie, Isabel
and
MJ

CHAPTER ONE

Eleanor Raven had used the room before, but not with the same guy. That would have been a mistake, and she didn't make mistakes: there was too much at stake. The room smelled of damp carpets, and the beige flock wallpaper was peppered with an ominous green mould in the corners, which all added flavour to the upcoming event.

Eleanor sat on the bed, looked around nervously and ran through the procedures once more. Her bag and everything that could identify her were safely stowed in the bottom drawer of the dressing table. This room was way too cheap to have a safe, which would have been preferable, but she'd carried out her risk assessment and let that pass. She had placed shampoo, conditioner, hand sanitiser and antibacterial body wash in travel-sized containers on a glass shelf in the small bathroom. There was also an emergency first aid kit, mouthwash and antiseptic wipes wrapped in her own towel and secured in a plastic bag next to the shower unit. She was scrupulous when it came to cleansing after the event, and over the past few years this was beginning to take on almost ritualistic proportions.

Eleanor took out the ledger-sized sheet that contained the rules and, in block capitals, 'THE SAFE WORD'. She had thought long and hard about the 'word' before finally committing to something old-fashioned that possessed legal and authoritarian implications, which gave it gravity. It had two syllables, which meant that its rhythms would grab attention in a way that 'Stop' or 'No' did not. It was also easy to spit the syllables out if she was gagged in any way. It put her back in control, kept her safe. But most importantly, it could not be misinterpreted as a plea for more rather than less.

The rules were efficient, succinct and binding. If they were abused or transgressed on any level, there would be consequences. Only one individual had ever stepped outside what had been considered acceptable by Eleanor, and he was very unlikely to break any rules again. Whatever either party believed in the room, before or during the event, it did not reflect the real Eleanor Raven.

The man arrived on time, which was a promising start. He was around thirty-five to forty years old, a comfortable six foot with a trim figure. His teeth were artificially whitened and cleanly straightened, which indicated a professional background, probably degree-level education and a fairly lucrative career choice. He wore a labelled suit and his cufflinks, platinum yin-yang circles, implied a man who had come to terms with his desires and was looking for another to share these proclivities. All these signs were encouraging, and Eleanor began to relax slightly and allow the familiar sensations to creep over her as she watched the man read the rules. Occasionally he glanced down at her, as if he had a query or an amendment to make, but when he had finished, he slowly and carefully placed the paper onto the dressing table and loosened his tie. Eleanor watched him silently, feeling the pulsing between her legs and the ache in her chest as the man sat on the bed next to her.

*

He assessed the curious woman lying on the bed, her head propped up by a large, strong hand. Her nails were unpainted and her fine chestnut hair was inexpertly plaited and hung languidly over her shoulder and across a small breast. Her green-blue eyes surprised him. They should have been cowed, but the sharp intelligence that scrutinised him made him nervous. Maybe this would be different, more… pleasurable. She wasn't girlish or particularly pretty to him; rather she possessed a functional face, pale skin, high cheekbones and small, imperfect teeth. But the event was not about appearance, affection or lust. It was about power.

*

The rules stated that only Eleanor's own equipment could be used. The handcuffs were heavy and convincingly authentic. She had positioned them before his arrival so that her hands and feet would be spread away from her body, fastening her to the bed frame via four chains that slipped over the bed legs, thus making her vulnerable to him, but not so much that she couldn't twist both her toes and thumbs and unclip the safety catch that would free her. This wasn't an easy manoeuvre, but what would be the point of that?

With slow and steady movements the man grabbed her wrists and ankles and locked her into the handcuffs; she held her breath, waiting. The handcuffs had been specially treated on the inner rim with a translucent plastic coating that reduced friction and ensured that chafing was kept to a minimum. Not that Eleanor didn't enjoy chafing, but any area not generally covered with clothing, such as her face, throat and hands had to be protected from her colleagues' intuitive gaze.

Eleanor had not given permission for a blindfold yet. That was at her discretion, and so far she didn't have sufficient information to gauge the man's character. She needed to watch his eyes carefully to see if he showed signs of losing control, and only if she was satisfied would she give the sign that would permit the move to the next level. So far the man's slaps were restrained and showed a practised hand. She decided to wait.

*

The man was getting into his stride; he was an expert in the administration of illicit pleasure. What he wanted was the absolute and complete satisfaction that came when a woman or man was taken to the limits of their desires. He would supply that; he had a gift for dispensing pain that could cleanse the soul of an angel. In fact he had long since understood that what he did, what he was able to do for another human being, was a gift from God. Had not Christ himself suffered untold agonies on the cross, thus purifying himself and mankind for the past two millennia? His gift – his calling – was necessary, and he took comfort and pride in knowing that the woman wincing, gasping and writhing as he slapped and pinched her was being liberated from her pride and sins. He respected this woman for recognising her frailties and turning to him for redemption. He would not let her down.

Time is relative, particularly when endurance is involved, and neither the man nor Eleanor knew how much time had passed since they had met. Aware that he was slipping into a regular rhythm, the man began to vary the strokes and combine them with some moderate asphyxiation. He pinched her nostrils between his index finger and thumb and used the palm of his hand to clamp her jaw firmly closed.

He looked at her face, seeing the initial flush of excitement, then the fear in her eyes, and finally – acceptance. Not too much. It took time, and the woman wasn't clean yet. He saw her eyelids flicker and her chest buck as her carbon-dioxide levels rose and the tunnelling of her senses began. He'd planned to take her a little further than she was used to, make this special.

He moved his face closer to hers and stared into her eyes, watching her pupils begin to dilate and lose focus. It was too soon. He slapped her face, waiting for a cue to move him on. There, a quick saccade of her eyes and he slowly released his hand, listening sensitively as she chugged greedy lungfuls of air.

The man saw the change in her. Her skin was hot to the touch, and dry, as if she had a fever. Now time mattered – each second would need careful control.

He stepped back a pace and watched her. Slowly, he undid his leather belt and pulled it free, letting the final inch crack the air. He watched her mouth beginning to form the word 'No'. He'd expected that and lowered his index finger to her lips, lightly grazing them.

'Shh,' he whispered. 'You've been so brave, and now it's time to finish.'

*

The word 'finish' triggered a jolt of adrenaline, slowing time and crystallising her thoughts. She'd made a mistake – the man was going to 'finish' her and she wasn't sure if she had enough time to act.

Eleanor twisted her index fingers viciously and began to work on the safety catch just as the first blow landed cleanly across her thighs. At first she found it hard to separate the sound of the leather strap flying through the air from the sound of the pain. A flash of heat burned her thighs, momentarily paralysing her, then the second blow sliced a band of red across her belly and she knew what she had to do. Her lips had just spread across her teeth and she was about to articulate when the man said, 'No!' The strap cracked over her hips and then her breasts. She heard herself scream.

The man had impeccable timing. While she shook and sobbed, he gently unfastened her hands and feet and, putting on his jacket, tiptoed out of the room with the leather belt in his hand. The door closed softly behind him.

Eleanor looked around her and confirmed that the man was gone, then smiled inwardly and stretched herself on the rough sheets before moving quickly into the bathroom and turning on the shower. What she should have done – what she usually did – was to make sure that the door to the room was locked from the inside.

*

The man had taken several steps towards the emergency exit when he stopped and methodically threaded the belt back through his trouser loops. He felt good, really good, possibly more satisfied and holy than he had in years. The woman had been an excellent player. She had recognised the nuances and responded to his 'dialogue', as if they were both Oscar-winning actors. He smiled.

'Always leave 'em wanting more.'

He'd heard that on the radio years ago and adopted it as a sort of light-hearted motto. But he didn't want this to be a one-off performance. Of course he'd read the 'rules', but rules were there if not to be broken, at least to be infringed. So he turned round and took a tentative step back towards the door. He listened carefully, his ear pressed to the plywood and smiled with satisfaction as he heard the irregular splashing of an occupied shower. The bathroom door was angled away from this one and the dressing table, so he knew he could step inside without alerting her to his presence.

He quietly tried the handle. It was open, which was surely a sign that she was still interested in continuing their journey.

He stepped back inside, pulling the door behind him, and looked around slowly. The room was empty of clothing or personal belongings, but that wasn't unusual. He slid open the wardrobe door and three bare metal clothes hangers swung lazily on the bar, then he turned to the dressing table and carefully pulled open the drawers in descending order. The first contained her clothing: a navy-blue trouser suit, polo-necked sweater, knee-highs, plain full panties and sports bra. He was a little surprised by her choices: not a hint of frill or tease. She dressed considerably older than her years, and he wondered if she was an accountant or teacher.

The last drawer revealed a small, black leather handbag, with a large clasp, which told him that she was a cautious, private woman. He liked that. A woman's secrets were something to be savoured and appreciated, and he felt a thrill of excitement as he opened the bag and felt for her purse.

The sounds from the shower were different now, as if she was rinsing off and preparing to step out. He opened the purse, noted that she kept a sensible amount of cash on her and turned to the cards – he wanted her driving licence. He found it amongst the credit cards and held it up to his face. 'Ms Eleanor Raven'.

The shower was turned off, and the plastic shudder of the curtain accompanied the sound of her feet being placed onto the linoleum. He needed to leave – now. His lips moved silently and childishly as he memorised her address and continued to mouth the information as he swiftly replaced her licence and purse before closing the handbag. A quick scan of the room to check he'd left it as he'd found it and then he slipped back through the door, closing it softly behind him.

*

Eleanor wrapped herself tightly in her towel and ran a comb through her hair, checking in the mirror for any bruises or scratches above her throat. Satisfied, she cleaned her teeth, rinsed with mouthwash and then rubbed hand sanitiser over every inch of her body. Her eyes watered as she daubed the wheals with gel.

Eleanor made it a point to leave the room and building within ten minutes of stepping out of the shower, and she was well on target. She scraped her wet hair into a braid and checked twice that she had removed all evidence of her presence from the bath and bedroom. She collected several long hairs from the shower, wrapped them in toilet paper and flushed them away. Satisfied that she could not be traced to the room in any way, she grabbed her handbag and cautiously opened the door, looking up and down the corridor. The man was nowhere to be seen and Eleanor headed for the emergency-exit stairs with a confident walk.

Once outside the rear of the building, she threaded her way through overflowing trash cans and re-entered the hotel from the street, dropped the key on the desk and left, all of this taking no more than sixty seconds and arousing no one's suspicions.

Her car was several blocks away, in a discreet, private parking lot. As she walked, Eleanor turned on her phone and discovered fifteen missed calls from her boss and colleagues, and twelve unread texts. She flipped through the texts as she unlocked the car, looked around only to make sure that no one was watching and then slid into the driver's seat. As she started the engine she pressed 'call back' and listened as the ringing threaded through the Bluetooth connector and filled the car's interior with urgency and normality.

'Where the hell have you been, Raven?' bellowed Marty Samuelson's familiar tones. 'Why do I even bother calling? Perhaps I should wait till you choose to slope into the office at your convenience?'

'Sir, I'm responding now to your first message which arrived fifteen minutes ago. I'm not due to be on duty for another hour and a quarter,' Eleanor responded flatly. 'I am therefore early... sir.'

'There's only one thing a homicide detective can be, DS Raven, and that is too goddamn late.'

CHAPTER TWO

The Westex power station had finally been abandoned in '98. Its giant turbines had been decommissioned two years earlier, every ounce of valuable metal had been legitimately collected and the more toxic of the waste products disposed of in a moderately responsible manner. The less discerning and more adventurous harvesting had taken place during night hours over the following three years until two deaths due to falls and a roof cave-in stopped business. This left considerable scope for the city wildlife, which moved in with enthusiasm and soon had their own little ecosystem established complete with raccoon, peregrine, rat and pigeon populations. What the demolition team had failed to dismantle, the native flora had, smashing through concrete with delicate stems and twisting cables until the whole edifice resembled a low-rent conservation area. All it lacked were some picnic tables and a couple of kiosks selling ice cream.

Eleanor stared at the entrance to the building. A uniformed officer stood guard, and on seeing her, he lifted the police tape. She ignored the gesture and studied the door, which was solid steel and secured with a heavy-duty new chain and padlock, which were hanging loosely from the bolt. A CSI was dusting it for fingerprints.

'Was this open?'

'Mr Heston over there opened it when he did his rounds.' The officer pointed at an elderly-looking man dressed as a security guard. The uniform was at least a size too big for him, so either he was ill or standing in for someone.

Eleanor walked over to him. 'Did you open this door, sir?' she asked.

'I did,' he replied calmly.

'Did it show any signs of being tampered with?'

'Not that I could see. It was locked, and I'm pretty sure no one had opened it since I'd locked it last night.'

Eleanor raised an eyebrow.

'I always twist the chains in a particular way, so it's easier to lock. The chain is heavy and' – he held up his arthritic hands – 'I do 'em in a particular way. They was in their usual position,' he said emphatically.

'You called this in?'

He nodded.

'When did you find the body?'

''Bout an hour ago,' he said. 'And I ain't got no idea how they got in or why they chose here,' he snapped.

Eleanor nodded and turned towards the entrance. 'Why did you say "they"? You think there was more than one person involved?'

'I meant her what's dead in there and him what took her in there. That makes "they" in my opinion,' he snarled.

'Hmm,' replied Eleanor. 'Any other way they could have got into the building.'

The man paused, as if thinking about that. 'Only if they could fly.'

'Thank you, Mr Heston. I will need to talk to you further.'

She caught his sigh as she stepped carefully under the police tape, nodded curtly to the officer who held it aloft for her and made her way slowly to where the tungsten lights had been positioned.

Once inside, Eleanor didn't rush; the victim had all the time in the world and she needed to gather her first impressions. She studiously avoided looking at the illuminated creation hanging from the cross-beam and channelled her energies into interpreting the surrounding environment.

The first thing she noticed was the intense cold in the building. It seemed at least three degrees colder than the surrounding lakeshore area, which didn't make sense to her. Although some sections of the building were exposed to the elements, the integrity of the external walls mostly remained. It should, in her opinion, be warmer.

She moved around the periphery of the violence and took in an impression of the space. This section of the building must originally have housed the turbines. The roof, or what remained of it, was at least fifty metres high and the space was the length of a football field. The walls, damp and pocked, sprouted twists of rusted steel and a huge gaping wound where a section of walkway had been removed for scrap.

She gazed at the floor, which was littered with fresh raccoon shit, and looked for signs of previous human activity. Unusually there were none: no butt ends, no condoms, needles or rags. Why?

She caught a glimpse of two white-gowned and booted CSIs looking at her impatiently; she would give the sign when she was ready, and not before.

She inhaled deeply, trying to capture another scent, something other than fur, mould and the ominous tang of airborne carcinogens, but there was nothing. Usually she could detect, or believe she detected, the pheromones given off by fear. Semen gave off the fishy tang of cadaverine and putrescine, but there wasn't a hint of that here, and the metallic stink of blood wouldn't hit them until the plastic cocoon was opened.

Why here? She took in a 360° slow turn and tried to capture the sense of the place and what it could mean to the murderer. Then she knew – it was a cathedral. The high vaulted ceiling, echoing chambers and implications of power. This was where a sacred act had been performed.

Eleanor turned her gaze to the suspended body, wrapped protectively in a transparent plastic liner, and moved a little closer. She snatched two bootie covers from the outstretched hand of the CSI and slipped them over her shoes before she walked into the light, taking care not to step on any scuff marks. A raised voice from the darkness indicated that the pathologist had arrived, which allowed her a few more moments before the wheels of crime scene processing began to turn.

The woman's body was partially visible in the plastic liner, but a build-up of blood and moisture made some areas difficult to make out. From where she stood, Eleanor could see that the body was suspended by a single chain, its links about three inches in length, without a hint of rust on them. It would seem unlikely that the chain had been located in the building; rather it had been brought in for a purpose. However, the hook that had been inserted between the cervical vertebrae looked rusty, though it was difficult to get a good look as it was hidden by the woman's bleached hair, which clung wetly to it. If the hook had been inserted while she was alive, it was unlikely that she would have continued breathing for long.

The woman's face was resting lightly against the heavy plastic liner. Her eyes were open, both pupils fixed and dilated. It was difficult to make out her features as her make-up had been smeared into black smudges beneath her eyes, which were beginning to flatten and take on a milky hue. Her mouth was an unnatural red gash, looking more like a clown's than merely smudged lipstick.

As Eleanor took in the surroundings, Dr Mira Hounslow, the chief medical officer approached. A petite woman, immaculately dressed, her hair elaborately piled and pinned into a chignon, she spoke in a deceptively quiet and controlled manner, but Eleanor and the entire city detective force knew better.

'What can you see?' asked Hounslow.

'Planning – lots of planning,' Eleanor replied slowly. Both women stared at the body hanging several feet above the ground.

The pathologist waited patiently for her to elaborate.

'Look at the mouth. Her face is bloody, but the red around her mouth hasn't oxidized, so it's not blood. It's lipstick and it's been applied by the killer – repeatedly by the look of the build-up,' said Eleanor.

Hounslow looked and nodded carefully. 'Meaning?'

'That he brought a lipstick with him for that purpose,' said Eleanor.

'Or?'

'Or he had the time to go through her purse, find hers and utilise it. Time equals patience, and patience…'

'Equals planning,' finished Hounslow quietly and stared at Eleanor.

'If he's organised and plans, then he'll do it again,' said Eleanor darkly.

A commotion was taking place in the ring of darkness outside of the arena, but Eleanor didn't need to investigate – Marty Samuelson always brought a halo of chaos wherever he went. Samuelson had been Eleanor's boss since she'd graduated ten years ago. He had nurtured her progress through the ranks in a clumsy but caring sort of way. A family man and proud of it, he'd never managed to slough off his disgust at the deeds of men and his desire to make the city a safer, more sanitised place.

'What the hell!' Samuelson's voice trailed off as he gazed at the murder scene. 'Are you not still mystified by the actions of mankind, Dr Hounslow?' he asked, leaving his mouth slightly ajar to emphasise his outrage.

'Beyond shockable – you know that, Chief Inspector,' she replied calmly as she took a temperature reading. 'It's colder in here than out.'

'Are you ready, Raven?' asked Samuelson. Eleanor nodded to the CSIs hovering impatiently on the periphery and waited as they began to spread across the scene, each one having had several minutes to coordinate their approach to the collecting.

'I want her ID'd as soon as possible, understand? You can have Timms, Wadesky and Smith when he's finished in court.'

Eleanor nodded while catching the eye of the patrol officer.

'I want constant updates and a debrief by lights out.'

'Sir,' she responded.

'Call me when she's in Autopsy; I'm coming down for that,' he said to Dr Hounslow and, with a final shake of his head at the outrageous nature of the crime, made to leave. 'One last thing, Raven.'

Eleanor knew what was coming and felt heavy. 'Sir?'

'No more temping with Wadesky.'

Eleanor frowned.

'For Christ's sake, she's seven months pregnant. I want her behind a desk, not backing you up.'

'It's just till Mo comes back.' She heard the infantile pleading in her voice and felt ashamed.

'Don't give me that shit!' hissed her boss. 'You've had three weeks to make some suggestions as to who you're going to partner and you've not said a thing. Mo isn't coming back!'

This was met with silence from Eleanor. Detective Artie Morris, known to everyone, including his six children, as Mo, had been her partner for the past seven years. He was short, ridiculously fat and where Marty Samuelson could see only the corruption of the human spirit, Mo just saw weakness. He seemed to understand with saint-like patience that human beings were meant to fall and keep on falling, no matter how many times they were picked up, dusted off and sent on their way. Not that he was an indifferent man – he had once knocked a man's teeth clean out of his head for declaring that his twelve-year-old murdered and mutilated daughter 'had it coming'. This in itself was quite a feat as the man was twice his height and Mo hadn't swung an arm further than the doughnut counter in fifteen years.

Eleanor had made the mistake of believing that a man like Mo was somehow above and beyond the commonplace ailments that afflict the rest of humanity, and when he'd keeled over in the canteen with a massive heart attack, the only person who hadn't seen it coming was her. In fact, the most mysterious part of the whole business was how Mo had managed to survive his own death. He'd been clinically dead for at least forty-five minutes before his abused organs had rumbled back into action, and now, after a heart bypass and gastric band, he was just about capable of staggering from the front door to the porch without the aid of his wife. Eleanor hadn't really come to terms with the fact that Mo's days in the force were over, but Marty Samuelson was working on it.

'Detective Whitefoot will be joining you later on this morning.'

With that, he turned on his heels, gathered his cloud of commotion and disappeared into the darkness.

At the risk of making another peevish comment, Eleanor decided that silence said more. She cleared her mind of troubled thoughts and directed it at the crime scene once more. Dr Hounslow moved away to talk to her assistant, who was directing a minion to point his camera on some minute marks.

Eleanor began to focus her attention on the obscene chrysalis that held the woman's body. The victim's body, from what she could see, was covered in a mass of cuts, bruises and possible burn marks. There was a fair amount of blood, though nothing she saw made her think this had been a quick kill; on the contrary, it looked as if it had been staged, but where? She looked around her and saw nothing to indicate that a violent crime had taken place here.

She examined the floor below the body and saw what looked like the regular furrows caused by a yard broom.

'Did he sweep before or after?' Eleanor asked the CSI, who was painstakingly taking samples from the floor and placing dust into a small plastic wallet.

'Stop!' came the authoritative tones of the unit head Susan Cheung. 'Did anyone walk over here, towards me?'

Everyone was listening; no one responded.

'Sure?'

There was a hum of conviction from everyone.

'Then our guy wore plastic bootie covers.'

Eleanor made her way cautiously over to where Susan was standing.

'See that?' She pointed at a line of ill-defined footsteps. 'The crease marks obscuring the tread have been made by some sort of covering, no visible fibres, so I reckon he had bootie covers on.'

'When can you confirm this?' asked Eleanor.

Susan shrugged. 'Depends whether I can get a chemical trace of the plastic.'

She stopped talking and returned to the floor. Eleanor followed the path taken by the killer with her eyes – it seemed to bank round sharply to the left, before heading towards a wall adjacent to where the team entered. She tried to visualise the killer and his movements.

'Are the footsteps entering or leaving?' asked Eleanor.

'That's the weird thing,' said Susan, waving her arm to elaborate. 'The feet are all facing the victim.'

Keeping clear of the footprints, Susan walked parallel to the killer's trail. 'They all face forward, but there are two distinct lanes.' She had nearly reached the wall. 'The footprints stop here and there's a cross-print as if he'd turned around, and then...' Susan looked perplexed.

'He backed away from his work, looking at the body. He walked backwards because he couldn't take his eyes off her,' said Eleanor with a note of excitement in her voice. 'Can you see any marks that could have been made by a ladder?'

Susan's head dropped as she examined the area around the footprints.

'Yes,' she said calmly. Her head rose and she scanned the wall.

'Get a light on that wall,' Eleanor called to a CSI standing near a lamp.

When the light levelled out, it revealed a window about thirty feet above Susan's head. There was no obvious way of getting up to it, though someone with a ladder could have climbed down. But with a body?

'I'm not seeing how he could have got through there,' said Susan. 'It's too high and too small. Wait – there's a wooden fascia. Maybe there's a pull-down ladder behind it?'

'I need to get onto that roof,' said Eleanor to an anxious-looking patrol cop.

He nodded and began to make his way towards the entrance.

'No!' yelled Eleanor. 'Go around!'

The patrol cop nodded again and looked around desperately for a way of getting to the exit without contaminating the scene further.

Away from the crime scene, Patrolman Stephen Ellis was notably calmer and more helpful. It was mid-afternoon in Toronto and the cold, grey autumnal day was making it difficult to distinguish the external features of the wall, a great amount being covered in a flourishing bindweed.

'How would you get up there, Ellis?' asked Eleanor, catching his name tag.

'Am I carrying the lady, ma'am?' he said eagerly.

'Let's say no, for the moment,' replied Eleanor.

He took a moment or two to look around the outside of the building, and then, with the boundless energy of a twenty-something, he climbed onto a low wall, walked several paces along it and then pulled himself up to a ledge to his left. He then disappeared behind a leaf-covered parapet, emerging moments later at least ten feet higher and only a couple of paces away from the window.

'Is there anything there? Footprints, some sign that someone climbed up there?' yelled Eleanor.

'No, ma'am, nothing I can see, but... hang on! Yeah, these look like partial footprints!'

'Ellis, watch where you're putting your feet! Don't over-tread, understand?'

'Got it,' he shouted back.

She watched, impressed, as he took a balletic leap of at least five feet to clear the tread marks and shimmied along the narrow ledge that led to the window. He peered at the window frame, took out his torch and expertly shone it around the casing and then through the window. He let out a low whistle and then shouted down to her. 'I think it's been opened recently.'

'Why do you think that? And don't touch it!' Eleanor yelled up.

'There's what looks like drag marks, like someone squeezed through. But I'm not sure.'

She watched as he pushed gently on the window frame, while trying to keep his balance on the thin parapet. The window swung open easily from a central pivot.

'It's been oiled, ma'am,' he yelled down at her.

Eleanor smiled to herself as she saw his head disappear out of sight. His torso twisted and then he let out another whistle.

'There's a ladder – one of those pull-down jobs. It's hidden behind a wooden cover; you'd never have known it was here.' He stared down at her. 'But I don't see how he could have carried her up here, alive or dead.'

'Can you see the body from the window?' she called up.

'Yes. It's parallel with my line of sight.'

'Come down,' called Eleanor. She watched him step off the ledge and, uninterested in the rest of his progress, walked back into the building.

'I need one of your guys to check out a possible means of entry. Patrolman Ellis is outside and will show you,' said Eleanor to Susan Cheung, who nodded. She looked at Dr Hounslow, who was standing next to the body and debating with her assistant Matt Gains about how they were going to release the body.

'Matt's going to cut through the chain with a bolt cutter and we're going to lower her—'

But before Dr Hounslow could finish, Eleanor had turned quickly on her heel and headed towards the entrance. She saw Patrolman Ellis explaining to a CSI how he'd accessed the window, but her attention was on the lock and chain. 'Get me the security guard,' she barked at Ellis.

Heston's expression was, in Eleanor's opinion, considerably shiftier than it had been when she'd spoke to him earlier about the lock.

'You're lying to me, and I want only the facts from now on,' she said bluntly.

'I dunno what you mean,' replied Heston, his voice trembling slightly.

'The lock and chain were replaced this week, am I right?' said Eleanor firmly.

'I don't know nothing about that,' he said, with a stubbornness that implied that a different tactic was required.

'You're ill, correct?' Eleanor watched his lip curl in disgust. 'Cancer I'm guessing, and you don't want to lose this job, right?'

Heston's lip was now quivering, a ghostly pallor beginning to spread across his cheeks.

'I like this job,' he said tonelessly.

'But you made a mistake, didn't you?'

He stared at her face, unsure of whether to continue.

'I need to know, Mr Heston, but the company doesn't,' she added more gently.

He licked his lips and leaned into her. She could smell the sulphurous compounds on his breath.

'The lock and chain. My key wouldn't work and I knew... I thought that someone had changed it. It was the same type as mine but the key just didn't work.'

'So you cut it off and replaced it with your own, right?'

He swallowed hard. 'They'll sack me 'cos I never reported it in. Look, I need this job.'

'When, which day?' Eleanor asked.

'Saturday. I found it out Saturday morning and replaced it in the afternoon.'

She nodded.

'She dead because of me?' he choked.

'Not unless you killed her, Mr Heston.'

He shook his head violently.

'Did you see anything else that might help me out here? Because you owe me some help at the moment.'

He sighed and shook his head. 'It's quiet here. I ain't seen no cars, no people. I'd...'

Eleanor held her breath as he considered something.

'The dust.' He seemed embarrassed. 'I went in to do my rounds on Saturday and I was surprised at how dusty the air was.' He shrugged.

'As if someone had swept the floors?' she added.

'I guess that'd explain it. It just seemed strange that there was so much dust in the air.'

Eleanor watched as the team, led by Matt, cut through the chain and gently lowered the body onto a gurney. Hounslow, satisfied that she had nothing more to contribute outside of the morgue, gathered her bag and with a final chat to the gurney men, headed for the exit.

'Give me till three; I've got another call to make before I can get back to the office,' said the pathologist.

Eleanor nodded.

'Matt and Susan will be here for a couple more hours I imagine.'

'Don't start without me,' said Eleanor.

'Then make sure you pick up your cell,' said Hounslow sharply.

Eleanor turned to Susan, who was packing evidence bags into a large plastic tub. 'What have we got?'

'Not much really. I got a couple of broom fibres, which could have been shed when our killer cleaned. They look new, so we might be able to get a manufacturing ID on them, but don't hold your breath. Very little in the arena here. We have photographs of the footprints, but they're indistinct; Manny's up on the ledge getting traces there. He's nearly finished if you want a quick check.'

Eleanor nodded that she would.

'I'm setting up a team to scour the building inside and out. Matt will head over to the morgue to prepare our lady for her physical examination.'

Whereas most of Eleanor's police colleagues employed terms like 'the vic', 'the perp' and 'the deceased', Susan and her team always referred to the body as being 'our lady' or 'our gentleman' or, in some hard cases, 'our baby', and if a name was available they were always prefixed with Mrs, Miss or Mister. Eleanor suspected it was a public relations ploy rather than a psychological prop.

Eleanor walked outside and looked at the white-clad figure moving cautiously along the ledge, trying to unroll a sticky tape in an increasing wind.

'What have you got?' she shouted up at him.

He turned round and cupped his ear. She waved her fingers at him. He shook his head.

'Shit,' she said quietly.

She stared at the proceedings and ran through the information she had acquired already. The lock had been changed sometime on Friday night after Heston's patrol. It was discovered on Saturday morning and replaced by the afternoon, which meant that when the killer came back with the body, he was unable to get in through the entrance. This must have been on either Saturday evening or the early hours of Sunday. He obviously hadn't brought his bolt cutters with him. Instead, he'd carried the body up to the window, lowered the ladder and carried her down. So, this place was important to him and he knew an alternative way in, which indicated that he had certainly worked the area in some detail before yesterday.

Eleanor speed dialled as she watched Manny placing a small object into an evidence bag. 'Timms?'

'I'm on my way – with you in five.'

Eleanor listened patiently as he swore imaginatively at the city traffic.

'You been briefed?' she said.

'Very brief… *Asshole!*'

Eleanor heard Timms give a quick blast of the siren. 'Is Wadesky there?'

'Yup.'

'Give her the phone.'

There was a brief rustle before Wadesky's shrill tones came down the line.

'Slow it down, Timms! Hi, Ellie; how're you doing?'

'Better than you by the sound of it,' replied Eleanor, smiling.

Sarah Wadesky was difficult not to like. Seven months pregnant with her third child, she refused to sit at a desk and push papers around. A six-foot black, empowered athlete, Wadesky loved the chase, a fight and her five-foot-six Polish husband Jozef, who ran a small impecunious business sketching people's pets while raising their two boys, Alex and Aaron. A constant source of jibes, Jozef had become a standard bearer for his sex by performing all household jobs without complaint, not suffering from jealousy and dedicating whole evenings to massaging his wife's feet. Women wanted him; men declared him 'a fag'.

Timms pulled his Taurus in behind the ME's van and stepped out. 'Where's the action?' he growled. 'Cavalry is here!'

Wadesky rolled her eyes and massaged her lower back with a grimace. 'What do you want us to do?' she asked Eleanor.

'Recce the site, and then I want you to start compiling names. Start with bad sex guys in the area – rapes, kidnapping and assaults, particularly if they were flagged. Prioritise adult hetero to begin with. Then start fishing names that may be connected with Westex, maybe an employee or someone who knows the layout of this place.'

'No problem. You looking for any particular flavour of flagged?'

Eleanor paused for a moment and then spoke carefully. 'He took his time. It was premeditated and he used his imagination.'

The gurney carrying the woman's body was being expertly trundled out through the main entrance.

'Who's leading the clean-up? Sue Cheung?' asked Wadesky.

Eleanor nodded, tapping her phone against her teeth as she pondered.

'What you thinking?'

Eleanor thought carefully for a moment or two. 'The killer may have had to carry the dead woman up there.' She nodded to where Manny was finishing up and passing some small evidence bags to Ellis, who was hovering helpfully on the lower parapet.

'How heavy was the vic?'

'I'd say about my weight, difficult to tell for sure, but mine, give or take,' Eleanor replied.

They watched as Manny picked his way slowly down to the parapet, where Ellis was lowering himself gamely onto the low wall and then fluidly to the ground.

Wadesky squinted at Eleanor. 'You wanna try?'

Eleanor nodded. 'Why not?'

They made their way over to Manny and Ellis. 'You got boot prints?'

'I'm pretty sure we got a couple of clear photos,' replied Manny. 'No signs of plastic, blood or fabric, and the surface had been handled with gloves.'

'Give me a guess on foot size.'

'I'd say he was a nine; nine and a half. That'd make him a little under six foot. But these are guesses,' said Manny.

'What's your boot size?' Eleanor asked, turning to Ellis.

'Um… ten, ma'am,' he replied uncertainly.

'You reckon you can carry a dead woman of about the same dimensions as Detective Raven here?' coaxed Wadesky.

Ellis looked at both of the women and then at the window.

'I guess,' he said non-committally.

'Well how're you going to do it?' asked Eleanor.

Ellis visibly relaxed as he realised they weren't asking him to physically go through the process, just to throw out some ideas.

'You're wrapped in the bag at this stage, ma'am?'

Eleanor nodded helpfully.

'Well I'm definitely wearing gloves because there's no finger-prints and I'd need them for grip.' He followed the route he'd take with his eyes and then looked at Eleanor. He frowned. 'Yeah, I could do it easily, but in a plastic bag? I'm not sure.'

'The vic didn't have any shoes and the bag wasn't torn.'

Ellis looked on in horror as Eleanor slipped off her shoes and coat.

'Manny, get me a body bag. Ellis here is reconstructing the crime.'

Ellis began to shake his head. 'I'm not risking your life, ma'am,' he said decisively.

'Are you expecting me to do this in my current condition, patrolman? You surely can't imagine that Detective Timms is capable of hauling his own fat ass up there, never mind Detective Raven's,' said Wadesky.

Ellis's gaze flicked over to Timms, who was in the process of bumming a doughnut and coffee off CSI. He shook his head.

'Take it easy, okay?' said Wadesky.

Ellis nodded nervously.

'I'm dead weight so it's going to be difficult, but I need to know if this is how he did it. It's going to save a lot of man hours,' said Eleanor.

Manny unfolded a body bag and helped Eleanor step into it. He zipped it up to her throat but left her head exposed, tucking the excess material into itself.

Timms strolled over, the doughnut sagging precariously from the side of his mouth. 'What the hell's going on?' he asked, yanking the doughnut out and waving it at the body bag.

'Police work, Timms. I'll explain if it gets too confusing,' snipped Wadesky.

'Ready?' asked Eleanor.

Ellis nodded, and then with one swift, practised manoeuvre, lifted Eleanor over his shoulder. He tried looping his right arm over both her legs, but when that proved too difficult, he grasped the plastic body bag tightly at her knees and shoulders.

Eleanor felt a strange mixture of complete vulnerability and, paradoxically, security. She smiled inwardly as she thought that in different circumstances, this would have been intoxicating.

Ellis made his way over to the wall, hesitating for a moment.

'You're going to be fine,' Eleanor said encouragingly. She felt his breathing change and was surprised at how warm he was next to her cooling skin. It took him a matter of seconds to climb onto the low wall and then step along to level himself with the ledge.

Eleanor glanced up. It seemed impossible that he could make it with her over his shoulder, but she felt him raise his foot and then started to clamber up. He grunted with the effort as she was hoisted higher, then he slipped back down to the wall level momentarily.

'Hang on,' he said. 'I can't see where I put my...' Then he was off again. It took him less than ten seconds to reach the ledge and pull himself up.

'Hey, Raven, if you fall off at least Manny won't have to go to the bother of bagging you.' Timms laughed uproariously but stopped when he saw Wadesky's expression.

Eleanor felt the muscles in Ellis's arm tense and bulge as he took the strain of lifting both their weights higher. There was a sudden, dramatic lurch of angle and her head and shoulder cracked painfully against the wall.

'I'm fine!' she hissed. 'Keep going!'

His grip tightened on her leg and sleeve, drawing her more protectively in as his knee gained purchase and he hauled them up to the ledge.

Eleanor felt the cold, wet smack of leaves against her face as Ellis moved sideways along the ledge in the direction of the parapet. Again, she began to tip dramatically to one side as Ellis climbed up the steep parapet, grabbing sections of the foliage to maintain his balance. For a moment, his foot slipped on the build-up of wet leaves, but he steadied himself and moved on. It took him one last heave and he was on the ledge, inching towards the window.

'Thank Christ for that! How's your head?' said Ellis, with obvious relief.

'Can you get me through the window?' asked Eleanor, looking at the thirty-foot drop between her and the figures staring up at them.

Ellis grunted, shifted her weight slightly and reached the window, pushing it open with his right hand.

'I've opened the window, but I'm not sure about the ladder,' he replied.

'Try.'

For a moment, Eleanor thought he'd let go of her and was hurling her over the narrow ledge to the ground. Instinctively she grabbed at him and tightened her legs, like the coils of a boa, round his chest.

'Whoa!' he spluttered. 'I've got to reach in and pull down the ladder. You're going to feel vulnerable, but if I don't think I can do it without endangering you, I'll stop, okay?'

Eleanor loosened her grasp and tried to relax. She steadied her breathing and listened to the calmness of his voice.

'I'm not going to drop you. He didn't and I won't.'

For a second time she lurched but managed to control her adrenaline surge and not grab him. She felt him fishing around behind the window frame, and then came a satisfied grunt, followed by the metallic scream of the ladder being pulled down.

'Ladder's down and I can get us both through the window and onto it, but that's as far as I'm going... ma'am,' said Ellis. 'Now the killer didn't do it in reverse so I'm going to swap round and lower you against the wall. Then you can get down under your own steam. There's not much wiggle room so try to keep yourself close to me.'

The wall was cold and damp against Eleanor's back as Ellis pressed her into it. She felt his knees bend and then straighten again.

'Ellis!' bellowed a voice from the ground.

Eleanor peered down to see who was shouting.

'Ellis, move back towards the wall end – you can lower her there more safely.'

It was difficult to see who the voice belonged to as her hair had been caught and loosened over her face by the wet foliage and the abrasion on her forehead was bleeding sufficiently to have glued a mass of hair over her left eye.

'Okay!' shouted Ellis.

She heard a sound and caught a glimpse of movement as someone began to work his way up to where they were standing. In a matter of moments, two strong hands supported her as Ellis lowered her gently to a standing position. Eleanor had a clear image in her mind of how ridiculous she must look to this man.

Incarcerated in a black body bag, her matted hair covering a head wound, there could be no dignity or even rationale to the situation.

'Can I unzip you, Detective?' came a soft, somewhat bemused voice.

'Yes!' she snapped back.

She heard the zip being opened carefully and felt Ellis steady her as the man helped her out. Her stockinged feet curled as she stepped onto the freezing parapet.

Eleanor brushed the hair from her face and peered at the man. He was at least six-foot-two, with short, dark unruly hair, blue-green eyes and a trimmed beard peppered with red.

'Who the hell are you?'

'I'm Detective Laurence Whitefoot. Your new partner.'

CHAPTER THREE

'Can I assume your new partner has asserted his dominance over you?' asked Hounslow in a deadpan tone. Eleanor grimaced as Laurence tried to smother his smirk.

'It was a wall and it came off worse than me,' quipped Eleanor, masking the irritation she felt at having a new partner foisted on her and a large, apparently very visual, bruise and swelling over her left eye. But the jokes were over – Hounslow had already had the plastic liner removed from the body of the victim after an initial investigation and had handed it over to Susan Cheung and her team. The X-ray team had taken their slides and departed.

The woman's body was lying on its back, her head supported by a metal headrest, the hook trailing several links of the chain, still deeply embedded in her spine. Hounslow tested her pen and then began to walk round the body for the external physical examination.

'Detective Whitefoot, you haven't had the honour of attending one of my physical examinations before, so I wish you to be absolutely clear of what is and what is not tolerated.'

'Yes, ma'am,' replied Laurence cautiously.

'If you wish to have a conversation with any of your colleagues, you either leave the room or wait till I have left the room. Once you have left the room, you are not invited back in. If you have some pertinent question, and by that I mean pertinent, you may clear your throat or raise a hand and wait for my response. Is that clear?'

For a moment, Eleanor thought that Laurence believed Hounslow was making another joke, and she waited with interest to see if the smile curling the edges of his lips would provoke a crushing verbal attack from the pathologist, but he seemed to cotton on quickly to the reality. Unsure as to whether the clock had started, he merely nodded.

'Good. Right, let's get started. White, unidentified female, five feet seven inches—'

Hounslow stood stock-still as Marty Samuelson crept through the swing door and meekly folded himself behind Eleanor and Laurence. With one raised eyebrow, Hounslow began again, her voice clipped with irritation. 'I would say well-nourished but too low a BMI for a young woman in her twenties. Starting at the head…' Hounslow peered closely at the woman's face, depressing the skin around her face gently with a gloved finger. She then peered at Eleanor. 'Our lady here is sporting an almost identical abrasion to yourself, Detective.'

Eleanor allowed herself an inward smile. As her eyes dropped to her notepad, she noticed Laurence's thumb gesture upwards. She caught his eye and he nodded encouragingly. Eleanor set her mouth in a hard line.

'The wound shows no sign of bleeding.'

Eleanor's hand shot up and she waited for the nod. 'You believe she was dead before she entered the building.'

'This wound would indicate that, yes. Passing down to the throat and shoulder region, there is bruising consistent with ligature marks, and what could be petechiae…' Hounslow's voice trailed off as she leaned in closer to the body. 'No… these look like tens of small stab wounds. Possibly from a darning needle… I'll know more when I perform the internal.

'Passing along to the chest region… both breasts have a great deal of bruising, and what could be pinch marks made by a mechanical device. Also, what look like old injuries. Maybe strap marks.'

Eleanor cleared her throat and waited while Hounslow indicated to Matt that he could photograph those areas.

'Yes, Detective?'

'Can you give us some idea of the age of those wounds?'

'Certainly not perimortem or anything like it. From the healing I'd say a week or so before,' replied Hounslow.

Matt stepped back and allowed the pathologist to approach the body.

'Okay, looks as though we have more old bruising, again possibly a week or so ago. There are more needle marks around the breast, stomach and thigh region, and what look like small burn marks.'

Laurence cleared his throat and waited.

'Yes?' said the pathologist testily.

'Are the burn marks consistent with cigarette or electrode attachments?'

'Can't be sure yet, but I would think that they were more likely to be the latter suggestion.'

Eleanor watched with interest as Laurence jotted down copious notes in a large ring-bound notebook.

'This might help ID our lady,' said Hounslow and indicated that Eleanor should step closer. Wedged tightly on the swollen fourth finger of the woman's left hand was a diamond engagement ring. Even though the ring was partially covered in skin and blood, there was no doubting the quality of the stone or the craftsmanship.

'When can we have it?' asked Eleanor.

'Call Susan – this needs a tissue scrape. Possibly today, but Matt will give you photos.' Hounslow nodded to her assistant, who proceeded to photograph and then remove the ring from the finger.

*

'You want to follow up the ring?' asked Laurence, trotting behind as Eleanor headed for her car.

'No, you do that,' she replied indifferently. Hounslow was performing the internal examination. That would take at least another hour, and the clock was ticking.

'Okay, where are you going?'

'Downtown.' Eleanor reached her car and, flipping the lock, began to climb in.

'Hang on! Eleanor, we need to talk.'

She waggled her cell phone pointedly before closing the car door and turning over the engine. Laurence rapped his knuckles on the window.

'I'd like to buy you a coffee now so we can discuss effective strategy on this,' he said emphatically.

She let out an audible sigh and contemplated driving off but didn't, because whatever Eleanor Raven was, she wasn't stupid. She would have to share the case, and if this was to be her new partner till Mo got back on his feet, then so be it.

Reluctantly, she opened the door and headed for the local coffee shop, noting that Laurence stayed several paces behind her.

D'Angelo's coffee shop was frequented by medical technicians, cops and morticians, much to the constant chagrin of the proprietor 'Big Al'. He had placed a large, handwritten sheet with the legend 'Wash your hands before you use the restroom!' on the wall that divided the ladies from the gents. Big Al had established the coffee shop in the days before the new city morgue had been built. Back then his customers had been mostly clerks and accountants from the financial district, a demographic he approved of; now the daily conversation consisted mainly of horror stories about murders, accidental deaths that defied imagination, natural law and the inevitable consequences of drinking and eating too much – both long-term vices of Big Al. So, in a small act of empowerment, Big Al always used butter and lard in all of his cakes, including those marked 'low fat', because if cholesterol was sending him skyward early, then he was going to take a few of those smug bastards from the county morgue with him. Homicide, he had decided, was a nebulous concept.

Eleanor took a window seat and watched as Laurence struggled to pull his wallet out of his pocket and hold on to the huge file of photographs at the same time.

'Sugar?' he asked.

She shook her head.

'You seem a little pissed at having to work with me,' he said quietly.

Eleanor leaned closer to him. 'Mmm, a little.'

'Why?'

Eleanor opened her mouth, and then closed it abruptly as she realised she wasn't entirely sure why she was so angry with him. It couldn't just be because he was sitting here instead of Mo, or maybe it was.

'Your partner Artie… he's coming back?' Laurence asked.

'Possibly,' she answered evasively.

'Well when he does, they're probably going to hook me up with Timms while Wadesky's on maternity leave. So maybe we could call this a temporary partnership and enjoy the experience?' He smiled encouragingly. 'I've not been in Homicide for very long, and you have the best solve rate in the county. It's a great opportunity for me…' His voice trailed off.

'I'm not won over by flattery, Detective Whitefoot; in fact it has a tendency to put me on edge and suspect I'm being manipulated. Is that your intention?'

Laurence hesitated. 'Yes. I want to work with you because I want to learn. I need this opportunity and I'm trying out a few approaches to win you over.'

Eleanor stared at him for a second or two before responding. 'Okay, let's run through what we've got.' Laurence visibly relaxed.

'Our victim is in her twenties, she has no tattoos, no needle marks, her legs are waxed, hair professionally dyed and her teeth whitened and capped. So…' Eleanor looked at him, wanting him to continue.

'She's no hooker.'

'It's very unlikely she's a hooker,' Eleanor corrected him.

'She's wearing a very expensive ring, which will make it easier to identify her.' He looked down at his notes.

'You don't need to follow up the ring to identify her.' Eleanor watched his eyes fasten on her with interest. 'What will be important is how long it takes her fiancé or parents to call in her disappearance. This woman comes from money and is marrying into money. Women like that are missed very quickly.'

Laurence's phone rang; he glanced at the number. 'It's Matt.'

Eleanor looked at him with interest as he took the call.

'Okay, autopsy's not finished yet but Matt's giving me the heads-up…'

'A heads-up from the ME's office? Have you got something nasty on Matt Gains?'

Laurence smiled and shook his head. 'We go back a long way.'

'How?' Eleanor pushed.

'We went to med school together,' he said quietly.

'Med school? That's not how I got into policing,' she stated.

'I'm a doctor… was a doctor,' he said.

'And now you're a cop? That's quite a sidestep, Detective Whitefoot. How qualified are, sorry, were you?'

'Qualified enough, just in the wrong thing. Now do you want to hear what Matt has to say?'

Eleanor nodded and made a mental note to investigate his strange and intriguing past later.

'There were no traces of semen or obvious sign of recent penetration.'

Eleanor's brow furrowed. 'So we've got a dead woman with obvious signs of healed strap marks that are at least a week old, and a collection of injuries that appear to have been received over the past twenty-four to thirty-six hours,' she said slowly. 'Are there any injuries that fall outside those two periods?'

'Not that they've seen, according to Matt,' he replied. 'Oh, and she does have a tattoo.'

'She does?' Eleanor was interested.

'Yeah, a yin and yang circle apparently.'

Eleanor grabbed her bag, stood up and began to leave.

'What's happening?' Laurence grabbed the photographs and notebooks and swung his coat over his left shoulder. 'Am I coming?'

Eleanor turned round and looked at him, puzzled. 'I don't know. Are you?'

'So what's the relevance of the tattoo?' he asked as Eleanor drove slowly through the building traffic. 'Doesn't it mean him and her? Opposites together?'

Eleanor was thinking and had pretty much pushed his presence from her mind.

'Opposites attract?' Laurence cleared his throat noisily, making her turn. 'Are we going to check out tattoo parlours?'

'Do you want one?'

'What?'

'A tattoo?'

'No, I just want to know what the hell we're doing and what the relevance of the yin-yang thing is?' he said with growing irritation.

'It symbolises complimentary opposites. Two people with opposite needs and desires who combine to form a dynamic whole.'

Laurence fell silent, clearly trying to piece together the implications of this information.

As Eleanor parked the car outside a dingy building, surrounded with litter and broken paving slabs, he was still obviously struggling to make the connection, as he'd said nothing further. But one glance at the torn poster adorning the entrance made it clear. The As You Like It club was a two-storey building with matte black painted walls and windows. The entrance was a large washroom door with an old-fashioned vacant/occupied lock, which was presently in the 'occupied' position. The poster, which rippled aggressively in the cold wind, showed an image of a young woman, hogtied on a wooden frame that resembled a mid-eighteenth-century weaving loom. The woman, her long red hair dragged tightly into a high ponytail, was rolling her eyes in apparent ecstasy, though the leather gag and ball made this difficult to ascertain.

Eleanor took out her badge and held it up to the discreet camera positioned above the door.

'Why here?' whispered Laurence.

'Somewhere's gotta be first,' she replied as she hammered again on the door with her fist.

'Police, Gary – open the door!' she yelled.

Ten seconds later a bolt was pulled and the door opened to reveal a tousled, grey-haired man in his late fifties, sporting an unlit cigarette in a long 1920s holder and wearing a stained and frayed silk dressing gown of the variety adopted by Hugh Hefner.

'Gary Le Douce is proprietor of this salubrious establishment and this' – she gestured to her new partner – 'is Detective Laurence Whitefoot.'

'I heard about Mo; how is he?' asked Gary in an affected British accent, which he seemed to have acquired from old Noël Coward movies.

'He's good; let's talk,' she said, walking past him.

Gary nodded soberly, turned round and began to limp his way along the gloomy corridor that opened out onto a gloomier bar and dance floor, lapped by a low-level mezzanine.

'I'm taking tea – care to join me?' asked Gary as his slippered feet flapped noisily across the beer-sticky floor.

Gary brushed the seat of a red velvet sofa with his hand, indicating that they should sit down. He gestured to the teapot, but both Eleanor and Laurence declined.

'Now, my dears, how can I help?'

'Someone's not playing nice, Gary,' said Eleanor emphatically.

'Oh dear. Have you received a complaint?'

'From the pathologist, yes. She feels that someone who doesn't understand the rules is a danger to everyone, and anyone with ideas as to who that might be would be performing a service both to their city and mankind in general.'

'Hmm. Well I would help if I could,' said Gary, cautiously sipping his tea. 'But all my girls and boys just have fun and no one really gets hurt.' He smiled encouragingly at them.

Eleanor leaned towards Gary, lowering her voice so much that both he and Laurence had to strain to hear her. 'But someone did get hurt, Gary, and as a man who makes his living from these little games, I expect you to furnish me with some information – rapidly.'

Gary placed his teacup on the saucer carefully and leaned towards Eleanor. She studied the lines around his mouth and eyes, covered patchily with ill-toned foundation.

Finally, Gary's indolent expression began to harden and his back straightened. 'Tell Daddy about the games… in detail.'

With snake-like speed, Eleanor leaped from her seat and, crushing his windpipe with her right hand, used her left to snatch a set of handcuffs from her back pocket. In a fluid manoeuvre, she flipped him over onto his chest and cuffed his hands behind his back.

Laurence stood up, clearly unsure what his response should be.

Gary was making little snuffling barks as he tried to twist his head away from the suffocating effects of the cushion, but Eleanor was pushing him down firmly between his shoulders. 'I'm not playing,' she hissed in his ear.

'Detective?' whispered Laurence, but he shut up when he saw her eyebrow rise.

Eleanor pulled Gary into a sitting position, noting that his make-up had left a greasy smear on the cushion cover.

'Now we've established who's in charge here, Gary, perhaps you'd like to have that conversation that eluded you before? So I repeat, who isn't playing according to the rules?'

'No one here, and I ain't heard of anyone neither,' he snarled, all pretence of English heritage having evaporated.

'Oh I find it hard to believe that a nasty old tabby like yourself doesn't know exactly what's going on,' said Eleanor.

'I don't talk from a compromised situation,' he snorted.

Eleanor waited for a second or two and then released him. Gary flopped onto the sofa.

'I'm telling you the truth when I say that there's no one getting out of line here.'

'Anyone new around?' asked Laurence.

'A few but no alarm bells,' replied Gary, finally lighting his cigarette and inhaling deeply.

'How about her?' Laurence held an enlarged black-and-white photograph of the murdered woman.

Gary showed not a single sign of repulsion or surprise at the image of the dead woman. He shrugged.

'Recognise this?' said Laurence, showing him an image of the ring. 'She had a small yin-yang tattoo under her armpit,' he added hopefully as Gary stared at the ring.

He snorted, blowing a line of smoke out of each nostril. 'Yeah, I've seen her.'

'When, and who was with her?' asked Eleanor calmly.

Gary settled back into the sofa. 'They've been in a couple of times.'

Eleanor nodded. 'Can you ID either of them?'

Gary stared at her silently.

'When did you last have an inspection, Mr Le Douce?' said Laurence.

'Oh please!' Gary laughed, and to the detective's obvious surprise, so did Eleanor.

She turned to Gary, leaning in closer to him. 'Give me something, Gary – let me believe you're cooperating, eh?'

There was silence as Gary seemed to weigh up his options.

'He drives a black Porsche, but I don't keep tapes and I don't look at plates.'

Eleanor nodded and placed her card next to the teapot. 'You've been a great help; let's keep it that way.'

*

Laurence waited till she'd started the engine and pulled into the traffic before speaking. 'Why'd you laugh when I threatened him with an investigation? And why didn't we push him on the car – he said he didn't keep the tapes, but how'd you know for sure?'

'Okay, have you met Gary Le Douce before?'

'No,' he replied, unsure as to where this was going.

'You should have,' she said simply.

'What do you mean I should have met him? When?'

'You want to learn? Want to be a better cop?'

He nodded.

'Then you should already have bought drinks for yourself and for patrons in As You Like It and found out who goes there, who owns it, what makes it tick. Then you would have seen which lawyers, politicians, teachers and pros go there. That's how you become a good cop – you research, remember and then use that knowledge to track down the bad guys. You don't use it to judge what people do or desire. Remember that next time you curl your nose up at something you don't like the look of.'

Eleanor set her jaw and accelerated through the traffic; there was to be no more conversation for a while.

On the face of it, Xxxstacy was considerably more appealing to the more daring and financially equipped. Where As You Like It had offered tawdry low-key BDSM, this club was awash with subtle lighting, plush furnishings and head-height cages sporting naked, leather-bound models gyrating lazily to the steady thump of an electronic beat.

Laurence followed Eleanor down into the gloom and noted with surprise that not only was the club open and serving in the mid-afternoon, it was busy with young executive types, swilling cocktails and wolfing down sushi.

Eleanor went over to the bar and spoke quietly to a woman mixing a complicated drink, who stopped what she was doing and nodded to a colleague to take over while she ushered them both into a small back room behind the bar.

Laurence handed her the photographs of the dead woman and an image of the ring. 'Jesus!' she said, with feeling.

'Do you recognise her, Bella?' asked Eleanor.

Bella shook her head. 'What happened to her? She looks like she got run over!'

'She was tortured to death,' said Laurence simply.

'You know who she is?' asked Bella.

'Do you?'

Bella shook her head energetically and looked at the ring. 'This left on her?' she asked with astonishment.

Eleanor nodded.

'Then you're dealing with some seriously messed-up dude. He just likes to kill, huh?'

'That's our thinking,' replied Eleanor.

Bella paused, her brow knotted.

'We think her guy may have a black Porsche,' said Laurence.

'Who doesn't have one would narrow it down round here,' said Bella. 'Guys that use this place don't think nothing of spending five hundred bucks on champagne and oysters.'

She peered at the woman's face again, her mouth turning down at the corners in disgust. 'You know what sort of a place this is.'

Eleanor nodded.

'But this is just fun stuff; it ain't for real.'

'It was real for her.' Eleanor let this sink in for a moment or two. 'You call me, huh?'

Bella nodded vigorously and took the proffered card. Eleanor turned to go. 'You still got the noticeboards?'

'Yeah, but the boss moved 'em down to the restrooms a couple of weeks ago – said it "lowered the tone".'

*

The restrooms were situated at the bottom of a set of glass stairs, illuminated garishly by green strip lights. Eleanor indicated that Laurence should use the men's room while she stepped into the ladies. She found a large noticeboard, and small business cards with women and men's names, cell numbers and sexual preferences were pinned all over it. There were a couple of out-of-date posters advertising burlesque and live sex shows, but most bills were aligned neatly and the board seemed to be managed.

She scanned the cards, collecting with a latex-gloved hand several that seemed worth investigating. '*Need it hard and dangerous! Call Sam*' and '*Gent seeks submissive woman for mutual pleasure*' seemed fairly typical.

Eleanor unpinned them and placed them in an evidence bag.

Her hand hesitated over an expensive embossed card: '*Seeking woman of exquisite need*'. Underneath the familiar cell-phone number was a small yin-yang symbol. It was identical to the one she had collected for her own use the week before. For a fleeting moment, something akin to concern rattled her self-composure.

*

Laurence was trying not to be judgemental about any of the cards and posters displayed on the noticeboard inside the restroom. Some had photographs and offers from what he assumed to be prostitutes; others had a more amateur appearance, the requests being more specific. '*Dominatrix, with own dungeon*' seemed more a business proposal than '*Desperate for man who knows how to dominate and teach willing slave girl*'. Laurence wasn't really sure what he was looking for and was almost tempted to grab the entire board's worth and work through them later, but that would alert anyone using the board to police involvement, so he studied the cards intently.

Suddenly the door swung open and a man in his mid-thirties strode in, speaking Italian noisily into a hands-free set. Laurence glanced at the man as he urinated into the trough.

Conversation and urination over, the man zipped himself up and walked back to the door. Stopping momentarily next to Laurence, he tapped one of the cards with his index finger and smiled. 'Very nice lady, very… accommodating.' And with that, the man walked out.

Laurence unpinned the card and slipped it into his pocket. As he did so, he inadvertently released a second card, which fluttered to his feet. It took him several seconds to process the information on the card and turn it into a believable scenario, and less than one to leave the restroom and stride down the corridor to where Eleanor was emerging from the ladies.

'We've got him,' he hissed, handing her the card.

Eleanor scowled and pulled on a latex glove. She took the proffered card and read the script, her astonishment clear on her face. '*Kidnappings Arranged*'. Below it was a cell number.

CHAPTER FOUR

Laurence wasn't surprised that Mo's desk was still dominating the workstation he was to share with Eleanor; he was just irritated that he wasn't allowed to use it. Eleanor had had a small, temporary table shoehorned into the corner of the room where movement was well-nigh impossible, and he'd had to find an extension cable to link his laptop to the power supply. So far he'd been unable to stretch the phone far enough so he could reach it, and every time it rang he had to lunge over the tabletop. It was ringing now, and after a gymnastic stretch, he heard himself snap into the receiver, 'Yes!'

'Whoa, back up there, Detective! Only the brave or those not wanting their AFIS report use that sort of tone,' said Wadesky tersely.

'Mea culpa,' he replied. 'What have you got?'

'Well there are three complete fingerprints; two are yours, because you weren't wearing latex gloves,' she said pointedly.

'And the others?'

'One partial index, unknown to database and a complete thumb and partial index, which are known,' she replied.

Laurence felt the adrenaline kick in and held his breath.

'The known belong to a Cheswell Barnes, a white male, thirty-four years old, who served three for forgery and tax evasion.'

'Is he on the sex crimes register?'

'Afraid not. Clean on that score, but he's got two DUIs and one domestic in 2007.'

'Domestic?'

'His wife beat him with a shoe,' she said, laughing. 'She was charged and fined.'

'Okay,' he sighed. 'Send it through and I'll go and check this guy out.'

He broke the call and typed the name into the record bank, sighing when he saw Cheswell's mugshot. Weighing in at slightly more than a bag of feathers, he didn't look capable of fighting off a sparrow, never mind hauling a dead woman thirty feet up a wall and then hooking her onto a cross-beam. Still, it was their first lead. Checking the address, he called Eleanor and left instructions as to where he was heading.

*

Eleanor stared at the middle-aged couple through the two-way glass and felt intuitively that they would now be able to identify the victim. The woman wrung her hands together and threw beseeching looks at her husband, who sat in stoic silence. It was time for them to move on to the next stage of their lives, knowing they would have to live with the anger and guilt of their daughter's murder; never quite able to talk to friends about what happened or ask for a full disclosure of the circumstances of her death. She sighed deeply before entering the room; watching grief hit people was a deeply unpleasant experience but one she had never shied away from.

'Mr and Mrs Greystein?' Eleanor asked and thrust out her hand to Mr Greystein first. His was dry and cold but his shake was solid. He was a tall man and stood rigidly to attention. His wife scrabbled to her feet, clumsy and desperate.

'My sergeant tells me that you've come to register your daughter as missing?' Eleanor said calmly.

'Lydia's dead, isn't she? Isn't she? That's why we've been brought in here instead of lining up like everyone else?' choked Mrs

Greystein. 'You're a detective and they don't deal with these sorts of things.' She looked to her husband, whose mouth was set in a rigid line, his jaw grinding his teeth together. 'Isn't that right, Harry?'

Eleanor considered her approach for a moment or two before deciding clear and honest would serve the couple best.

'Mrs Greystein, the body of a young woman was discovered this morning and it's protocol for the primary on the case, myself, to deal with all enquiries that could be matched to that case. We have no reason at this stage to believe the young woman to be that of your daughter Lydia.'

The woman's wrinkled, gem-laden hand hovered in front of her mouth, as if that would stop the flow of misery.

'Was your daughter engaged, Mrs Greystein?' asked Eleanor carefully.

'Yes she was! How did you know?' gasped Mrs Greystein. 'Harry, how do they know?' She turned to her husband, grabbing his hand in hers.

'She's engaged to be married to Eric Stollar; he works for Delacroix and Stansfield,' he said slowly.

'They're a law firm, a good company. Eric is a good man,' said Mrs Greystein, falling into what Eleanor could tell was a comforting mantra.

'Perhaps you could give us Mr Stollar's address before you leave?'

'Why? You think it's her, don't you?' Mrs Greystein's voice had risen an octave.

'Mrs Greystein, you came in to tell us that your daughter is missing and we need as much help as possible if we are to find her,' Eleanor said firmly.

'Yes, yes, I understand,' she whimpered.

'Mr Greystein, I'm going to ask you to accompany me to the morgue. Do you feel able to do that or would you like us to contact another member of your family?'

His eyes widened with fear, but he spoke clearly and with strength. 'I can do that on my own. Thank you.' He gently disentangled his wife's hands from his.

'I'll come – she's my daughter!'

Eleanor registered the fear on Mr Greystein's face and took a step towards his wife. She spoke slowly and firmly. 'Mrs Greystein, if this isn't your daughter, you'll have exposed yourself to an unpleasant experience. If it is her, you'll see her later when you can have quiet moments and see her in the right environment. Do you understand what I'm saying to you?'

Slowly the woman nodded. Tears loosened her mascara and ran down her cheeks, leaving rough tracks.

'I do,' she whispered.

'I'm going to get someone to bring you a drink and sit with you till we come back.' Eleanor nodded to Mr Greystein, who kissed his wife and then followed her.

Eleanor walked in silence along the corridor, taking the emergency exit to the car park so Mr Greystein would not be exposed to the bedlam that was reception. He needed to compose himself, and a few moments would help.

She drove fairly quickly to the morgue, which was less than five minutes from the station. Parking in the reserved bay, she turned and picked up the manila envelope containing the photograph of the ring. 'Sir, can you describe your daughter's engagement ring?'

She saw his lip tremble, knowing that this would be the decisive moment. If his description matched the one in the envelope, his life was over.

He cleared his throat. 'It was a large diamond solitaire mounted on white gold…'

His voice trailed off as Eleanor's eyes began to reveal the truth to him.

'Can I ask you to look at this photograph and tell me if you recognise it?' she said.

He nodded. There was no need for him to say anything because his face gave his answer.

'I thought it was rather showy myself,' he said quietly.

Mr Greystein, Eleanor noted, no longer held himself ramrod straight but let his shoulders slump and his back curve, as if his body was succumbing to the inevitability of what lay behind the glass partition.

A curtain was drawn across the viewing window, enabling the bereaved to take the identification process in a series of small steps.

'Are you prepared, Mr Greystein?'

He nodded.

Eleanor tapped lightly on the window. Matt Gains pulled open the curtains and then stood behind the gurney where the woman's body was covered with a green surgical sheet. He gently lifted the corner of the sheet and folded it neatly across the woman's throat. Eleanor was relieved to see that Matt had washed and arranged her wet hair and removed all traces of make-up, making her look younger and less abused.

Mr Greystein made a choking sound and seemed to sway a little before regaining his composure.

'Mr Greystein, can you confirm that this is the body of your daughter Lydia?'

He nodded and then realised Eleanor needed more. 'Yes. This is my daughter, Lydia Rachel Greystein.'

'Could she have been in an accident?' asked Mr Greystein desperately as Eleanor drove them both back to the station.

'No, I'm sorry. We're looking for her killer now,' she answered, quietly but firmly.

'I'll need to tell Eric,' he said vaguely.

'Perhaps you wouldn't object to talking to him after we have? We'll be visiting him this afternoon.'

Mr Greystein turned to look at her, his brow knotted with concern. 'Do you think Eric had anything to do with Lydia's death?'

'At the moment we're gathering information, not making any assumptions,' she replied. 'Mr Greystein, what are your impressions of Eric Stollar?'

Eleanor thought she could detect a rise in colour in the man's cheeks.

'He's a…' He paused. 'A slimy little shit.' With that, he clamped his jaw tightly closed and stared ahead.

*

Cheswell Barnes stood shivering on his front porch, his arms wrapped tightly around his chest. He stared aggressively at Laurence Whitefoot.

'I don't know who the hell you're talking about. I ain't never seen no woman and I ain't done nothing wrong,' he said peevishly.

Laurence took in the pathetic spectacle that was Cheswell Barnes. Standing no more than five-foot-five, with patchy, sand-coloured hair and a fourteen-year-old's attempt at a moustache, he was sporting a large cold sore on his upper lip and crusted sleep around his bloodshot eyes. His clothing had a 'slept in' appearance and an aroma to match. Cheswell wasn't convincing as a murder suspect, but he was certainly up to something, as his eyes continuously flickered to the left as he spoke.

Before Laurence could pursue matters, a female voice boomed from within the confines of the house.

'Chessie! Who's there? Chessie?'

'He's leaving now, honey,' said Cheswell, with an edge of hopefulness.

'He's not I'm afraid,' Laurence replied firmly. 'Perhaps it would be better if we went inside, Mr Barnes?'

Cheswell groaned as he led the way into the house. The hallway was narrowed by a wall of cardboard boxes, each sealed with parcel tape and advertising its contents as televisions and stereo equipment.

'May I take a look in the boxes, Mr Barnes?' asked Laurence.

'No you may not, because you haven't got warrant,' came a terse, heavily accented response.

'And you are?' asked Laurence, recognising the woman's face from her arrest photograph.

'Sashia Irina Yesikov, but you already know that.'

Sashia was as round as she was tall, a cigarette clamped between her uneven teeth, which she puffed enthusiastically as she stared at Laurence. Her ill-fitting, low-cut T-shirt revealed a bosom covered in tattoos of surprising artistry. Laurence felt an unseemly desire to stare but fought it. The nasty smirk on Sashia's face confirmed he hadn't fought hard enough.

'What do you want?' she spat.

'We have a dead girl in the morgue who was kidnapped and tortured, and this' – he held up a plastic evidence bag with the 'Kidnappings Arranged' card clearly visible within – 'has Mr Barnes' fingerprints all over it.'

'Metaphorically or literally?' asked Sashia, sneering.

Laurence noted that Cheswell's shoulders were slumping lower than he thought physically possible. It was clear that he was neither the brains nor the brawn of whatever enterprise Sashia was running.

'Literally,' replied Laurence.

Several seconds passed as Sashia pondered matters.

'That cell phone is not registered to either of us, and there is nothing other than Chessie's fingerprints to link him to it, correct?'

Laurence nodded, pleased that Sashia was feeling more relaxed and confident – it meant she was more likely to make a mistake. He waited patiently for it. It didn't take long.

'So, for all you know, Chessie could have been planning a little fun for his beloved Sashia, correct?'

Again, Laurence nodded. 'But the card was left on the noticeboard; surely if that was Mr Barnes' plan he would have taken the card with him,' replied Laurence, catching the hopeful expression flitting across Cheswell's face.

'He just note the number,' said Sashia, casually miming a pen motion on paper.

Laurence nodded. 'Again that's possible. Were you?' he asked Cheswell, who glanced nervously at Sashia.

'Maybe,' he answered cautiously, hedging his bets.

Recognising the signs that Cheswell was about to start digging a hole for them, Sashia began to draw matters to a close. 'We have done nothing wrong; you must leave now.'

'Do you recognise either the girl or the ring?' asked Laurence, handing Sashia the photographs. She looked at both, raised an eyebrow and shrugged.

'Never. You find this on the girl?' She tapped the photograph of the ring with a long, painted nail.

'Yes,' Laurence replied.

'Then it definitely can't be Chessie,' she said emphatically.

Cheswell nodded in agreement at the notion that having taken the time and trouble to kill, anyone would leave a ring of such value on the corpse.

Gathering the photographs, Laurence prepared to leave.

'The televisions?' he asked.

Sashia smiled. 'Gone by the time you get the warrant.'

Laurence nodded sagely. 'IRS?'

'Listen, Detective,' Sashia hissed, leaning towards him, 'women like that get killed every day because they play dangerous games. I run business here with Chessie, make okay living and pay tax to—'

'What do you mean they "play dangerous games"?,' Laurence cut in. He noted with interest that Sashia, previously unconcerned and confident, began to fidget. Cheswell was staring at her, his brows knotted.

'What games?' Laurence added, more firmly.

'When a woman wears expensive ring and ends up dead, she is playing a dangerous game,' said Sashia. 'We cannot help you any more. Perhaps you will be good to leave now.'

Laurence stared at her for a moment and then made his way along the narrow corridor. He opened the front door and stepped out onto the porch, turning to face Cheswell, who was gratefully ushering him out. Laurence slammed his hand on the door. Cheswell's frightened face appeared in the slim gap.

'I don't care about this nasty little enterprise you've got going here, Mr Barnes, but I will happily turn you over to the department that does. Do you understand?'

Cheswell nodded imperceptibly.

'I want to find who killed this woman, and everything about your body language tells me that you know something.'

Cheswell's head remained rigidly set.

'Think quickly about how you can help me, and by doing so, help yourself.'

Laurence slipped his card through the gap and felt it taken by an invisible hand. He gave the worried eyes a final glance and then turned and walked back to his car. Mr Barnes, he concluded, would be costing the city some serious police overtime.

CHAPTER FIVE

'I thought we had a meeting with the boss?' noted Laurence as he followed Eleanor across the parking lot outside police headquarters. An increasingly cold wind was yanking off the last of the sugar-maple leaves, sending them into a manic vortex, accompanied by plastic wrappers and scraps of litter.

'Well if you look behind you, you can wave to Marty as we leave,' replied Eleanor as she swiftly unlocked the car and jumped in.

Laurence peered up at the third floor and saw Marty Samuelson's angry face as he banged expressively on the window pane, and then stabbed at his watch in a gesture that could only mean he'd thought the same too.

Laurence watched as Samuelson put his phone to his ear and pointed at Eleanor, who had started the engine and was about to pull away.

Laurence hopped in. 'I think the boss is—'

Eleanor's phone started ringing. Laurence stared at her as she calmly pulled into the heavy city traffic.

'Are you going to answer him?' he asked.

The phone stopped and, almost immediately, Laurence's sprang to life. Sighing, he answered.

Samuelson's voice filled his ear. 'What the hell are you doing? We had a meeting arranged.'

'Sir, we're following a lead,' replied Laurence calmly.

'To hell with the lead! Where's my debrief?' Samuelson snapped. Laurence saw Eleanor roll her eyes.

'An email was sent to you before we left outlining our knowledge so far. We've identified—' began Laurence timidly.

'I know that!' railed Samuelson.

Laurence opened his mouth and then closed it again; it seemed more prudent to leave his boss to do the talking. There was a pause as Samuelson waited for bait, but when none came he snarled, 'Neither of you clock off tonight without giving me a face to face, understand?' and hung up.

'Jeez!' groaned Laurence. 'First day in the department and I've pissed off the boss.'

'What do you care?' asked Eleanor.

'Unlike you, I don't have a gold standard solve rate. I'm a grunt.'

'You think I've just adopted rebellion as a recent ploy? I've been pissing Marty and everyone else off since day one. If you stop to care, you're losing sight of the fact that you only have one boss.' She slipped through the sluggish traffic, making an illegal turn onto Queen's.

'The city?' he replied.

She turned to him with disgust. 'The victim!'

*

Eleanor stared through her windshield at the enormous glass tower that housed the most expensive legal advice in Toronto. Delacroix and Stansfield was sandwiched on the eleventh floor, in between merchant bankers and two other legal firms. She tapped in a number she read from a Post-it note and waited for a second before it was answered.

'Delacroix and Stansfield. How may I help you?' trilled the enthusiastic tones of what could only be a recently employed receptionist.

'This is Marilyn from Burbage Heights. Can you tell me if Mr Eric Stollar is still there as his order is ready for immediate dispatch?' cooed Eleanor.

'Yes he is! Let me see if he's available to take your call,' she chirped.

'No, that's alright, honey. It'll take us less than an hour to get it to him. Will he still be there or should I send it to the second nominated address?' Eleanor spoke quickly.

'Um… wait, I can see him putting on his coat. Should I ask?' The receptionist sounded worried now.

'No, I'll just deliver it to his home. Thank you,' replied Eleanor, breaking the call.

'Why don't we just go up?' asked Laurence.

'I'm interested in why this guy wasn't the first to call it in that his girlfriend was missing. Let's see whether he goes straight home or needs to pop in anywhere first? You watch,' said Eleanor, as she handed Laurence a photocopy of his driving licence, along with his car make, model and registration number. 'We'll give him five and then swing round to the parking lot.'

'No need – that looks like our guy,' responded Laurence, instinctively climbing out of the car and following him. Eleanor started the engine and after a few seconds swung out into the evening traffic.

*

Eric Stollar was about five-foot-eight and appeared to possess, from the discrepancy between his waist and shoulder breadth, an unnatural preoccupation with the gym. Strangely, Laurence noted as he followed his brisk step along the street, he wasn't carrying either a briefcase or laptop, essentials for a man pulling six figures in a top law firm.

He moved quickly, almost at a jog, barging through the commuters with indifference. This wasn't the way to either the subway or his apartment complex, so maybe Eleanor was right.

It only took Laurence one more block and a crossover to realise where Stollar was heading. He felt his cell vibrate. 'He's heading for Xxxstacy isn't he?' he blurted into the phone.

'He might be,' came Eleanor's calm tone. 'I'm going to stop on Victoria and get there first, okay? If we're wrong, keep with him and I'll catch up.' She broke the call.

Laurence noted her car slip past him and make another illegal left onto Yonge ahead of him. If he was right, Stollar would cross over Yonge Street and then take another left at The Cheese Factory.

He couldn't help smiling when Stollar did just that.

Laurence walked into the club and looked around for Stollar. He was talking animatedly to the bartender, who shrugged and then turned away and picked up a glass. Laurence followed as he moved quickly in the direction of the basement, watching as Stollar looked around anxiously and then entered the restroom.

Laurence was about to follow him in when he felt a hand on his arm. He barely recognised Eleanor; she was wearing sunglasses, a leather jacket and had piled her hair up in a messy ponytail and drawn a thick smudge of dark colour on her lips. She thrust a pair of what looked like non-prescription reading glasses at him.

'Take off your tie!'

Laurence put on the glasses quickly and yanked off his tie as he entered the room.

Stollar was so preoccupied frantically rummaging through the cards pinned to the noticeboard, it took him several seconds to register Laurence's presence. By that time, Laurence was peeing into the urinal and not of any further interest.

Stollar yanked a few of the cards off, glanced at them and then dropped them to the floor in frustration before storming out of the restroom, trampling the cards underfoot.

Laurence gave him a second or two as he adjusted his clothing and then followed him up to the bar, where Stollar talking to the bartender again. Eleanor was sitting at the bar playing with her phone.

Laurence made his way out of the building, taking off the glasses as he walked out, and tucked himself in behind the adjacent doorway, where he put his tie back on.

*

Eleanor listened carefully to Stollar.

'You see anyone putting up one of those cards, or you see a card appear with any variation of that on it, you call me straight away. You hear?'

The bartender stared coldly at him as he was handed a business card and a fifty. Then Stollar walked briskly out of the bar, leaving behind him a heavy tang of sweat and fear.

*

Laurence watched Stollar launch himself into the busy traffic and head back in the direction he'd come from. He was about to pursue when Eleanor put her hand lightly on his arm and turned her back on the retreating figure. 'He'll be going back to the office to finish off his day. We'll wait. I want to get an invite into his apartment.'

*

While they waited for Stollar to complete his business in the office, Laurence and Eleanor sat patiently in the car.

'Why the disguise? Bit nineteenth century, eh?' quipped Laurence.

'Research proves that the chances of anyone recalling a face after only a couple of seconds of exposure is low to negligible. What we tend to remember are non-natural features such as glasses, heavy lipstick and hats. I don't want Stollar to recall seeing either of us in the club, so I just scrambled our images a little, so to speak,' replied Eleanor.

Laurence smiled at her. 'You got a trunk-load of accessories in the back?'

'No,' said Eleanor flatly, watching with a certain amount of pleasure as the smile faded from his face.

They had followed Stollar's erratic drive back to the apartment and now stood at his front door, Eleanor insisting that allowing him only a few moments to enter the flat would place them at an advantage. He opened the door cautiously, his face falling on recognition of what they represented.

'Can I help you?' he asked coldly.

Eleanor took in his features. His eyes were small and deep set, but reflective. His lips were thin and his face slightly overlarge, his brows furrowed more deeply than was typical of a man of his age.

'Mr Stollar? I'm Detective Inspector Eleanor Raven and this is my colleague, Detective Laurence Whitefoot. May we come in?' She leaned her body a little closer, anticipating a positive response.

'What do you want?' Stollar snapped.

'Mr Stollar, we have an extremely delicate matter to discuss and I don't believe the corridor is the best place for it,' replied Eleanor, pushing gently past Stollar.

Before he had a chance to prevent her, she walked straight into the lounge area, which seemed to make Stollar extremely nervous.

'What's the problem?' he asked testily.

'Do you know a Miss Lydia Rachel Greystein?'

She watched as Stollar swallowed hard, a paleness creeping over his collar line.

He nodded. 'Yes – yes I do.'

Eleanor watched him silently as he waited for more. His next words would have a direct bearing on how she tackled the next part of the investigation.

He fidgeted. 'Has anything happened to her?' he said quietly.

Eleanor furrowed her brow but still didn't say anything.

'Has there been an accident?'

'An accident, Mr Stollar? What kind of accident?' she said, knotting her brow in puzzlement.

'A… a car accident?' he said. Now there were beads of sweat appearing on his brow.

'No, I don't think so,' she replied.

'Then why the hell are you here?' he bellowed, losing any attempt at composure.

'Because Miss Greystein has been murdered.'

At that, Stollar staggered backwards and slumped onto his white leather sofa.

'What happened to her?' he asked, his voice shaking.

'Haven't you heard this from her parents?'

'What? Her parents? No, I haven't. When did this happen?' Stollar's hands were now shaking.

'Would you like a drink, Mr Stollar? My colleague will bring you a glass of water.' She nodded to Laurence, who slipped out of the lounge. It would give him a chance to have a quick look around.

'No, I'm fine,' Stollar moaned, but they ignored him. 'I really don't need a drink.'

'When did you see your fiancée last? She was your fiancée, wasn't she?' asked Eleanor.

'What? Yes she… was?'

'Was. She's dead, Mr Stollar. Murdered.'

'I don't… recall,' he said vaguely.

'You don't recall what?' she asked quickly, noting that the window of opportunity was closing. Eric Stollar was a lawyer and thus savvy to interrogation techniques.

He sat himself upright and took a deep breath. Eleanor watched this with interest.

'I don't recall when I saw her last. It was in all probability Friday or Saturday night,' he said calmly.

'Mr Stollar, are you due to make any court appearances this week?' she asked.

'Yes. Why?' He was confused.

She slipped out a small thin notebook and opened it, giving the impression she was checking availability.

'Can I ask when? It would be helpful,' she added politely.

'Tomorrow at 3 p.m. and Friday at 11 a.m.'

'Then why, if you can remember these details, can you not remember the time and date when you last saw the woman you were intending to spend the rest of your life with?' She stared hard at him.

'It was Saturday night at around six. We met at The Rodeo Club and had a couple of drinks and then we parted.' He looked angry.

'Why did you not spend the rest of the evening together?'

'She had a dinner date with her friends.'

'Where?'

'I don't know! Some restaurant on Bloor Street. And no, I don't know who she was meeting,' he snapped.

'How strange,' she added.

'Not at all!'

'When were you due to meet her again?'

'I don't know. We hadn't made any plans.'

'None at all?' replied Eleanor 'Surely you would have some plans to meet this past weekend, or maybe tonight. Did you call her? Were you confused as to why she wasn't answering?'

Stollar's eyes narrowed and he stood up. 'You don't have a search warrant!' He made for the door, but at that moment Laurence walked in, an innocent expression on his face as he handed him a glass of water with several ice cubes in.

'Sorry, couldn't find your glasses,' he said soothingly.

Stollar looked at him in disbelief for a second or two, then took the water and gulped it down. He sighed deeply.

'I need to come and identify her... body,' he said quietly.

'There's no need to do that, Mr Stollar; her parents have already done it,' Eleanor said.

'What! They saw her?'

Eleanor narrowed her eyes. 'Shouldn't they have? They reported her missing this morning. Why didn't you?'

For a moment she thought that Stollar had fallen for the bait, but he had regained sufficient professional sense to close his mouth and keep it closed.

'Here's my card, Mr Stollar.' She handed over the small piece of paper, watching with interest as he hesitated slightly before taking it. 'Please call me if you remember anything that may help us in our investigations. My colleague will make arrangements for you to be formally interviewed at Headquarters. Thank you for your time.'

She turned and headed for the door but stopped when she heard what sounded like a sob. She turned and looked at the man curiously. For a moment she was almost convinced that he was genuinely crying.

'Okay, apart from knowing where he keeps the glasses, what did you find?' asked Eleanor as they both climbed into her car.

'Well his refrigerator had an interesting collection of fountain syringes and other douching equipment. Some weird-looking creams with a high capsaicin content. Do you think he's a hygiene nut or into the kinkier stuff?' asked Laurence.

'What do you mean?'

'Well the label on the cream indicated it was from "The Punishment" range!'

'That can be purchased on the high street. It indicates an interest, not a lifestyle,' snapped Eleanor.

'You said observe. I observed,' replied Laurence.

'I didn't say impose a value judgement on it,' stated Eleanor. 'You start judging people and you're not investigating. You want to evaluate morals then take another sideways move into the judiciary.'

Laurence seemed about to launch a defence but then settled on a different option.

'Okay. I judged… How about a coffee?'

Eleanor set her jaw and then let it relax a little as she wondered whether she wasn't indulging in a bit of hypocrisy herself.

'How about D'Angelo's? I'll pay,' he added as a sweetener. Eleanor tried a smile and turned over the engine.

'Hey, I did see something else. Not sure if it's of any relevance, but he withdrew five grand's worth of cash from his bank account last week. I saw his bank statement on the breakfast bar,' said Laurence.

Eleanor glanced at him. 'And why did that seem relevant?'

'Because that was the only cash withdrawal; he pays for everything on the card. Even his milk and papers.'

Eleanor smiled. 'Now that is interesting.'

CHAPTER SIX

Laurence let out an exaggerated moan as Eleanor drove past D'Angelo's and then took Wellesley in the direction of Police HQ.

'At least let me have a coffee before the boss chews me out,' he muttered.

Eleanor reached into the glove compartment and handed him an energy bar and a can of soda.

'It's not the same!' he whined theatrically.

Eleanor smiled. 'Listen, I have to go and see someone. You need to go and personally make sure that there's a twenty-four-hour solid watch on Barnes. Make sure the paperwork is logged; I don't like wiggle room for the defence,' she said.

'You're not leaving me to go and tackle the boss on my own?'

Eleanor grabbed a page from her reporter's notebook, scribbled a sentence, folded it and stuffed it into his jacket pocket. 'Okay, you go meet Marty and call me if he gets shirty. When you get up there, check the note and see if I'm right.'

She tapped his pocket and ushered him out of the car. 'I'll meet you in D'Angelo's at 7 a.m.' With no further discussion, she drove off.

'What about the debrief? The development of a strategy?' he muttered, and, taking a look up at the third-floor window, made his way into the building.

'Honey, he left at six for his dinner,' said the woman fiddling with a malfunctioning photocopier outside Marty Samuelson's office.

'He did?' Laurence replied, a little astonished that his boss should have left so early in the middle of a major case like this one. Well at least he wouldn't have to face Samuelson on his own.

He was just contemplating his next move when his cell phone rang. 'Hello, Detective Laurence Whitefoot speaking.'

'It's Mags. Just to let you know I let Monster in and I'm back on the eighth as we discussed,' his ex-girlfriend chirped into the phone.

Laurence felt his chest tighten and his heart rate double. 'No! We did not discuss that! You left Monster unattended in the apartment?'

'Oh he's fine now; Sully has been working on his little peccadilloes.'

Sully was Mags' latest 'significant other' and his general approach to dog calming, as it was to all things, including Laurence himself, was to ignore it.

'Peccadilloes? What sort of phrase is that? The dog's a psychopath – he'll destroy my apartment,' raged Laurence.

'Your apartment? The apartment you're squatting in belongs to me, Sully and yourself!' she hissed down the phone.

'How the hell does Sully have any ownership? This is some sort of goddamn joke, isn't it?'

'What's mine is Sully's and vice versa. I'll be back on the eighth!' And with that she disconnected.

'Bitch!' bellowed Laurence as he redialled and heard the answer message kick in. He stared wildly around the corridor and saw the woman looking at him, her mouth open. He inhaled deeply. 'I'm sorry. My ex-girlfriend.'

'No shit!' replied the woman.

Laurence felt his blood pressure rise exponentially as he stood outside his flat and listened to the steady brain-numbing bark of Monster. His hands shook with rage as he tried to insert the key. At this the barking stopped and some heavy, hysterical movement began to take place from somewhere in the flat. For one tantalising moment, Laurence had a fantasy that Sully had actually tamed Monster and he would be sitting obediently in the kitchen, but on opening the door and seeing the chaos through a cloud of drifting feathers, reality hit. Laurence heard a strange whining noise but suspected it was emanating from him rather than Monster, who was keeping a low profile.

'Monster?' he called, through gritted teeth.

The German shepherd burst happily from the bedroom, carrying one of Laurence's Italian brogues in his mouth. Laurence whipped his pistol from its holster and levelled the barrel at Monster, who, suspecting that manners were required, duly flipped onto his back, tail wagging.

Laurence tried to calm his breathing and was lowering the weapon when he caught sight of the photograph pinned to the refrigerator. It showed Monster, his tongue lolling out of his stupid face, Mags and Sully arm in arm behind him, waving like the bloody Waltons, and a handwritten note proclaiming 'Back on the eighth!'

Laurence fired one shot at the photo. It tore through Monster's temple, just above the right eye, and then, as he would later discover, embedded itself in a risotto that had been sitting between two ancient and unloved bags of seasonal greens. The sound ricocheted around the flat, triggering the real Monster's bowels to open alarmingly and pungently.

*

Eleanor sat on Minnie's small occasional chair in her sitting room and stared at Mo. His face was an alarming porcelain shade and the weight he was losing, due to Minnie's strict dietary regime and the gastric band, seemed to be slipping from his face and neck down his chest and arms and into what could be mistaken for a flaccid tyre around his waist. His breathing was erratic, punctuated by a slurping cough.

'So, why do you think Stollar didn't call it in?' he gasped, settling himself into a more comfortable position. Eleanor had given Mo a complete debrief, probably one she should have presented to her boss and new partner, as Mo had sagely observed. 'You think he's guilty? Statistics say he is,' he added.

'Not sure,' she replied slowly. 'I think there's some sort of link between him and her death but I don't know what it is yet.'

'What about the cards? The kidnappings to order?'

'Again, I'm not sure. We've got a tail on Cheswell Barnes and hopefully he's going to give us a lead in that direction.'

'You think this is a kinky kidnapping that went wrong?' Mo asked.

Eleanor thought for a minute before answering. 'I don't think this kidnapping went wrong at all. It was minutely planned, and our perp covered his tracks.'

'You think some guy's advertising for murder volunteers?' Mo asked, bewildered. 'Well it takes the guesswork out of selecting a victim! It seems to me that there's the key. Find out who's behind this kidnapping business and you'll find your guy.'

Exhausted, Mo slumped back into his seat and belched loudly. 'Goddamn gastric band!'

Eleanor stood up. Seeing Mo was a double-edged sword: he looked like he was about to keel over and die, but talking through the case had helped clarify it for her. 'Time to see what Mr Barnes is up to I think,' she said quietly.

'You keep me up to speed, okay?'

Eleanor nodded and made her way to the door. 'Sure will, boss.'

'Hey, you never told me what this new guy's like?' asked Mo, but Eleanor carried on going, slipping quietly out of the house into the night.

*

Laurence wasn't sure how long he'd been sitting staring at the stinking pool of dog faeces. Monster had slunk under the dining table to freshen his nether regions noisily while Laurence came to terms with his arrival. He became aware that where a bowl of apples and citrus fruit had been, there was now an empty bowl, and he could only deduce that Monster had eaten every unsuitable item of food he could find, which had led to the explosion.

Sighing, Laurence pulled himself to his feet and tried to mentally organise a cleaning strategy. Failing to do that, he flung his jacket onto a chair, opened the now ominously hissing refrigerator and reached for a beer. As he tipped it down his throat, he caught sight of the piece of paper that Eleanor had stuffed into his pocket and picked it up cautiously. It read: 'Samuelson went home for his dinner at six!'

He smiled broadly, and then his face sank as he remembered the other task that he'd failed to carry out.

With the sudden flurry of activity as Laurence grabbed his coat and holstered his pistol, Monster recommenced his insane barking.

'No! Shut up!'

At this, the panicking dog began to intersperse the barks with yowls of misery.

'Oh my God!' yelled Laurence as he unclasped his belt and threaded it violently through Monster's collar.

It was with the anticipation of a walk that Monster trotted complacently alongside Laurence as he headed for his car.

'You're saying that there isn't a single patrolman or detective that can cover a watch? Really? Really?' snapped Laurence.

'Honey, you heard me say that! If you want surveillance then you apply through the proper channels and don't leave it till the night shift when I ain't got no officers free!'

'But this is part of a major murder investigation,' Laurence whined.

'Then you had better do it yourself, Detective,' answered the duty sergeant and rang off. Laurence flung the cell phone onto the passenger seat and accelerated through the traffic in the direction of Cheswell Barnes' home.

CHAPTER SEVEN

Laurence found Eleanor watching with interest as he made his way over to her table, precariously balancing two cups of coffee and a tray of mixed pastries on one arm and holding a pile of paperwork in the other. 'I've got a coffee thanks,' she said.

'They're both for me,' he growled.

He saw her take in his appearance – his uncombed hair, slept-in shirt and the dog hairs covering his trousers.

'How long before Patrolman Ellis turned up?' she asked innocently.

'You sent him?'

'I checked with the duty sergeant. She said you hadn't organised a watch so I did.' She sipped her coffee.

'He turned up at six. When did you call?' he asked suspiciously.

Eleanor grimaced. 'You really need a shower and some deodorant.'

Laurence contemplated making a snippy comment and asking her whether she could have got the surveillance earlier, but it had been his job and he'd forgotten. He'd been so damned grateful when Ellis had tapped on his car window and explained that he'd been sent to take over watching Barnes' house, but now he was flagging and twenty-four hours without sleep was taking its toll.

'Thanks… sorry, I should have—'

'The cell number on the card is registered to a Miss Evelyn Strange. It's a pay-as-you-go account and so far has never been topped up. So it's used for incoming calls only,' she cut in. 'We've left two messages, one by Wadesky and another by Timms, hoping we'll get some feedback.'

'Was the phone purchased locally?'

'Molto Electronics, city-centre branch. Smith's going over today with mugshots, but don't waste hope on that one,' she responded.

'Hmm.' Laurence shovelled down another pastry. 'Okay, we know that Cheswell Barnes is in some way connected with this.'

'We think he is,' Eleanor corrected him. 'We have his fingerprints and a plausible explanation from his girlfriend as to why they're there. You said yourself it seemed unlikely that either Sashia or Barnes could have dragged our victim's body up the side of a thirty-foot wall.'

'So what is the connection?' he heard himself snap.

Eleanor raised an eyebrow. 'Icebergs. Whatever's visible above the surface, there's ninety per cent we can't see underneath.'

Laurence looked at her with incomprehension.

'You've met Sashia and Barnes, but I bet there are a few individuals lurking under the surface that we haven't got on our radar.'

'Shall I get onto that this morning?' Laurence asked, polishing off the last of the pastries.

'Wadesky's working on that. You are going to shower, make yourself look and smell presentable and join me for an eight-thirty meeting with Mr Stollar and his legal representation,' she said, rising to her feet and grabbing her bag. 'Bum a shirt off Smith; he's about your size, and ditch the dog hairs.'

Laurence looked at his trousers, which were coated in black and tan hairs. He groaned, swilled down his coffee and, remembering that he'd left a toiletries bag in his trunk, headed off to the car.

Monster had filled the car with humidity and methane, and was now draped lethargically over the driver's seat, whimpering miserably. Hearing the trunk being opened, he began to bark hysterically, causing several officers heading over to their vehicles to look over in alarm.

Laurence gritted his teeth, snatched his bag and was just closing the lid when he felt a firm tap on his shoulder.

'How long has your dog been in the car, sir?' asked a young officer wearing mirrored sunglasses.

'What?'

'Your dog, sir? He seems distressed,' he stated calmly.

'I'm distressed!' snapped Laurence. 'He's not my dog.'

He saw the patrol officer's eyebrows rise with interest and felt that now was not the time to launch into the saga of his relationship with Mags.

'He's coming with me,' said Laurence, opening the car door and watching as Monster leaped out, buried his head in the officer's outstretched hand and began to shudder dramatically.

'You're lucky to have such a nice dog, sir,' said the patrolman while patting Monster's head, his voice laden with subtext.

'Hmm,' said Laurence, yanking out his trouser belt, threading it through Monster's collar and pulling him inside and in the direction of the lift. The patrolman followed him.

'May I suggest you purchase the correct leading equipment, sir?' he said as the lift doors opened.

Laurence stared at him with undisguised anger. 'May I suggest that you go—' His trenchant advice was swallowed into the lift as the doors closed.

*

'What the hell are you eating?' asked Wadesky, her face displaying her disgust.

'This,' responded Timms happily, removing a moist, dangerously tiered beige-coloured item from his mouth, 'is the nectar of the gods.'

Wadesky appraised Timms' flabby backside, which had plonked itself uninvited on the edge of her desk. 'You are gonna die… soon,' she said, glancing at her laptop screen and huffing.

'Honey, we is all gonna die, but on whose terms, eh?' Timms smiled smugly.

'You're an idiot! Get your ass off my table before it collapses and don't speak to me until your mouth is empty.'

Unoffended, Timms lumbered over to his desk to gather his thoughts.

'Whoa! Well look what mama's just found!' said Wadesky. 'Cheswell Barnes has been networking, and look who he's chummed up with?'

Timms, still chewing, leaned over her shoulder to read the information on the screen.

'Now that is nasty,' he replied, looking at the image and curriculum vitae that had appeared. 'Mr Feodor Yesikov, aged thirty-eight, served ten of an eighteen-year sentence for the rape of a minor. Released in 2010, and when we look at who his bunk mates are we see… Cheswell Barnes!'

Wadesky typed rapidly and they both waited as the city probation service confirmed that Feodor had left prison and moved in with Sashia Irina Yesikov – his paternal cousin – and Cheswell Barnes, whom he had shared a cell with at the penitentiary.

Timms peered at the screen and jotted down the number of the assigned probation officer and headed off to his desk. Wadesky pressed 'print' and carried on digging.

Timms dialled the number and waited.

'Hey…' said a doleful voice.

'This is Detective Timms. Am I speaking to Samson Orbrook?'

'Uh-huh!'

'You are the probation officer assigned to Feodor Yesikov?'

'Uh-huh.'

Timms felt his dangerously high blood pressure notch a little higher. 'You can speak, can't you? Or are you one of those token "special needs" appointments the city has to make to get the minorities vote!'

He noticed Wadesky rolling her eyes from the opposite desk.

'I can speak,' sighed Samson wearily.

'Well if you can spare the jaw time, I'd like to ask you about Feodor?'

'Uh-huh… yup, what d'ya wanna know?'

'Where is he? Have you been in regular contact? Where does he work? You know, the sort of information you'd have at your fingertips, eh?'

There was a pause, followed by another sigh.

'I haven't seen Feodor Yesikov for three months now.'

'Why not?' replied Timms.

'He disappeared.'

'What d'ya mean "he disappeared"?' snapped Timms dangerously.

'Look, Detective. I have at least seventy per cent of my clients missing at any one time. You know how difficult it is to keep track of people who don't want to be kept track of?' Samson's voice trailed off as he heard Timms growl. 'Last time I saw him he was working at the Ford dealership on Dundas. He was staying with his cousin; can't remember her name… He kept most of his appointments and then, about three months ago, he disappeared off the radar,' he ventured more helpfully.

'What did you do?' asked Timms.

'I spoke to his cousin – Sashia, that's her name! And she said he'd upped and left without paying her rent and that she'd let me know if he showed.'

'And you believed her?'

'Of course I didn't! But I don't have surveillance capacity, and the city police – that'd be you – said they were too busy to put out a watch.' There was a meaningful pause. 'Look, if you want me to forward my files I'll send them today, and I can make another call to Sashia, but experience tells me unless he gets pulled for another crime, you ain't gonna find him.'

*

Laurence moved swiftly towards the interrogation suite, ignoring Lucy, the civilian typist, who was pointing meaningfully at Monster – who was lying across her feet snoozing, having consumed her lunch uninvited. As he opened the door he hoped that the shirt he'd borrowed off Smith, who was at least six inches shorter than him, didn't look quite as ridiculous as he suspected it did.

'This is Detective Laurence Whitefoot,' said Eleanor.

'Rudy Suchet,' the lawyer said, thrusting out a hand to Laurence. Eric Stollar sat at the table, his hands folded on his lap and his back rigid.

'Mr Stollar has asked me as his colleague and friend to accompany him today and assist with the provision of information which hopefully will bring the killer of his fiancée, Lydia Greystein, to justice.'

'Hmmm,' said Eleanor, staring at him.

There was a pause as Stollar gradually met her eye. Eleanor looked steadily at him, apparently waiting for the uncomfortable shifting around that went with silences and the anticipation of interrogation – but Stollar had had time to draw on his professional reserves and wasn't going to be broken so easily.

'Detective? Do you have any questions?' asked Suchet slowly.

'What do you know about the death of Miss Greystein?' asked Eleanor.

Suchet's mouth moved to open, but Stollar broke in.

'Nothing,' he replied. 'Absolutely nothing.'

'Why not?' she asked, leaning towards him and keeping her unblinking eyes fixed on his.

'Because no one has felt it appropriate to share any details with me, despite the fact that Lydia was my fiancée,' he said, with a hint of anger.

'Is it because you already know what happened to her?'

'Are you implying that my client—'

'I thought you said you were here as a colleague and friend, Mr Suchet?' said Eleanor.

'I am, but your tone is becoming more accusatory and—'

'Decide what your role is and stick to it!' Eleanor snapped and turned back to Stollar. 'This is what I think, Eric. You arranged a kinky little session for your girlfriend, and during the fun and games, things got a little out of hand and you killed her. Am I right?'

Stollar's face began to redden. 'I have an alibi for the night she was killed.'

'Why?'

'What do you mean why? I was out with friends,' he spluttered.

'Why weren't you with Lydia? We've called several of her friends and she hadn't made any plans to meet them. Was she having an affair?'

'No!'

'Are you sure?'

'Yes,' he hissed, leaning closer to Eleanor.

'Then you knew where she was, didn't you, Mr Stollar?' said Eleanor quietly as she placed the card they'd found in the restroom, still in its evidence bag, in front of Stollar. His breathing became shallower and his shoulders began to slump. She had him. It was only a matter of minutes now.

Suchet leaned over Stollar's shoulder and whispered a command to stop talking now.

'You arranged a kidnapping for Lydia. Thought she'd have a sexy time; a bit of fun. But something went very wrong, didn't it, Eric?'

'I am advising my client to—'

Suchet's voice was drowned out by the scream that emanated from Eric Stollar's throat. Everyone jumped, apart from Eleanor, who had obviously been anticipating some sort of reaction.

'It was a present. That's all. She was totally into… bondage and she'd wanted me to dress up and do it, but I'm a lawyer; if I got caught kidnapping her on the street I'd never work again!' His voice was almost a shriek, and it took Laurence a great deal of control not to put his hands over his ears at the sheer impact of the noise in such a constricted space.

'And now she's dead!'

Eleanor stood up and pressed a hand onto his shuddering shoulder. 'Look at me, Eric!'

Slowly he focussed on her.

'You've messed up, but now is the time to start making things right again.' She paused, clearly wanting to ensure he absorbed her next words. 'I need to catch this murderer, Eric, and in order to do that I want your complete cooperation. Do you understand what I'm saying?'

Suchet cleared his throat and made a move towards Stollar but froze in his tracks as Eleanor shot a warning finger up to him.

'You will tell me everything.'

Stollar made small glugging sounds as he nodded carefully.

'Everything,' he whimpered.

'Why did you go back to Xxxstacy yesterday?'

Stollar looked confused.

'We watched you,' said Eleanor.

'I went to see if there was a number: a card, anything that would tell me who she was with.' Stollar's voice cracked as he spoke. 'I needed to know what had happened, so I tried to get the number of the guy she spoke to, but there wasn't—'

'Lydia spoke to him?' interjected Eleanor.

'Yes. She arranged it and I left the money at Xxxstacy.'

'Do you know how she got the contact number?' asked Eleanor. Laurence noted a trace of excitement in her voice.

'Her friend did it and recommended it to her.'

'Did it?' asked Eleanor.

Stollar's voice began to rise in pitch. 'You know, experienced a kidnapping party. I went to the club to see if there was a business card. I don't know what I thought.'

'What's the friend's name?'

Stollar shook his head. 'She sometimes went to the club.'

'Xxxstacy?'

'Yes, I met her once. But Lydia had known her from somewhere else… her gym, that's it. She went to the same gym, on Wellesley.'

'When did Lydia first run the idea past you?'

'I don't really remember; a couple of weeks ago. It was a sort of anniversary and I wanted to treat her.'

There was a pause as Stollar tried to regain control. 'Lydia told me to drop the money off at the bar, give the barman a fifty as a handling fee and then wait for a call on Saturday. She was so thrilled with the idea. Look.' He leaned closer to Eleanor and dropped his voice. 'Lydia was a goddamn princess. I'd have done anything, *anything* to make her happy. Do you understand? If she wanted a huge diamond ring, it was hers. Likewise, if she wanted to explore the boundaries of her sexuality then so be it!'

Eleanor nodded slowly.

'You catch the bastard who did this! Promise me!'

'I will,' replied Eleanor. 'You have my word.'

CHAPTER EIGHT

Ellis was bored; monumentally bored. He had watched the front of the house for the past seven hours and not a bloody thing had happened, except for a cat being booted out through the front door. He'd felt pretty good when he'd received a call from Detective Raven. It had indicated to him that she trusted him, recognised that he was an officer capable of thinking 'outside the box'. However, the reality of surveillance work was beginning to hit him; it was a snore. He had let his bladder accumulate what felt like several litres of urine in the belief that the discomfort would prevent him dozing off, and so far, it seemed to be working. Unfortunately, the safety margins of his bladder retention were being passed, and after a quick glance around, he opened the driver's door and gingerly stepped out. If he kept low, he could scoot round the side of a hedge, opposite the Barnes' house, and unload.

He had emptied about a quarter when he saw the front door open. A white van drew up in front of the house and the two suspects emerged quickly from the house. A stocky figure climbed out of the driver's seat and went round to the back of the van, where he and Sashia were ushered in by Cheswell, who then climbed into the driver's seat and revved the engine. With a lurch, the van headed off in a northerly direction, leaving Ellis to leap into his car and swerve into the road behind them, still a good half litre short of comfort.

There were several cars in front of Ellis, but by the clouds of burning engine oil, he imagined keeping up with the van wouldn't prove too challenging. He called in and was patched through to Timms.

'What've you got, buddy?'

'I'm following a white van, reg Alpha Bravo Echo Sierra 189,' said Ellis.

'Uh-huh?' said Timms, nonplussed.

'Three individuals travelling north along Queen's. Hang on, it's making a left at the next junction… yup, we're on Elmore Avenue now.'

'Well who's in the van and why am I interested?' snapped Timms.

'Oh sorry, Cheswell Barnes and Sashia Yesikov. I was put through to you because Detective Raven is interrogating—'

'Who's the third?' interrupted Timms.

'I don't know.'

'He look Russian, ugly?'

'I didn't catch a good look. Pretty sure it was a male, but the windows to the back are blacked out. Hang on…'

He heard Timms let out a sigh of exasperation.

'Okay, they've cut off the main street and are parked in an alley next to Hunca Munca Vegan Foods and—'

'What the hell is a Hunca Munca?'

'Whoa something's happening.' Ellis watched as Cheswell Barnes stepped out of the van and looked around. He had what looked like a photograph in his hand and was glancing at passing women and then the photograph. 'I think he's looking for someone.'

'Cavalry's on its way, buddy.'

*

Eleanor watched with interest as Laurence extracted a twenty from his wallet and paid Big Al. He seemed to have accepted that he would be paying for all coffees and lunches in this partnership for the foreseeable future, a position encouraged by Eleanor. He placed the cup in front of her.

'You think Stollar was telling the truth?' asked Laurence, emitting a shower of pastry crumbs.

'He was consistent in the facts, and I suspect that he's striving for forgiveness. So logic says he's being subjectively truthful, if not entirely accurate,' she replied.

'You think he's holding back?'

'Not at all. But the mind protects us. Particularly if we're motivated by guilt or fear of being judged, and events may become warped, tipped in our favour. It's our job to tease out the objective truths.'

Laurence absorbed this. 'So where do we start?'

'How do you think?' she asked Laurence seriously.

He paused. 'Um.'

'Do you absorb verbal facts or do we have to visualise the data?' she asked curtly.

'I'm sorry. I didn't... visualising helps,' he spluttered, obviously unsure of her meaning.

Eleanor turned over one of the paper menus and began to draw a spider diagram. In the centre, she wrote 'perp', circled it and linked it to the name 'Lydia'. Laurence smiled encouragement and nodded. Eleanor handed him the pen.

'Lydia likes her sex rough, but Stollar doesn't want to be caught doing something nasty,' said Laurence, pen poised.

'Nasty? That's a judgement call, Detective,' said Eleanor coldly.

'Sorry, yes. Well they were both into BDSM...' He waited till Eleanor nodded her approval. 'But Stollar didn't want to... didn't feel he could role-play a kidnapping on the street in case he was caught and compromised. But then she sees the ad in Xxxstacy and phones the perp. He then arranges to leave five thousand in cash behind the bar where it's collected—'

'How do you know it's been collected?' asked Eleanor.

'Shit!' Laurence gulped his coffee dregs and, grabbing the menu, they headed out.

*

Ellis tried to formulate a possible scenario as to what the hell Cheswell Barnes was doing. So far he hadn't come up with anything plausible.

Barnes, after having presumably memorised the photograph – his tongue sticking out as he gazed – was now hiding behind an upside-down newspaper and peering over the top, watching as the occasional woman passed along the street. He hadn't given men a second glance. A couple of the women he had scrutinised carefully and made little hopping movements as if unsure whether he should act.

There had been no sign of either Sashia or the unknown male in the back of the van, and despite the fascination of watching Cheswell Barnes acting like the dumbest asshole he'd ever seen, Ellis was beginning to worry that he'd called Timms out prematurely.

Suddenly, Barnes stood straight and stared intently at a woman who had appeared at the entrance of the avenue and was now walking casually towards the van. Barnes gave the photo one last check and then made his way rapidly to the driver's seat and started the engine. Ellis saw that the white van would go straight past him, so he lowered himself in his seat, trying to look as if he were taking a nap.

'Timms? This is Ellis.'

'Yeah, nearly with ya!' came the response.

'The van is making a U-turn and seems to be heading towards a white woman, twenties – no, definitely thirties – wearing…' Ellis stared hard at the woman's attire; it consisted of a gabardine raincoat tied loosely at the waist, fishnet stockings and black patent high-heeled shoes.

'I think she might be a prostitute,' said Ellis weakly, not really convinced that this would be acceptable amongst the hookers he knew. They had a tendency to dress for a fast getaway: Nike trainers, joggers and sports tops.

'What the hell's happening?' bellowed Timms.

'The van's slowing next to her. Should I attempt an arrest?'

'No, just keep on their tail. We're two blocks behind you. Keep on this channel. Got it?'

'Yes, sir,' replied Ellis, turning over the engine.

As he did, he saw the woman spot the van and then begin to trot away on her impossible heels. The back doors flew open and the stocky man leaped out, grabbed the now struggling woman and flung her into the back. The doors were pulled shut, and the vehicle accelerated in a cloud of black smoke before swerving dangerously into the traffic stream.

'Oh Christ, they've got her! This is a 10-35! I repeat: a 10-35!' shrieked Ellis, as he accelerated towards the van. 'He's turning onto Dayton Street!'

'Dayton? That's gonna get him boxed in,' replied Timms.

'Yes, Dayton. I'm following. He's turned into an unnamed alley between two warehouses, opposite the tyre place. Should I park?' Ellis asked nervously.

'We're pulling in to your right and backup's sealing off their exit, okay?'

Ellis looked to his left and saw Timms and Wadesky moving quickly across the street, both hands wrapped round their weapons. Wadesky approached Ellis's window and tapped lightly.

'Okay, buddy, you armed?' asked Wadesky.

Ellis nodded and stepped quickly out of the car.

'You follow Timms' lead; I'm behind you both.'

With a quick glance at Wadesky's belly, Ellis followed Timms to the corner of the alley. Using rapid finger movements, Timms gestured that he would move in first and Ellis would follow. Ellis had made arrests before, and several had required a quick fist to a drunken jaw, but this was big-league crime and he felt his adrenaline levels soar.

The van was squeezed next to a small fire door, which had been left slightly ajar, a brick preventing it from slamming to in the wind. Ellis's gaze flicked from the van to Timms, who was peering around a brick wall, waiting for the sign that would activate the operation. When it came, Timms held up three fingers and counted down by the second.

Timms moved more stealthily than Ellis thought possible for a man of so many years and calories. The younger man dropped in behind him and took up a hostile position ten feet clear of the van door.

Timms indicated that Ellis should open the vehicle's doors; Wadesky covered the driver's door from the entrance to the alley. Ellis reached out his hand and touched the door handle, but before he could surprise the kidnappers, the van doors burst open, revealing Feodor Yesikov with the kidnap victim draped over his shoulder. Her gabardine raincoat was now missing and she was clad only in high heels, fishnet stockings and a black satin basque, which was doing sterling work holding in her ample figure.

'Hands up!' shrieked Ellis.

Feodor's mouth fell open in complete surprise as he tried to understand the scene in front of him. Not having either the wit or imagination to do that, he dropped the woman and shot both hands into the air.

Ellis watched in horror as she rolled off Feodor's shoulder onto the floor of the van and then bounced noisily onto the tarmac. Forgetting protocol, he leaped forward and tried to help the groaning woman.

'Step out of the van!' yelled Timms.

Wadesky had moved forward and was gesturing to Cheswell Barnes with her gun to step out of the driver's seat. Feodor lowered himself to the ground and walked towards Timms, followed by Sashia, clad in thigh-length leather boots, leather catsuit and studded gauntlets.

Gently, Ellis pulled the blindfold away from the woman's eyes. 'Are you injured? My name is patrolman Stephen Ellis and—'

'You bastard!' screamed the victim and swung her fist in a confident arch; it landed with an explosive impact on Ellis's cheek.

'W-What the…' he stammered, vaguely aware that both Timms and Sashia were sniggering.

'You absolute bastard!' repeated the woman, staggering to her feet.

Bemused, Ellis tried to dust her down in a caring yet appropriate manner. He was rewarded by a second bone-crunching smack to the face.

'I've been saving since Christmas for this!'

CHAPTER NINE

Eleanor stared at the bartender's face. His eyes flicked nervously and he curled his sweaty top lip under his teeth as he evaded their questions. 'You're telling me that the package left by Mr Stollar has disappeared. You don't recall who collected it, but someone did. Is that right?'

'Yup, that's it,' replied the bartender.

'Why don't I believe you then?' said Eleanor, her voice taking on a dangerous edge.

He shrugged. 'I dunno.'

'It's because you took the money and that makes you our lead suspect in the murder investigation,' said Eleanor pointedly.

'Look, *he* said—'

'Who's he? Stollar?'

'Yes, Stollar. He said the money would be picked up by Saturday.' The bartender's expression was changing from shifty concealment to the hangdog misery of the cornered. 'But no one came. I worked all Friday and Saturday and no one came and asked for it!'

'So you stole it,' said Laurence.

'No! I borrowed it.'

'Uh-huh, so you've put it back then?'

'No, I owed money to Rico Martinez and I thought—'

'That if you bet the money on Rico's notoriously fixed mutt races then you'd replace the five K and pay off Rico?'

The bartender nodded enthusiastically, pleased that they appreciated his logic.

'But being the only idiot still sucking breath this side of Mars, you didn't realise that you never pay off a gambling debt to Rico Martinez. He's a doper.'

'I... I... not necessarily,' stammered the bartender weakly.

'Bet big on a dog and pup gets a diazepam mixed in with his kibble,' said Eleanor. 'So now we've exhausted all the things you don't know, what *do* you know?'

'Nothing,' said the bartender miserably.

'"Nothing" gets you eighteen months to three and a cosy meeting with Rico's buddies inside,' said Eleanor.

'Look, I dunno what happened, but all the money that got left here before always got collected.' He leaned towards Eleanor. 'Some Russian guy collected. Big guy, nasty, but he always collected same day they dropped it. This time, nothing, so I figured...' His voice trailed off.

'You figured he'd been arrested or knocked off and the money was there for the taking,' said Eleanor helpfully.

He nodded.

'How many times has this happened before?' she asked.

'Three, four maybe... about once a week.'

'Did you know the people who dropped off the money?'

'Yeah.' He nodded. 'Regulars, you know.'

Eleanor nodded. 'You need to get your ass down to the station and tell all of this to my colleague Detective Sarah Wadesky. I want names. Today!' she said emphatically, handing him her card.

*

'Soooo,' drawled Timms, taking a seat next to Ellis in the canteen, 'this is what our "victim"' – Timms waved air quotes – 'has agreed to.' He paused. 'If you apologise for spoiling her spa day in the dungeon of Madam Yesikov, she'll drop charges.'

Ellis's mouth dropped open in disbelief. 'She *what*? What charges?'

Timms flipped open his notebook and read them out. 'Endangering her person while making a false arrest... um... oh yeah! Causing actual bodily harm by forcing the lovely Feodor to drop her several feet onto the ground and, finally, she wants her five thousand refunding.' Timms folded his notebook and grinned.

'I saved her!' Ellis raged.

'No you didn't,' replied Timms, wagging a finger at him. 'Miss Stone was engaged in a prearranged consensual sex act, which constituted no breach of the peace and did not infringe anyone's human rights.' He let this outrage sink in. 'You could also be charged internally with improper use of police resources.'

'What the hell! I thought she was being raped and murdered,' bellowed Ellis, launching himself to his feet.

Several patrolmen turned to stare at him. Timms reached over and helped himself to Ellis's half-eaten sandwich and cold coffee.

'Relax. No one here's gonna press charges against one of their own.' He pulled a face as he tasted Ellis's coffee and stirred three more sugars in.

'What about Miss Stone?'

'Depends whether she's willing to pay out for a good lawyer.' He took a bite. 'Oooh nice,' he said, chewing appreciatively.

*

Wadesky rubbed her tender back as she listened to Sashia run through the details of her sordid enterprise for the second time. Both women were bored and in need of a hot bath. Sashia's leather apparel must have been chafing due to the amount of fidgeting she was doing.

'I tell you once more and this is the last time, okay,' said Sashia peevishly, pulling indiscreetly at her crotch. 'I run very legitimate business. I have full year's lease on property in Dayton Street.'

'Your dungeon?' asked Wadesky, without a hint of irony.

'Yes,' snapped Sashia. 'My dungeon. Which observes health and safety regulations.'

At that, Wadesky couldn't suppress a snigger.

'What? I am conscientious citizen who has business degree and pays taxes. I find niche in marketplace and exploit it. Women want to be kidnapped and have big strong Russian man dominate them, and they pay for pleasure. No one gets hurt!'

Both Wadesky and Sashia looked up as Eleanor slipped into the room.

'This is Detective Inspector Eleanor Raven and she's in charge of the investigation into the murder of Lydia Greystein,' said Wadesky.

'That is nothing to do with me!' hissed Sashia.

*

Eleanor appraised the woman sitting in front of her and found her intriguing. Her assured manner and blaring sexuality had a dangerous appeal to her – a thought that didn't appear to be lost on Sashia, whose lips curled cat-like as Eleanor took a seat opposite her.

'Ask your questions,' purred Sashia.

'I've got a dead woman tortured to death after her boyfriend bought her a "red letter" kidnap day. You have been arrested carrying out an identical activity. I'm assuming you're not going to deny that?'

'Of course not! But did my lady complain about her treatment?' Sashia leaned towards Eleanor.

'She complained mostly about the arresting officer,' responded Eleanor.

'Exactly!' Sashia banged her hand on the desk. 'There are no complaints from my customers.'

'But this is the problem,' said Eleanor. 'Lydia Greystein didn't make any complaints because somebody killed her. Someone using your business card, or one similar, picked Lydia up and murdered her. Now, convince me that it couldn't have been you, Cheswell Barnes or your delightful cousin Feodor.'

'Depo-Provera,' said Sashia smugly.

'How do you know he's taking it?' asked Eleanor.

'Because I inject him myself!' barked Sashia. 'I control my employees!'

'What is Depo…?' flailed Wadesky.

'Depo-Provera, aka medroxyprogesterone acetate,' answered Eleanor.

'Birth control?' said Wadesky, confused.

'Chemical castration for Feodor,' replied Eleanor.

Sashia nodded and smiled, inhaling deeply on a cigarette. 'Such a nice boy now. Very accommodating.'

*

Laurence hovered around the doorway of the Bodyworks Gym, observing the clientele for several minutes before entering. The atrium was decorated with large black-and-white photographs illustrating what the management considered the perfect human frame draped appropriately across various pieces of gym equipment. Unlike the station gym, which reeked of sweat, trainers and nicotine, this gym was bathed in flattering lights and perfumes. It was Laurence's considered opinion that only gay guys and wealthy bitches frequented this sort of establishment, probably because they were the only ones who could afford the monthly fees.

The brilliant white smile that had greeted him at the desk disappeared instantly the moment Laurence wafted his badge under her nose like a bad smell.

'We don't discuss our clients with outside agencies,' she snipped.

Laurence sighed deeply. 'Look, a member of your gym has been murdered under extremely unpleasant circumstances.'

He paused to stare at the receptionist, whose eyes didn't even flicker. Perhaps, he thought, client murder was an everyday occurrence here. He waded further.

'The victim had a friend here who supplied her with some information that may prove vital to solving this case. So your cooperation would be both appropriate under the circumstances and appreciated.'

He softened his expression and raised an eyebrow in what Mags had always claimed to be a winning combination, but it obviously lacked universal appeal as the receptionist added another layer of frost to her already icy expression.

'Or I could just hang around the entrance and piss your clients off when they come in,' said Laurence stonily.

Two jocks, clad in at least fifteen hundred bucks' worth of anti-sweat, anti-blister attire, bounced over to the desk. The receptionist's face was instantly suffused with radiance as she handed over a pile of thick, white towels.

'Hey, honey, is Tracy here?' asked one guy.

'She is, but she's just finishing with a client. Shall I page her?' purred the receptionist. The jock smiled and blew her a kiss as he wandered towards the changing room with his buddy.

'You and Tracy are on my radar,' he cooed as he disappeared inside with his smirking buddy.

Laurence watched the receptionist simper and had to make a titanic effort to prevent his eyeballs rolling skyward.

As soon as the door swished closed, the icy expression returned as she focussed her attention on Laurence once again.

'Give me her name,' she hissed.

'Lydia… Lydia Greystein,' he said.

'I can confirm she was a member of this gym,' replied the receptionist, with finality.

'Uh-huh. Who was her friend here?'

'I have no idea as to her social networking,' replied the woman, with a hint of outrage.

Laurence turned from the desk and walked purposefully towards the main door, flipping open his badge with the obvious intention of accosting the next individual to cross the threshold. He heard a scurrying sound and turned to face the receptionist.

'Lydia always booked with Tracy,' she spat.

'Tracy, as in "with a client" Tracy?'

Her eyes narrowed. 'Yes.'

Laurence paused, his eyebrows rising. 'She one of the personal trainers?'

'She's a posture therapist.'

'A what?'

'She's in the main gym on the first floor. They finish in ten, okay?'

'Thank you for your cooperation,' said Laurence, with minimum irony.

Laurence had prepared himself for a similarly frosty reception from Tracy but was pleasantly surprised by her open manner and very appreciative of her sculpted frame. Laurence estimated her to be around five-foot-eleven, and her figure was a testament to healthy living and a lifetime of excessive exercise. Her thick blonde hair was expensively cut and curled round her strong features.

'I didn't know Lydie terribly well. I've got a few clients and run one or two classes, so I don't get much time to build up meaningful relationships, but she's okay... why?' asked Tracy, daubing the negligible sweat from her brow with a towel.

'You seemed to have several interests in common,' said Laurence carefully. He watched her expression harden slightly.

'Such as? And what's this all about anyway? Is there a problem with Lydie?' asked Tracy.

'She's been murdered,' replied Laurence.

'Oh my God! How?' gasped Tracy, leaning back against the wall for support.

'She decided to take your advice and have a kidnapping arranged,' said Laurence, gauging her reaction.

A look of complete incomprehension glazed her expression. 'I don't understand. You mean she met up with Madam Sashia? But—'

'We don't know who she met up with. Her intention seemed to be to experience the same...' Laurence felt himself flailing a little. 'The same kinky kidnapping as you did.'

Tracy was beginning to look a little nauseous and asked in a quiet, trembling voice if Laurence minded carrying on his questioning in the staff canteen where she could get a coffee.

A short while later, Tracy stared at her coffee, her long manicured fingers wrapped tightly around the cup.

'I've been to Madam Sashia's place a couple of times but only did the kidnapping once. It's a great way to get turned on and relax, but it's expensive.'

Tracy studied Laurence's face and smiled. 'I know it sounds a bit sick, but it's just a game, and the master is kinda sexy but not too scary.'

'You mean Feodor?'

She nodded. 'Look, I've never been injured. A couple of pinches and bruises but nothing nasty.'

'How does it work? How do you determine what's going to happen to you?' Laurence was trying not to appear salacious but was genuinely interested in how the enterprise worked.

'You have a consultation with Madam and she determines how far you want to go and what sort of thing it is that gets you off. Then you arrive at her dungeon and that's it.'

'How do you pay?'

'It cost a thousand a session, but the kidnapping was five thousand in cash. I had to leave that behind the bar at Xxxstacy. The other sessions I always paid for when I got there.'

'Why was this a different arrangement?'

'I guess because you weren't really sure when it was all gonna kick off. I chose the day and was told to walk along Elmore Avenue near to that vegan restaurant. There was an alley there and I should maybe walk up and down it. So, I walked around and then suddenly I was blindfolded and chucked in the back of a van. Next thing I was in the dungeon. It was fun but kinda overpriced for a ten-minute drive with Feodor sitting on top of me. I was hoping they'd arranged a new venue.' She giggled lightly and sipped her coffee.

'So under what circumstances did you get talking to Lydia about your interest in masochism?'

Tracy smiled at the term. 'I met her and her boyfriend in Xxxstacy by accident and we had a couple of drinks together and I mentioned it. Lydie just went crazy and said it sounded fantastic. I said I'd bring her in Madam Sashia's cell number for Monday's gym session, but when I saw her she'd already got the number and arranged it.'

'Is it possible she found the card pinned to the noticeboard in Xxxstacy?' asked Laurence.

Tracy thought about it. 'Yeah, maybe. I really don't know, but I didn't give her the contact details, and I just can't imagine Madam Sashia going that far.' She sipped her coffee.

'Why not? Feodor has served time for going a little too far with someone not of the right age,' said Laurence, noting Tracy's eyes widening.

She leaned towards him. 'Because what goes on there is fun, but kinda lame. Understand? It's sexy and safe. You wanna look to the places that don't advertise.'

'This one did,' replied Laurence softly, 'and it wasn't "sexy" or "safe" for Lydie, okay.'

Tracy stared at him, nodding imperceptibly.

'Give me something, Tracy. Anything that might help,' said Laurence quietly.

Tracy knotted her brow and appeared to be about to shake her head when she paused. 'Okay, come with me.'

Laurence followed her along the corridor, past a glass-fronted room where toned bodies pushed and pulled ridiculous weights under the watchful eyes of a bank of television screens and into an atrium leading to the changing rooms. The walls were fitted with lockers identifiable as such only because of a discreet metallic number next to a small electronic key swipe. Tracy looked around her and, seeing there was no one around, opened locker 492 with a master key.

'This is her locker, okay?' whispered Tracy and stood back. 'I have no authorisation to do this, so be quick.'

Laurence peered into the empty locker and sighed. He ran his hands around the box in a futile gesture, but there was nothing, not even a stray hair.

He nodded to Tracy, who closed and reset the lock.

'By the way,' asked Laurence as he turned to leave. 'What is a posture therapist?'

Tracy smiled. 'I make people stand up straight.'

CHAPTER TEN

'Malcolm… MALCOLM! Where is he?' screamed Cassandra Willis to no one in particular.

'Didn't you ask him to fax through those résumés?' responded Aria calmly as she placed a neat pile of documents, each bearing several coloured sticky tabs indicating where a signature was required, in front of her boss. Aria sighed and began to walk back to her office.

'Tell him I need him here, not by the goddamn fax machine!' bellowed Cassandra.

Aria didn't bother to reply but moved slowly through the glass partitions that only nominally divided the recruitment staff from each other.

Cassandra Willis, who had taken over the company nineteen years ago, was a great believer in always reminding her staff who was in charge and in keeping visual tags on all comings and goings. It was believed by all seven staff members that she had a stopwatch that calculated exactly how much time was taken for restroom activities and lunch breaks. She had even mooted that the fax and photocopier should be brought in from the walk-in down the corridor and placed within eyeline, a measure strongly discouraged by everyone who used it as a last refuge for an illicit text, quick gossip and for general time-wasting. Cassandra Willis had always run the company with a rod of iron, never doubting that bullying and criticism were tried and tested means of making money. Unfortunately, her recruitment agency had always turned a very tidy profit, which cemented these beliefs.

*

Malcolm had been idling by the fax machine for the last thirty minutes and, so far, had only managed to achieve one sent fax and a deeply bitten fingernail. He'd had a lot on his mind recently, and now that the day of reckoning had finally arrived, he was consumed with doubt, fear and inertia.

Aware that the finger in his mouth was becoming ominously salty, he withdrew it and watched dismayed as a neat red bubble began to swell in the corner of the nail bed.

'Shit!' His boss hated chewed nails and sighting this one would most likely bring on that lemon-sucked expression she adopted when she was about to tear him off a strip.

He was just about to pop another finger in his mouth when the door swung open.

'Hey, Mal,' said Aria, wearing the sympathetic smile that told him Cassandra was on the warpath.

'I've only been in here for ten minutes.' he whispered angrily.

'She needs you, buddy,' said Aria as she gently steered him in the direction of the main office. 'I'll finish these off.' She smiled and then tutted gently when she saw he hadn't made an impression on the tide of papers.

'I owe you one,' gasped Malcolm appreciatively as he hurried off.

'Doesn't everyone,' she said, flipping the fax machine switch to 'on'.

Malcolm gazed longingly at a large glass paperweight on Cassandra's desk as she vented her disappointment, frustration and general disgust at his incompetence. The voice ricocheted around the less conscious areas of his brain as he waited for the phrase that would herald his dismissal from her presence. He didn't have to wait too long.

'Why the hell do I put up with you?' she wailed.

Malcolm knew exactly why she 'put up with him', and he her. They had been working in the same office for the past eleven years, ever since his grandfather knocked a zero off the cost of purchasing the company. Cassandra had signed the cheque and the paperwork, brushing away the caveat as if it was nothing; a trifle. The conditions of sale demanded that Malcolm receive a quarter of the director's wage, plus an annual proportional bonus, but to qualify he had to complete a ninety-seven per cent attendance record.

Cassandra, on the other hand, needed to find him lawful employment and the agreed wage or forfeit the fifty per cent shareholding held in trust to a myriad of charities – most involving the preservation of small domestic mammals. They had both tried in the early years to find a way to minimise this arrangement, but she'd signed and Malcolm would never find other employment that would pay as well or tolerate his less-than-ethical approach to work. So for as long as he or she was alive and the company remained profitable, the situation would be unchanged, and this was, Malcolm concluded, the only course of action left to either of them.

Malcolm nodded and turned to leave. He had almost reached the relative safety of Aria's desk when the voice started up again. 'I assume that you've remembered to order the car. Or should I do that myself?'

Slowly, he turned around to face her but couldn't quite meet her eye. 'It should be here in thirty-five minutes… or so,' he corrected himself. He shouldn't be too prescriptive; it would make her suspicious.

She was raising her eyebrows to question this when she noticed his fingernail.

'Je-*sus*!' she squealed.

Malcolm turned around, scurried out of the office and headed for the in-house coffee shop.

Willis Recruitment was situated on the third floor of the Northtec Building; the other three floors were home to a mixture of accountants and stockbrokers. The eatery was tucked into an alcove as you entered the building and served pastries, great coffee and panini at lunch time. It had been serving local office staff in the surrounding buildings for several years now and had a professional buzz about it.

Malcolm loved it and spent considerably longer than the allocated lunch hour there, chatting and sipping coffees. In fact, it was on a lunch break a week or so ago that he'd met Cindy, and he'd been drawn into her world immediately. She was vibrant, attractive and talked about the smuttiest of things. He'd only known her for ten minutes and she was asking him what sort of sex he liked. Malcolm had been so shocked and amused that he'd spluttered the froth off his cappuccino all over her croissant, but she hadn't cared – she'd thought it was funny too and proceeded to lick the froth off the chocolate glaze with long, lazy tongue strokes. Malcolm was convinced he'd stopped breathing for the entire fifteen seconds it took her to perform this act.

Cindy didn't work in the buildings, just liked the coffee and company she said. In fact, he didn't know very much about her, just enough to know this was a woman he could trust; spend time with. She seemed to have a complete understanding of his problems and had been hinting that she knew someone who, for a price, would be willing to 'take care' of Malcolm's problem. For a mere five thousand, he could give that bitch Cassandra a taste of her own medicine and nothing could ever be traced back to him. It had sounded perfect, too good to be true even! This utterly gorgeous woman with the unbelievable figure, long brunette hair and wicked sparkle in her eye was offering him a way to get revenge for his godawful existence. She had even hinted strongly that a man that was capable of taking those sorts of decisions was of extreme interest to her.

So, after a great deal of internal debate, Malcolm had accepted the offer and given a padded manila envelope stuffed with his savings to Cindy. It had to be said that the most recent debate he'd been having with himself was mainly concerned with whether his savings might be lost, but it was too late to worry now.

Malcolm had spoken to Cindy yesterday and told her that Cassandra was going on a business trip the following day, and that it might be a great opportunity for Cindy's 'friend' to pick her up. Cindy had appeared to think about this carefully as she sipped her coffee, and said that it might be possible and what sort of time would his boss be expecting a car?

Malcolm had tried not to get too excited by all of the planning, knowing he had a tendency to fidget and fuss with objects. He had deliberately sat on his hands when the arrangements had finally been made and he'd watched Cindy stand up, slip on her sunglasses and sashay towards the exit on ice-pick heels.

It hadn't really occurred to him until an hour ago that there might be any moral concerns as to organising the kidnapping and sexual humiliation of a woman. In fact, he'd been considering calling the whole thing off, but he'd heard nothing more from Cindy, and she hadn't been around today in the coffee shop, even though he'd made several unscheduled visits throughout the day.

Malcolm checked his watch; it was 4.40 p.m. He scanned the coffee shop wildly in the hope of seeing Cindy, but she still wasn't there, so with an uncharacteristic burst of speed, he headed back to the office. He stabbed energetically at the elevator button, noting that it was on its way down from the top floor.

'Come on!' he shrieked at the lift, causing a couple of executives to turn round and frown at him.

Malcolm didn't like drawing attention to himself. His small, untidy presence was more suited to conservative tasks and situations, and bellowing at the elevator was uncharacteristic.

His hand shot to his mouth, as if shocked at his own behaviour. He had to remain composed and focussed. He took a deep, calming breath and closed his eyes. Nothing he could do would change the speed at which the elevator arrived, so he relaxed. He smiled when he thought of what Cindy would say if she saw him so flustered.

The elevator made a 'donging' sound, accompanied by the sucking swish of the doors, and when he opened his eyes, he found Cassandra standing directly in front of him, her face thunderous.

'Why are you never where you're supposed to be?' she hissed, barging past him and wheeling her overnight bag over his foot. He suppressed a squeak.

'I was checking that your car was here,' he answered peevishly.

'No you weren't! You were lolling around the coffee shop. Waiting for the tart you've spent most of this week chatting to, instead of doing anything resembling a working day!'

Cassandra glanced out through the glass entrance doors. They both saw the car at the same moment, its blacked-out windows and polished black exterior proclaiming its role. Cassandra waved a gloved hand at the car and turned towards him, lowering her voice.

'Listen carefully, Malcolm,' she spat, poking him in the chest with her index finger.

'Maybe you shouldn't—'

'I've had just about as much as I can take with your apathy and incompetence. When I get back, I'm going to meet with my lawyer and get rid of you. Something I should have done years ago. To hell with the consequences; I cannot stand another day of looking at your moronic face. Consider yourself terminated.' She grimaced, and with a vicious twist of her heel marched triumphantly towards the door.

Malcolm had to call on all of his reserves of self-control not to burst out laughing. He waited till the door swung shut behind her and then stepped into the elevator.

As soon as the doors closed, it was as if a huge weight had been lifted from his chest, and the relief manifested itself in a huge guffaw of laughter. Tears ran down his flabby cheeks, and he had to ignore the stitch-like pain grabbing at his sides as he sniggered.

The elevator drew to a stop and the doors opened onto a new world. A world without Cassandra Willis and a new regime where he, Malcolm Stringer, would become the boss everyone in the office had always longed for. The sort of boss who would not make unreasonable demands of his workforce and would listen to their needs. He also believed he'd make a pretty decent partner to the lovely Cindy, who was going to be treated to a fabulous wine-and-dine evening complete with roses and champagne, all at his expense.

*

Cassandra Willis barely registered the man who was going to kill her. He stepped lightly out of the driver's seat and opened the rear passenger door for her, gently extracting the overnight bag from her hands and placing it in the trunk. He closed her door carefully as she slid down into the back seat.

She was exhausted but resolved. She would phone her lawyer Harry Chen on Friday and arrange a meeting, and then hope that between them they could minimise the financial impact of breaking her contract. Harry made a tidy packet doing routine contractual work for her; it was about time he earned it. Yes, this was it for Cassandra – it was time to turn her life around and take control.

It was whilst mulling these matters over that she became aware they were no longer heading east in the direction of the airport. She leaned forward and addressed the driver, noticing his strong jawline and smooth, perfectly shaven cheek. It was a handsome, muscular profile but not of particular interest to Cassandra in that moment.

'You know I've got a six-thirty flight?' she asked, irritated.

'Yes, ma'am, but there's been an accident and the road ahead's closed. I'll get you there in plenty of time – relax,' he said calmly.

Cassandra didn't like the word 'relax'. It implied that she was overreacting to the situation, and the irritation that she'd been trying so hard to dampen exploded.

'What do you mean relax?' she screeched. 'You will—'

Any further thoughts on what he should or shouldn't do were lost as the driver twisted round with snake-like speed and punched Cassandra in the face. The combination of shock, pain and utter incomprehension silenced her for several seconds. Her immediate thought was that it was a mistake – what had happened couldn't have happened. But as her brain began to process the event and pain started to bludgeon its way across her fractured cheekbone and shattered nose, one clear thought emerged. She had to get out of the car.

Tearing at the door handle and only dimly aware of her own screaming, Cassandra tried, but neither door yielded. Frantically she tried to strategise: she was too afraid of the man to launch an attack, but logic told her that as she was heading in the opposite direction to the airport, she wasn't likely to be let out at the next available drop-off.

She stared wildly out of the window, smearing the blood across her face as she tried to clear her vision, but the sudden movement of her hand caused her eyeball to shift alarmingly in its socket.

By now she was bordering on complete hysteria. The car was a wall of sound as Cassandra's opportunity to turn her adrenaline flood into defensive action began to slip away.

She hammered on the windows with her fist. There was a means of escape – her cell phone!

Rummaging through her pockets and finding them empty, she ran her hands around the seat. Nothing! She moved her feet around, trying to maximise the distance between her and the man. It had to be there! Her handbag had been knocked to the floor and she grabbed it, tipping the contents onto the seat next to her, but it wasn't there.

And then she saw it.

The driver had placed it on the dashboard. He must have lifted it from her pocket as she'd entered the vehicle. Knowing she was doomed to failure, Cassandra lunged towards the phone. She managed to clumsily snatch it and savoured a fleeting moment of satisfaction as the possibility of escape teased her. But she was so focussed on the phone that it took several seconds to work out what the sudden sharp pain in her arm was and why it was accompanied by an icy sensation. Victorious but dizzy, she slumped back into her seat, trying to remember the emergency services' number.

Darkness.

*

The driver waited till he was sure the woman was unconscious, carefully pocketed the hypodermic needle and then swung the car around and headed back to the city.

He had, he concluded, a great deal to thank Cindy for.

CHAPTER ELEVEN

Eleanor watched Laurence through the window of D'Angelo's with interest as he manhandled the dog through the evening traffic. She sipped her coffee and speculated on why Laurence was hauling the enormous, unloved creature around with him.

It took Laurence at least thirty seconds to realise that the dog was not going to be fobbed off with being secured to a bike rack while his master conducted a debrief in the coffee shop and he was left in the now torrential downpour. The bark was unremitting and Eleanor wondered whether Laurence was going to thump the dog in front of the steadily increasing audience of law-enforcement agents.

Despite a momentarily balled fist, Laurence managed to maintain his calm and yanked the sodden creature into the coffee shop. Big Al's expression made it clear to Laurence that this plan was unlikely to reach first base.

'Sit outside!' commanded Al. 'You have coffee there.'

'And a house panini?' Laurence asked desperately.

Laurence's expression drew something akin to pity from Eleanor, who indicated that he sit at the table adjacent to her so they could communicate through the open window. Big Al looked as if he was going to complain about that too, but seeing Eleanor's slow eyebrow raise, decided to slam some plates around instead.

'Here,' said Eleanor, passing Laurence a napkin through the window to wipe the rain-saturated plastic seat.

'Thanks,' he muttered. 'For God's sake! I'm getting soaked!'

'You'll live,' Eleanor responded. She turned to the dog. 'He looks hungry.'

'How can he be?' snapped Laurence. 'He ate everyone's lunch in Admin, and Timms gave him a chilli burger. He's already a threat to global warming. God only knows how he's going to process that!'

Eleanor shrugged; she'd lost interest in the dog saga. 'What've you learned?'

'Hmm?' Laurence was craning his neck to see if his order was on its way. It seemed improbable as Big Al was chatting to a more favoured customer.

'Focus, Detective!'

'Sorry.'

'Tell me about the gym,' she said, catching Big Al's eye and nodding in Laurence's direction.

'I met Tracy Earnshaw, Lydia's personal trainer, who claims she bumped into her and Stollar at the Xxxstacy club and enthused to her about the kidnapping day trip.'

'Enthused?' asked Eleanor.

Laurence thought for a moment or two. 'Perhaps not enthused. She said she'd "mentioned it". She told me she'd only done the kidnap thing once and thought it a bit "lame". Tracy said she'd taken Madam Sashia's contact details into the gym for Lydia, but apparently she'd already got them and had contacted a man. Tracy felt it was possible that she could have got the number from the club.'

'What was her relationship with Lydia like?' asked Eleanor as Big Al delivered the food.

Laurence tucked in hungrily. The dog had slid his huge head onto the wet table and was staring at the panini with intense concentration. Eleanor smiled as Laurence slammed his arm between plate and snout in a gesture reminiscent of a kid fearful that someone would copy his exam answer.

'Whitefoot!'

'Sorry! Tracy said they didn't have a meaningful relationship. I guess she meant they were acquaintances, but she called her "Lydie", not Lydia,' he spluttered through a bolus of cheese, bread and coffee.

'Lydie's kind of a personal address. What else did she have to offer?'

'Not much, but she opened her locker for me.'

'Lydia's locker?' asked Eleanor.

He nodded.

'How many lockers were there to choose from?'

He made a gesture that implied a great many.

'Then how did she know which one was Lydia's?'

Laurence chewed slowly and swallowed. 'I don't know. The locker was empty; nothing in there at all.'

Eleanor nodded slowly. 'I think Tracy had a more "meaningful relationship" than she's admitting to. We should pay her a second visit.'

'What do you know?' asked Laurence, yanking his coat collar higher to prevent the rain running down his back.

Eleanor paused and drank the last of her coffee. 'I know that we have a dead woman, killed by a sadist for pleasure rather than material gain. He found a way to cream off a customer from Madam Sashia and kill her. It's possible that he left identical contact cards in one of the clubs that Lydia picked up. If so, we haven't found that yet, and Lydia's phone records show no unrecognised outgoing or incoming calls.'

'How the hell did she contact the guy? Could she have used a phone booth? Maybe there's one at Xxxstacy? But why would she do that?'

'Maybe there's poor coverage there or maybe she didn't need to call. Perhaps she met him there?' Eleanor said, rising to her feet and checking the time. 'I think I'm going to have a drink at Xxxstacy tonight; do a bit of fishing. Fancy a date?'

Laurence smiled. 'You betcha.'

Eleanor pulled on her coat. I'll pick you up at eleven.'

*

Laurence had been feeling tired but magnanimous on the drive home and had stopped at the local pet supermarket, purchasing a fifteen-kilo bag of medium-quality dog kibble and a leash. Monster seemed aware that concessions had been made and didn't whine or break wind on the way home. Unfortunately, any good will towards the dog evaporated when Laurence found a note attached to his front door. It read, 'What died in there, buddy?' and was signed, 'The poor bastard that lives next door.' Laurence groaned as he remembered the turd that was still sitting on the kitchen floor.

The smell rivalled anything he'd encountered in the morgue, and it took considerable presence of mind to scoop it, bag it and take it out to the street bin. By now, it was 8 p.m. and Laurence had been awake for the past thirty-six hours and was desperate for sleep, but he decided that a shower and a steak would be the best option; he could doze afterwards.

*

Eleanor knew that she was missing something. She'd been soaking in the bathtub for the past hour and barely registered the fact that the water had dipped to slightly above blood temperature. The key, she believed, lay in where Lydia had obtained the contact details. The killer had observed the protocol of Sashia's kidnap routine and managed to convince Lydia that she was going to have the same experience as Tracy Earnshaw.

Eleanor sighed and squeezed out the flannel, laid it over her face and tried to get a little deeper into the mind of the killer. Why had he gone to such elaborate lengths? Surely he could have snatched Lydia at any time? He didn't take the five thousand in cash but still went through the process of having it delivered to Xxxstacy by Stollar. By not collecting it, he was drawing attention to the fact that he wasn't part of Sashia's enterprise – that and not taking Lydia's ring.

Another question that had been eating away at her was why, when he'd gone to all the trouble of changing the lock on the Westex door, he didn't have the bolt cutters with him when he came to deposit the body? It didn't make sense that he wouldn't be prepared for that event, as he was clearly so determined that Lydia should be displayed in that place and manner.

In her mind's eye, Eleanor stood in front of the Westex power station and stared at the lock. Maybe he tried his key and found it didn't work; was he frustrated, desperate to find another way in?

She dipped her head below the water line, opening her eyes and looking at the scattered lights reflected on the surface. Where were the signs? Every event was heralded and garlanded with little signs, and it was her job to find and interpret them. It was because she hadn't always picked up on the cues that would save a life that she'd dedicated her adult life to searching for them.

Caleb had been a year younger than her, and at twelve was just beginning to stretch and fill out into the adult body he would never acquire. He'd lived on the next street to her in Cabbage Town, but it could have been another planet for the lack of similarities between their upbringing. Where Eleanor's life was nurtured with books, sports, love and indulgence, Caleb's was filled with fear, secrets and desperation. But she hadn't understood those signs until after the events had played out.

He and Eleanor caught the same bus, and on the days when she missed it, he'd wait for her so they could walk the two kilometres to school together. He was uncommunicative, lonely and vaguely unhappy, but as he'd walked next to her, his blazer collar yanked up and head sunk into his shoulders, she'd sensed their companionship. He'd seemed to like listening to her chatter about friends and family, never contributing any thoughts of his own.

This should have been the first warning sign. Eleanor's father had been a patrol officer for twenty years and he'd often told her that if you kept your eyes open and listened for sudden changes to the mundane everyday occurrences then you could spot the danger coming. But she hadn't listened to her nagging doubts when Caleb had said he needed to tell her something. His timing had been dreadful – registration had been about to start and Eleanor had wanted to sign up for a new kickboxing class. She'd said she'd catch him later, but as she'd turned, she'd seen something in his face that she'd never seen before – a sign.

Eleanor had been sore but triumphant the morning after, and eager to detail each blow delivered and received, but Caleb hadn't been there. She'd debated whether to miss the bus as he frequently did, but if he was ill and off school she'd have to walk alone, a thought that held little appeal for her.

He'd been absent for three mornings before she finally decided to walk Rusty, their ageing spaniel, round to his house. She wasn't sure why her father had found it surprising that she was walking the dog. Perhaps it was something she rarely did as a teenager – she couldn't remember. Neither could she remember the walk there, but every pace and sound of the run back was etched into her memory.

Eleanor hadn't liked Caleb's house. She had only been in once, and the smell and tension that had pervaded every room had made her feel uncomfortable, so it was an unspoken law that the only house visited was hers. Caleb hadn't liked to touch anything in her home; he'd just sit quietly in the kitchen and always took too long to finish any food or drink put in front of him. A gesture that seemed more poignant now, though it had irritated her beyond measure at the time.

The three minutes that separated her childhood from adulthood were, in her mind, a timeless entity. Eleanor had angrily looped Rusty's lead over a fence when his braying bark could not be shushed or threatened out of him. This she recalled but not her approach to the house or what prompted her to investigate the basement steps. Protocol demanded that she knock at the door and announce her presence to Caleb's stepfather, but something had told her these niceties were no longer required in this breached world.

Caleb's naked body lay curled underneath a hastily rearranged pile of household garbage bags, which his stepfather had piled in a pathetic attempt to hide his actions. The adult in her knew instantly that he was dead and had been for some time. Possibly the mottled pattern on the alabaster skin, or his obscenely bloated stomach and genitals, which had pushed the bin bags to one side satisfied the question, but the child in her still spoke and called to him.

Even now.

Pulling herself upright and breaking the surface of the water, she tried not to see the red wheals on her thighs and stomach but failed. An image of the man in the hotel room flicked into her head. The man had been good and, for a moment, she even considered contacting him again but crushed that thought quickly. Rule number one stated categorically that: '*There will be no second contact.*' With this in mind, she grabbed a towel and launched herself quickly out of the bath, rubbing vigorously at her stomach and breasts. Maybe you could wash away your sins?

An hour later, Eleanor stood outside Laurence Whitefoot's apartment and readjusted her clothing. She wore a shoulder-length platinum-blonde wig and numerous studs that were attached to her lips, chin, cheeks and nose. Each was held in place by a magnetic contact inside her mouth. Hazel contacts and heavy bronze liner and shadow gave her a feline appearance, and she doubted if even Mo would recognise her. It had been tempting to don full rubber latex fetish gear, but the object was to blend and hide her identity, and that meant not drawing too much attention to herself.

When Laurence finally opened the door, it was obvious from his confused expression that, firstly, he'd been asleep and, secondly, he had no idea who she was. He peered at her and began to splutter an introduction query when he froze, letting his jaw loll open like a kid with a big thought.

Eleanor swept past him and Monster, stopping only to breathe in the barely concealed scent of dog shit and note the bullet hole in the refrigerator.

'Is the dog your ex-girlfriend's?' she asked, pointing at what remained of the photograph.

Laurence sighed, yanked open the fridge and grabbed a beer. 'Yup,' he replied.

'But you bought the dog together?'

Laurence stared at her and nodded, taking a deep swig of beer. 'I don't need psychoanalysing,' he snapped.

Eleanor shrugged. 'Stop drinking, I need you alert and capable of driving.'

Laurence smiled and looked at her appraisingly, his eyes dropping from her mouth to her breasts and lingering on her crotch.

For a moment, Eleanor felt a heat between her thighs and a desire for him to grab her arms and push her down – but that was not a game she was willing to play now or ever with a colleague. She hardened her expression and snapped, 'Get ready. Dress down.'

'Yes, ma'am,' he answered stiffly, but his eyes twinkled, and she felt her own drop for a moment, despite her resolve.

CHAPTER TWELVE

Laurence had followed Eleanor's instructions to the letter. He'd entered the Xxxstacy bar at least five minutes after her and had propped himself up at the bar, cradling a bottle of beer in his left hand and tucking his right into his front pocket. He couldn't help an inward smile when he saw at least four other guys adopting the same posture, all surreptitiously stroking their members, while gawping at the cage girls.

The atmosphere felt very different to that of the midday sushi crowds. The lighting was low and the heavy metallic grinding of the music felt oppressive and unnerving. The girls who had seemed so languorous and sanitised earlier were now sweaty and enervated. Their bonds looked tighter, their expressions more convincing.

Laurence felt uncomfortable and censorious. He watched as a hand groped through the bars of a dancer's cage and stuffed what looked like a fifty into the girl's panty line, pinching her flesh and digging in with his fingernails. The girl groaned theatrically and shuffled away from the hand, straining against the leather wristbands and chains that pinioned her.

She looked, Laurence thought, like an ad for an animal-welfare charity. He took a pull of his beer and searched for a sign of Eleanor, trying not to let the stress of the situation prevent him from detecting. But what was he looking for? Suspicious behaviour? It all looked suspicious to him. Guys stroking their dicks as they imagined a pretty girl in pain.

He took another long gulp and called for another. This evening was certainly going to test his mettle.

*

Eleanor glanced at the bar from the dark and overpopulated alcove that housed the basement stairs and wished that Mo had been standing there rather than the sanctimonious rookie she'd had dumped on her. He was drinking too much and noticing too little. She sighed and determined that she would speak to Marty Samuelson tomorrow; maybe he'd swap him for Smith. But now wasn't the time to be distracted.

She moved through the crowd, pausing occasionally to meet an eye or tilt her head in a gesture of submission. She got several return looks but no one she considered interesting enough to pursue. It was time to move deeper into the building.

The stairs were illuminated by black lights and reminded Eleanor of a ghost ride she'd been on as a child at the local fairground. The teeth around her glowed an intense white, making the feral scene even more eerie.

Muffled sounds from rooms secreted behind seemingly doorless walls put her senses on high alert. A man brushed against her as he hurried up the stairs, the heavy stench of sweat and fear causing her to stop and watch him as he stumbled ahead of her.

As she turned away from him, she saw the outline of a face in the shadows. It was too dark to make out any features, but she watched, mesmerised, as the face split slowly open to reveal glowing white teeth in a smile the Cheshire Cat would have been proud of.

The basement corridor writhed with movement, but there was too little light to distinguish between individuals or even identify body parts. Eleanor made her way carefully to the restrooms, sliding cautiously past a couple grinding noisily against the adjacent wall.

As she stepped inside, the sounds and smells changed instantly. Heavy perfumes and piercing fluorescent strips above the mirrors gave the women within a ghostly, surreal appearance. Immediately Eleanor divided the group into three prostitutes, two trans women and one very unconvincing cross-dresser.

She walked over to the mirror, observing the scene whilst applying a heavy coat of purple lipstick. One heavy woman in her thirties with tattooed eyebrows peed into the bowl as she chatted to her friends with the door open. As she struggled to pull up her complicated panty arrangements, a second friend pushed past her and settled her ass onto the seat. They were discussing the apparent merits of a girlfriend's latest surgical reconstruction.

Eleanor wanted to single out some attention. One of the prostitutes was writing a comment on a card on the noticeboard.

'Is this safe?' asked Eleanor with exaggerated concern, waggling the 'Kidnappings Arranged' card cautiously in front of her.

The prostitute gave her careful scrutiny. 'You a cop?'

Eleanor looked confused and giggled. 'Only on the last Saturday of every month.'

The woman grinned her approval and leaned into her. 'How hard d'you play, honey?'

Eleanor drew in her breath and leaned a little closer to the woman. 'Hard,' she whispered, meeting her eyes.

'Hmm, well I heard it was okay, but expensive. There's a woman comes in every so often, Bella something or other. She's got a dungeon and rents it out for a reasonable rate. If you've got a private party in mind I'm very flexible,' she cooed, leaning even closer.

'You wanna watch who you go with honey.' One of the trans women had sashayed over from the mirror to join in the conversation. She was identifiable as such by her bulging biceps, enviable flat stomach, slim hips and huge silicon breasts. She'd applied foundation with a trowel but otherwise would be pretty convincing to anyone other than prostitutes and cops.

'You stick with who you know, honey. There's some bastard that's killing girls round here lookin' for the same fun as you, darlin'. You take Mandy's advice and stick to who you know!'

'Girls?' whispered Eleanor, in a shocked tone.

'Uh-huh. One of them came in here last week…'

'Who's that, Mandy?' asked a second woman, engaged in reapplying a wayward false eyelash.

'That posh girl with the blonde hair. You know, Tracy's friend?' responded Mandy.

'You mean Tracy Earnshaw? I know her! She works at the gym on Wellesley Street,' gasped Eleanor.

'I don't know about that, hun. But I was sitting on the pan when—'

She was interrupted by the eyelash woman. 'Honey, you don't sit on the pan.'

She and the first woman burst into shrieks of laughter. Mandy looked theatrically offended.

'Oh, you nasty bitches.' She shook her head with disappointment. 'Anyhow,' she sloughed off the insult and continued with her story, 'I was sitting on the pan, doing what a *girl* needs to.' She ignored the sniggering. 'And I heard them talking. The blonde girl was asking Tracy all about her being dragged into a van and whipped and all, and Tracy was saying that it was great and fabulous, and she came all over the place about a hundred times.' Mandy was well into her storytelling now and emphasising it with eye rolls, hand gestures and flips of her long glossy hair. 'And the blonde girl was just lapping it all up and said how'd she get all turned on and everything.'

Now several other women had gathered round to listen. Mandy was enjoying the attention.

'So who got killed?' asked the heavy woman.

'For God's sake, Lu, just listen,' responded another.

'Who got killed? I missed that bit,' Lu repeated, undaunted.

'Some posh blonde girl, looking for rough,' sighed the first.

'Okay, I shall re-continue… so posh blonde girl is telling Tracy how much coming she's gonna do and Tracy says if your boyfriend—'

'Who's her boyfriend?' asked Lu, much to the irritation of the other women.

'Shut the hell up and listen, you fat bitch! Mandy is telling us.'

'I dunno, some guy with money girl 'cos Tracy said the guy'd want five thousand bucks for roughing her up.'

'What the hell? I do it for two hundred,' snipped Lu, outraged. 'And they go home afterwards!'

'Not if you sit on 'em,' sniggered the first woman.

'Skinny bitch who'd…'

'Shut the hell up! I'm telling this or what?' snapped Mandy, theatrically exhausted. The women settled down.

'Soooo, Tracy says to her that she'll do the organising, you know phone the guy and after posh girl's bitch boyfriend drops the money off, then she'll get the deal.'

There was a pause as the information sank in. 'But how'd you know she's dead?' asked Lu.

''Cos I recognised the picture in the paper. They never said how she was killed, but you can read between the lines.' Mandy nodded knowingly.

'You said "girls",' coaxed Eleanor.

'Huh? Oh yeah! Remember that European girl who used to work Gary's place?'

The other women looked blank.

'You know, she had one eye.' Mandy slapped a hand over her eye as a visual aid.

'What happened to her eye?' asked the first woman, concerned.

'How the hell should I know? What am I? Her mother?' shrieked Mandy.

'Oh I remember her,' said Lu. 'Brenda or Deirdre or some such… she got murdered down the railway, didn't she?'

'Yeah that's right… six months ago, wasn't it? I heard about that! One trick too many.'

'Why'd you think she was murdered by the same guy?' asked Eleanor, trying to conceal her excitement.

'Well,' drawled Mandy, 'they found her in a plastic bag too, didn't they?'

CHAPTER THIRTEEN

Laurence sat in the cramped office and gazed at the information on the screen. The photographs of Belinda Myrtle were spread haphazardly across his desk, in a manner not dissimilar to that of her body on the rail track. It had been difficult to ascertain exactly how Belinda had been killed, as her body had been hit by a freight train travelling at close to ninety. The resulting soup had been reconstructed as best as possible by the pathology department, but Belinda had been identified mainly by her jewellery and the presence of a Daffy Duck tattoo on a small section of midriff. There had been evidence that the body had been wrapped in a plastic bag, which had made the likelihood of this being an unlawful killing rather than a suicide or accident all the more likely. However, it had been shredded and had provided little in the way of clues.

Eleanor pushed the door to the office open with her back and manoeuvred a large cardboard evidence box onto her desk.

'Okay, this is everything apparently,' she said, yanking some wipes out of her desk drawer and rubbing her face and eyes vigorously.

Balling the wipe and flinging it into the trash, she selected a knife from her office tidy, slit open the evidence tape and opened the box. It contained a small plastic handbag, heavily stained with dried blood and tissue. The items within had been separately bagged and recorded as a purse containing filter papers, chewing gum, and thirteen bucks and eight cents in loose change. There was a broken compact, containing a well-used compressed powder in a beige tone, several condoms and a small penknife. Also, a paperback romance novel stained with blood and dirt, with a sadly dog-eared page that gave a human veracity to the unidentifiable mess in the photographs. No cell phone or keys had been found on or near the body.

'So the tranny you met in the washroom was convinced that the two murders were connected?'

Laurence looked at Eleanor's stony face. 'Sorry, I meant the gender reassigned but politically egalitarian...' He sighed theatrically.

Eleanor looked puzzled and then smiled at him. 'I was just thinking about the same thing. Why would she think the two murders were connected?' Eleanor rubbed her neck and closed her eyes for a moment.

'She probably didn't see the first body because she'd have mentioned that rather than the plastic wrapper, so she must have got her information from the newspaper or TV coverage,' said Laurence.

Eleanor's eyes snapped open.

'Give me the date of Belinda's murder,' she said, activating the media archive that County had been trialling for the past eighteen months and hurriedly tapping in the victim's name.

Eleanor began to scan through the pages. 'I've twenty-three articles, three of which are front page...'

She read quickly, her lips occasionally jumping as her eyes travelled faster than her ability to process the information.

The printer whirred into action, spitting out a steady stream of heavily inked images and text. Laurence squeezed past the edge of Mo's desk and strained to lift the papers out of the tray. The articles had been collected from the two local tabloids and three nationals, two of which were broadsheets. The headlines varied from 'Prostitute Minced by Train' to the more conservative

'Body Found on Track'; Laurence scanned them looking for any mention of plastic bags. He found a couple of oblique references to its presence and a few page-two suppositions that the body had been wrapped before being dumped on the track, but the reports petered out after the first week or so as a lurid dope and party death was linked to a mayoral candidate.

Laurence was halfway through the papers when he saw the link. Someone from a local paper had managed to see a morgue shot of Belinda's face, or rather the remaining third of her face and had written a rather florid account of what he'd seen. The paper hadn't had either the nerve or the material to print the image, but the description of the victim's smeared red lipstick set off alarm bells.

Eleanor glanced up at the sound of Laurence rummaging through the morgue photographs until he found what he was looking for. The woman's face had a coronal severance, leaving the face as an eyeless mask. Most of the underlying tissue was missing, as was the left cheekbone and zygomatic arch, and the skin had a white pallor, which made the thick smear of dark lipstick appear even more obscene. Laurence twisted the print so that Eleanor could see for herself.

'Shit,' she retorted, snatching the autopsy prints from Laurence's desk and banging her elbow on Mo's desk. 'For God's sake will someone get rid of this bloody table!' she barked, and on catching sight of Laurence's satisfied expression said, 'Stop smirking and find the corresponding revelation on Lydia Greystein.'

Laurence had a pile of recent newspaper articles on the Greystein murder. It didn't take him long to find an article in both the *Toronto Sun* and *The Star*, which pointed out that the victim's face had been heavily smeared with red lipstick. None of the papers had made a connection between the murder of Belinda Myrtle and that of Lydia Greystein.

'Maybe we should recruit Mandy and her observational powers?' said Laurence, but Eleanor wasn't listening – she was calling their boss.

*

Wadesky was the first of the team to arrive, followed by Timms.

'Why'd she connect the two deaths?' asked Wadesky, puzzled. 'If she told you it was the plastic bags, I'm not buying that. Surely she'd have mentioned the lipstick as a more likely connection?'

Wadesky compared the two articles that mentioned the smeared lipstick. 'You think she could have seen the first body or maybe the morgue photos?'

Eleanor stared at her. 'You're right, and I'm going to send some patrols to do some casual digging. But first let's put all the circumstantial evidence from both cases together and run a link to any other earlier crimes that might fit the bill.'

Wadesky nodded and began to wade through the paperwork.

Timms sauntered in swigging a huge coffee and brandishing a box of doughnuts. 'What we got?' he addressed the room.

'Hey puppy, you still here?' he said, ruffling Monster's furry head roughly, much to the dog's delight. Monster's loyalty was being gradually won over by Timms' liberal application of rough love and junk food.

'Some bitch with an ability to detect what we couldn't,' growled Wadesky.

'Well send her an application form!' Timms snorted, offering Monster a doughnut.

'Pass me one, Timms,' snapped Wadesky. 'I haven't had any breakfast.'

'No waaay!' drawled Timms. 'And have your Jozef telling me off for feeding his unborn child carbohydrates and E numbers? No way, girl! Your body is a goddamn temple to reproduction and I ain't gonna foul it.'

'You know what Jo is gonna say?' hissed Wadesky. 'He's gonna say why'd you shoot the nasty fat detective, honey? Was it because he didn't share his food when you were starving?'

Timms giggled. 'Whoa! Steady on…'

He passed the doughnut tray in her direction. Wadesky shoved one into her mouth and placed a second on her notebook. Timms put out a hand to retrieve the box but Wadesky waggled it in Laurence's direction.

'Hey, honey, you want one?'

Laurence smiled and grabbed a couple, much to Timms' distress.

'There's going to be a bloodbath before this night is through!' said Timms ominously.

From the sudden slamming of doors and sound of raised voices, it was clear that Marty Samuelson was on his way. The door to the incident room flew open. 'Why are we here at five in the morning?' exclaimed Samuelson. 'It better be fabulous!' He stared pointedly at Eleanor.

'Whitefoot and I trawled the Xxxstacy club this evening and in conversation with a prostitute, she proffered a link between the killing of Greystein and Belinda Myrtle last February.'

'The prostitute found on the railway line?' Samuelson asked.

'Yes.'

'What's the link?'

'Both were wrapped in plastic bags and both had heavily smeared lipstick that had been applied by their killer.'

'Why didn't we pick this up, and why did she?' queried Samuelson.

'We don't know yet. The link seems tenuous, and apart from the circumstantial, very little links the two,' replied Eleanor thoughtfully.

'But you think the two crimes are linked. You see the same MO?' Samuelson stared at Eleanor.

She thought carefully for a few moments and glanced at the morgue shots of Belinda and those of Lydia. 'Yes, I believe it's the same guy,' she said decisively.

'Okay, then why'd this one get dumped on the railway lines to be pulped?' Samuelson tapped the photograph of Belinda with a thick finger. 'Meanwhile this one gets to be displayed?' He tapped Lydia's photograph.

'Because he wasn't happy with Belinda's final appearance. She didn't look right, and our killer's all about the appearance. I believe that Belinda was probably his first victim, though I'm not one hundred per cent on that one. But he destroyed her, rather like an artist will burn or rip a canvas that they don't like or that fails to convey their meaning.'

'What meaning?' asked Samuelson, moving closer. The room was silent as Eleanor ran with her thoughts.

'It's a show of power and taste. He kills the women, but it's more than just his control over life or death; it's about his skill as a performer… he's an artist in his mind. And as such his gallery has just opened, and there will be more to view soon.'

'How many more?' asked Samuelson, his voice low.

'As many as he can create before we catch him,' she said simply.

There was a pause as he took in the implications. 'Je-*sus*. What's the plan?'

'Whitefoot and I will go and talk to pathology, see if there's any lip tissue left from Belinda Myrtle to run chem tests on. Maybe we can match lipstick. Then we're going to talk to Tracy Earnshaw about her role. She seems to have been more proactive in Lydia's kidnapping than she let on to. I'm going to send in a couple of patrol officers to track down Mandy and find out what else she knows. Wadesky and Timms need to dig harder – there's more there. Focus on intrusion without theft, stalking and maybe animal abuse with display…'

'At least narrow it down to a demographic,' moaned Timms.

'Is Ruby Delaware still our go-to profiler slash psychologist?' Eleanor asked Samuelson. He nodded.

'Then let's get her to give us a profile. And we need immediate transfer of any missing females reports and any break-ins that don't fit conventional patterns. There's not enough staff for this, boss. Give me Smith and Rutger from Vice.' Eleanor stared at her boss.

'You can have Smith and first call on Ellis and Paget, but I can't call in Rutger yet.' He leaned towards her, lowering his voice. 'You sure we've got a serial killer on our hands?'

She nodded slowly.

He sighed then turned to the team. 'Okay, let's get this moving and I want debrief... regularly!' He pointed menacingly at Eleanor and then stood up and looked at Wadesky. 'What the hell are you eating?'

Wadesky lowered the doughnut, embarrassed.

'Did Timms give you that shit?' he said angrily.

'Not voluntarily,' Timms snorted.

'I'll send up breakfast okay?'

He'd reached the door and turned round to face Eleanor. 'You going to charge Sashia Yesikov and that mutt Barnes?'

She shook her head. 'Nothing doing there.'

'Okay, they get released end of the day, but I want them eyeballed. The DA is working on a way to shut them down, and Feodor is being shipped over to the Feds due to his misconstruing the terms of his parole.'

The door slammed noisily after him.

CHAPTER FOURTEEN

The killer stood still and drew in several deep breaths. The cold air made his chest contract, and he watched intently as his exhaled breath condensed in a thick cloud and drifted slowly towards the trees. If he were to analyse what his favourite part of the whole proceedings were, he'd have to say this part. All of the screaming and begging was over; not that he didn't enjoy that aspect of the performance, but it was so predictable. All his victims so far had made the same noises, which were generally too loud, and made the same pleas. Not one of them varied their performance, and he felt that maybe a future scenario might require some considerable thought if he was to maintain his enthusiasm for the whole thing. After all, when a thing became commonplace, he generally walked away from it; he'd done that plenty of times before. But here, in the clearing, he was flushed with success and pride. His last presentation had shown a considerable improvement on the first couple, but this one really did deserve some appreciation from his audience.

The moon had been unusually bright as he'd set up his tools and had made the clearing operation considerably easier than he'd imagined. He had selected the area several months earlier whilst walking in the park. The trees formed a natural auditorium, and the red oak tree that stood in the middle of the arena had been scarified by decades of love carvings and dates. He knew that there was at least an hour's work required to tailor the space to his needs, but he was prepared and had made sure that after

such a strenuous twenty-four hours he'd have sufficient stamina
by drinking several litres of isotonic sports drinks.

He began pruning back the lower branches using a handsaw
and dragging them over to the periphery of the arena, but this
was taking too much time and energy; he really wanted to have
the preparation finished before dawn broke. It was always going
to be a risky business using a chainsaw, but he'd selected a battery-
powered one, which although massively underpowered for the
task in hand, was considerably quieter than the motorised version.

Early recces of the site had proved that there was very little in
the way of pedestrian traffic during the night, and any clandestine
trysts took place closer to the car park, where both shelter and
a getaway could be secured. The site was at least eight hundred
yards from the nearest house and the single elderly resident wore
a hearing aid. No, it would be okay to use the power saw for a
limited amount of time.

*

Mrs Needermeyer had lived in the small house overlooking the
park for the last thirty-five years and she took endless comfort in
watching the seasons change the trees' appearance. The rhythmic
arrivals of migratory birds held a fascination for her that had also
filled many a lonely hour. At eighty-three, she seldom felt the need
to sleep for long periods of time; in fact her cat naps generally
lasted for two or three hours at most, which was why she was
sitting on a small oak occasional chair watching a pair of screech
owls hunting mice in the brilliant moonlight.

Mrs Needermeyer seldom bothered to put in the new hearing
aid her son had bought for her, but she was so tickled by the
petulant shrieks of the owls that she turned it up to maximum.

It had taken her at least three minutes to work out exactly
what the hideous racket was that was now accompanying the
owls. Who could possibly be chopping down trees at this time of

the night or, for that matter, who could possibly have permission to commit such an act?

She picked up the phone and called emergency services. The gentleman on the end of the call line had been extremely sympathetic and admitted to being very fond of owls himself. He said that a police vehicle would be dispatched immediately to investigate the matter.

*

Ellis was sulking. He hadn't spoken to his partner Eva Paget for at least an hour. Not that she cared very much. It was a slow night and all Ellis did was bitch about the horrible consequences of trying to be a decent cop and saving ungrateful bitches who should be spending their hard-earned cash on shoes rather than kinky sex. So she focussed on her sudoku and waited for the inevitable call from control.

She didn't have to wait long. The call was succinct and short. They were to go and locate a trans woman known as Mandy, last seen at the Xxxstacy nightclub, and find out where she lived, her group of friends and any information she might have on the murder of Belinda Myrtle and Lydia Greystein. But before that they needed to investigate a possible tree crime in Jubilee Park.

'Tree crime!' Paget said, laughing as she turned over the engine. Ellis said nothing.

*

It was just before 6 a.m. and there would be at least another hour before sunrise. Dr Hounslow disliked entering the sunless morgue before sunrise and leaving in the dark, which was why she had recently purchased three desk lamps, each one fitted with a bulb that mimicked natural light. She was just pondering whether she could manage to carry at least one of them from the car in with her when Eleanor and Laurence arrived. 'Matt will fax the final report through this afternoon. I did say that to Detective Wadesky last night,' she said tersely.

Eleanor nodded. 'It was on another matter regarding the case.'

Hounslow pointed at the three large boxes sitting on the back seat and handed the car keys to Laurence while pulling out the handles on her wheeled trolley box and heading towards the morgue at a brisk pace.

Eleanor followed her into the building, leaving Laurence to manhandle the boxes and catch them up.

'Did you perform the autopsy on Belinda Myrtle last February,' asked Eleanor as they walked. 'A prostitute hit by a freight train.'

'I did. Poor lady. Not very much to examine,' responded Hounslow thoughtfully. Eleanor held the door open for her.

'Why?' asked the pathologist as she moved swiftly towards her office, nodding politely at colleagues.

'We think there might be a link between Myrtle's and Greystein's death,' replied Eleanor.

'Really?' Hounslow unlocked her office door and indicated that the two officers should take a seat. They sat silently as she plonked her briefcase heavily on the table and rammed the trolley box snugly against the banks of grey stainless-steel filing cabinets. She flipped on the coffee maker, whilst unlocking a cabinet and selecting the relevant file, then flopped it onto her desk, tantalisingly close to Eleanor. Hounslow gave her a knowing smile as she set out three cups.

The only sounds in the room were the intermittent splutter of the coffee maker and the odd sigh and tut from the pathologist as she leafed through the file on Brenda Myrtle.

With the last drip of coffee into the pot, Hounslow closed the file and stood up. She didn't bother to ask how each officer liked their coffee; rather she added a drop of milk to each cup and placed them in front of Eleanor and Laurence. She noted a flash of disappointment on Laurence's face – perhaps he craved sugar but judged that the woman in front of him was unlikely to warm to any request for sweetener, so he said nothing; just sipped his coffee and waited for Eleanor to kick-start the conversation.

'Dr Hounslow…' she began, but the pathologist held a finger up. Eleanor fell silent and waited. Suddenly, with a shake of her head, the pathologist stood up and made for the door.

'This will take a few minutes, as I have to access stored materials from the basement archives.' She opened the door. 'Probably the same amount of time as it would take you to unpack, assemble and plug in one of my wonderful new lamps, Detective Whitefoot.'

*

The killer stood silently, his head cocked to one side studying his latest creation. Cassandra Willis had irritated him beyond measure by screaming incessantly, even when nothing was happening to her. He had wanted the experience to be enlightening for both of them and had planned to take his time and savour the smells and sounds of her torment. However, the awful woman had screeched like a pig, which was why he'd been forced to adapt his programme and slice her tongue out. He'd contemplated a less drastic alternative, but it was crucial that the outward appearance of her mouth wasn't damaged in any way.

After this event she seemed to calm down considerably and even gave the impression that she was quite enjoying the whole experience. Well that was often difficult to gauge because the artist couldn't trust what his canvases truly meant when they were being created. They always lied, trying to second-guess what he wanted from them, but how could they understand his needs? This was anathema even to him, a man 'in touch' with his inner self.

He sighed deeply and felt the momentary warmth of self-pity wash over him. He could not be understood in his own time; no artist of true stature and vision ever was. His motives and meanings would be his legacy, studied and debated years after his own death; it was possible that he'd even appear on university syllabi. He smiled at that idea.

The woman's body had been repositioned at least three times before it met his approval. He knew that if his canvas was readjusted too many times, the large hook that had been inserted between the second and third vertebrae had a tendency to snap through the spine and leave the body to stretch away from the head like a piece of old-fashioned taffy, especially problematic in a heavier woman. He had first looped three metres of heavy-duty titanium link over one of the primary oak limbs, which dipped into a generous curve about ten feet from the ground. The lowest chain link had been fitted with a carabiner, which would accept the smaller part of the double-ended hook.

With the mounting device in position, he then had to lift the woman higher than the carabiner and carefully lower the hook onto it, whilst supporting her weight. It was an extremely delicate operation and one that he'd spent a great deal of time perfecting with the use of dead pigs and, later, for a more authentic experience, weighted shop mannequins.

However, when he'd first hung the canvas he'd been distressed to see that the head was rather unattractively mounted. It leaned precariously to the left and caused the plastic to stretch the woman's features so that she looked comically malformed. He had wrapped his arm round her pelvis and lifted it slightly, using his right hand to readjust the hook and freeing the plastic so he could obtain a more relaxed expression. Unfortunately, as a perfectionist, he had to make another minute adjustment to the hook and heard the sound his artist's sensitivity feared the most: the cracking of vertebrae.

Telling himself firmly to leave well alone, he forced himself to take several paces backwards. He looked critically and tried to see none of the faults, only the beauty. It was at that moment that he saw the torches and heard the sound of footsteps. He watched silently, weighing up whether this was a good or bad thing. He wanted his latest creation found and appreciated certainly, but he wasn't entirely finished. The viewing arena needed to be cleared of all twigs and debris and any materials likely to be counterproductive to both the enjoyment of the experience and a threat to his freedom.

He took in a deep, considered breath and studied the light beams as they criss-crossed the wooded area near to the solitary house of the old woman. The beams appeared to be positioned at shoulder height, which meant they were likely to be police officers who held their torches that way and were therefore, in all probability, searching for him. He would go; leave them to it.

Resolved, he started to walk backwards, admiring his work and checking that he hadn't left anything too incriminating. The power saw had already been positioned at the entrance to the arena ready to be collected as he headed back to the car he'd hidden in the trees.

His arms full of twigs and branches, he stepped reverently backwards, giving his masterpiece his final appraisal when he noticed that the woman's feet, which previously were clear of the plastic bag's sealed end, were now straining and bulging the plastic. In a moment of horror, the killer recognised immediately what the problem was and sprinted back to the woman.

As he'd feared, the vertebrae had dislocated and the lower part of the torso was beginning to collapse, the neck obscenely stretched and showing evidence of internal tearing. The familiar sensation of disappointment and anger began to flood his system with unwanted hormones. He clamped his jaw tightly and tried to think of a redemptive plan, but the sounds made by the police officers crashing through the woodland made him even more frustrated. All this planning and effort was going to be flushed down the pan. He'd be a laughing stock!

*

'What the hell are we looking for?' carped Ellis.

'Not sure… you smell that?' replied Paget, swinging her torch round.

'Like what?'

'Fresh sawdust. Someone has been doing a bit of late-night tree management, but why?'

Ellis thought he didn't care very much why, and was trying to remember whether he had any leave left this year, as he was well overdue a bit of R & R on a foreign beach, when the bullet struck him in the chest. It had been silenced, and without the aural cues neither he nor Paget were completely sure of what had just taken place.

'Ellis? What the hell?' hissed Paget as she watched his face twist into a grimace; his knees buckle.

This time there was a palpable hiss and thud as the second bullet hit Paget in the side of the face and silenced any further thoughts.

In a final neural explosion of lights and comprehension, Ellis was able to understand that they had both been killed, but as to why and by whom there was insufficient time.

*

Laurence had managed to unwrap, connect and position all three lamps in the time it took Dr Hounslow to visit the basement. When she entered the room, she was carrying two slightly dusty folders bulging with photographs. Sitting down quickly, she opened the first and spread the materials in front of them. 'Twenty years ago I was working my post-grad internship with Dr Reznor. That was when the morgue was attached to St Anselm's,' she said in a low voice.

Eleanor nodded, remembering the old building, which spent proportionally more money on disposing of rats and roaches than people.

'This was one of my first cases,' Hounslow said, pointing to a photograph of the face of a young girl lying on a concrete floor. The girl's eyes were open and beginning to take on the milky hue of the recently deceased. Her lips were strangely dark and her perfect skin and halo of blonde hair made her look angelic.

'Carin Hughes was one of two bodies found by neighbours on the fourteenth of November 1992. An older woman, her mother Marilyn Hughes, was found in the vehicle.' Hounslow pointed to several other photographs showing a woman's body slumped against the wheel of an ancient Ford pick-up. Eleanor looked at the pathologist with raised eyebrows.

'They were suicides,' said Hounslow. 'The garage doors were shut and the car had been running for some considerable time before the alarm was raised.'

'What's the connection?' asked Eleanor, her eyes bright with anticipation.

Slowly Hounslow pushed another photograph towards the two detectives. The black-and-white image showed Carin's body. Eleanor drew in breath and held it for a moment as she worked out the implications of the image. Carin Hughes' body was wrapped tightly in a plastic sheet. Only her head was exposed.

'She was murdered?' stated Eleanor.

Hounslow nodded and raised an eyebrow. 'But not by the individual who placed her in the plastic.'

Eleanor and Laurence both stared at the pathologist as she began to narrate the events using the series of photographs in the folder. She pointed at the figure slumped inside the Ford's driver's seat.

'Marilyn Hughes, Carin's mother, suffered from a schizophrenic disorder and had recently been sectioned for displaying suicidal tendencies. She appears to have persuaded or forced Carin to accompany her into the garage where the doors were locked and the car's engine started. The keys to the garage were found in Marilyn's pocket.'

'They died at the same time?' queried Laurence.

'There or thereabouts,' the pathologist replied. 'Carin had been dead for several hours when her body had been repositioned by a third party. From the lividity patterns, it was obvious that she'd been seated next to her mother in the car while the engine ran. Her blood analysis indicated she died as a result of carbon monoxide inhalation, as did her mother.'

'So someone lifted her out of the car and placed her on the floor in a plastic wrapping,' said Eleanor.

Hounslow nodded. 'There was no proof that Marilyn's sixteen-year-old son had any part to play in the death of either female.'

'Did he report the deaths?' asked Eleanor.

Hounslow shook her head. 'No, that was a neighbour. As I said, there was no proof that the son had been culpable for any of these events.'

There was a pause. 'So what's triggered the connection in your mind?' asked Eleanor, leaning towards the doctor. 'It's more than just a plastic bag, isn't it?'

'When we performed the autopsy, both women had been subjected to physical abuse. They had the sort of bruising associated with prolonged sexual abuse. However, Carin was still a virgin when she died. Her hymen was still intact and no vaginal penetration was evident.'

Eleanor looked puzzled. 'That's unusual, isn't it?'

'In my experience yes,' replied Hounslow.

'Was there a father? Stepfather?'

'No one had ever been reported or seen entering the family home.'

'No one except the son?' said Eleanor slowly.

Hounslow nodded slowly. 'Lee Hughes was interviewed by police several times, but he confessed to knowing nothing, and there was nothing that could be pinned on him.'

'Dr Hounslow, were there any colour photographs taken of the crime scene?' asked Laurence anxiously.

The doctor smiled and nodded. 'I wondered when you'd ask.'
Eleanor frowned and looked at Laurence. 'Why?'

'Carbon monoxide poisoning,' said Laurence with excitement as the pathologist handed a slim envelope to Eleanor, who immediately slid the contents out and laid them in front of her. What she saw caused her gasp with shock.

'Carbon monoxide poisoning turns the cheeks and lips a beautiful cherry red,' said Laurence. 'An identical shade to those of Lydia Greystein.'

CHAPTER FIFTEEN

Eleanor accelerated through the early morning traffic, her fingers drumming restlessly on the wheel as she finished her call to Wadesky. '… I want a complete timeline on Lee Hughes… C-A-R-I-N Hughes… Yes, we'll be there in five. I need to know who the primary was on the case.' She rang off.

Laurence gave her thirty seconds before speaking. 'Well? You think this is the guy?'

'I think it's an interesting possibility. But I've had these coincidences before. You put your hopes into a lead and then find out the guy's been dead for years.'

'The lips and the plastic bag. That could be his first murder and he's been perfecting his methods over the years.'

'You heard Dr Hounslow say that there was no evidence that they had been murdered by anyone other than the mother,' replied Eleanor, trying to keep her excitement to a minimum. 'We need to find out if Lee Hughes could have left the school at any point and if so why?'

'But they'd both been sexually abused. It could have been him. Maybe that's why they killed themselves.'

'You've made an assumption that a fourteen-year-old girl was a willing partner in her own death. You need more concrete evidence before you leap into scenarios like that,' said Eleanor. 'If the primary is still alive and can remember the case, we should get a better picture.'

Eleanor's cell phone rang. She listened with a growing smile. 'Thanks. Well there's a piece of luck. Mo was the primary on the Hughes case,' she said with enthusiasm. 'We'll get into the office, pick up the files and I'll head on over to talk to Mo and you can go and talk to Tracy Earnshaw again.'

'Whoa! Why am I excluded from talking to Mo?' said Laurence peevishly.

There was a pause as Eleanor considered this matter. 'You're right. We'll both go together.'

*

Sergeant Andy Harrison had spent the last eight hours dealing with paperwork so, when the second call came through from Mrs Needermeyer to say that the two officers who'd been sent to investigate the woodland crime hadn't returned to their car for two hours, he was more than happy to haul ass down to the park and investigate. He'd tried to raise both Paget and Ellis on their radios, but wasn't worried yet. He'd learned over the years not to fear the worst, as it was proportionally most likely the worst hadn't happened yet, and it played havoc with his acid reflux. So, easing himself into his car, he drove through the early morning traffic with the window down, enjoying the cold, wet autumn wind.

The patrol car had been parked next to Mrs Needermeyer's front lawn. It was locked and there was no sign of either officer. Mrs Needermeyer pointed out the direction Paget and Ellis had taken and, putting on his overcoat, Harrison headed off into the wood. Where the hell were they? He knew that cops often stopped for a coffee, but none of the stalls were open and they'd been missing for at least two hours.

He chewed a couple of antacids as he made his way along the leaf-strewn pathway that bisected the park. He'd been walking for about five minutes when he heard a cacophony of dog barking followed by screaming. Now was the time to fear the worst.

It took him several seconds to comprehend the image in front of him. He knew exactly what was hanging from the tree, as he'd seen the images taken from the Westex power station. It was probably a woman, wrapped in a heavy-duty transparent plastic bag. But the base of the plastic bag had stretched and was beginning to tear where the weight of the body had collected.

He raised his weapon and began to walk slowly around the clearing towards the two kneeling officers. The dog, a long-haired collie, sprang up and down below the hanging woman, barking incessantly. Fortunately, it couldn't reach and destroy valuable evidence. He'd deal with the dog in a moment, but first he had to reach Ellis and Paget.

The two officers knelt with their heads bowed in what appeared to be an act of supplication to the woman hanging from the oak tree. Harrison knew he had to secure the site and that both Paget and Ellis were dead, but he couldn't calculate how they were both in a kneeling position.

He looked around cautiously as he approached the nearest figure, which he assumed was Ellis due to the size differential between the two officers. Edging nervously forward, he pulled off his glove and gingerly pressed two fingers against the carotid artery whilst keeping his gun raised; Ellis's skin was cold and there was no detectable pulse. Hunkering down, he saw that several large oak branches had been roughly pared down and used as a prop to prevent Ellis's body falling forward.

Paget's body was at least ten feet away. Still on high alert, Harrison moved slowly towards her, his legs heavy and hands shaking. Like Ellis, her body was resting on an A-frame of oak branches. He reached out his fingers but withdrew them gratefully when he saw the bloodied mess and knew that her injuries were too catastrophic.

He pulled the metallic tainted air through his nostrils and pushed it through his mouth in an effort to stabilise his inner chaos. In the distance he heard sirens gathering momentum as they sped towards him; the dog owner must have called 911. Breaking through the sirens he could hear the dog and felt the comfort that familiar procedure presented. Moving swiftly towards it, he grabbed the dog's collar and firmly rolled it onto its back. He felt it relax under his commanding hand, the bark subsiding to a whimper.

*

'When are my officers going to be released?' hissed Marty Samuelson to Dr Hounslow, his back to the figures of Ellis and Paget.

'Marty, we're going as fast as we can but I will not allow sentiment to cloud my judgement. When Susan Cheung has finished, these officers will be escorted to the morgue where we can look after them properly. You will not serve them by rushing my department,' said Hounslow firmly.

Samuelson turned to Eleanor and Laurence. 'Get this bastard! You understand?'

Eleanor nodded. 'Give me the manpower.'

'You have whatever and whoever you want. You have unlimited overtime, but you report in.' His voice quavered with exhaustion and emotion. He lifted a warning finger; there was so much more to say but now wasn't the time to open those floodgates. He turned and walked towards the mayoral Mercedes, which was parked ominously on the periphery of the police taped line.

Eleanor stared at Ellis and Paget and then fixed her attention on the woman. Laurence followed her over.

'Did you expect him to murder again so quickly?'

Eleanor slowly shook her head. 'There's always a reason.' She turned to Laurence. 'Give me some.'

Laurence opened his mouth to speak.

'Don't rush your thinking,' she said quietly.

He nodded and took in the whole scene. 'Opportunity.'

Eleanor let the corners of her mouth turn slightly. 'You don't think this is well planned?'

Laurence shook his head. 'No, there's something missing… something's wrong about it. He had to have carefully planned and selected this site but…' He fell silent as he tried to put his finger on what was wrong.

'Look at her first. She was selected and presented,' said Eleanor. She held a hand up to Matt, who was moving towards the body with removal equipment.

Laurence circled the body. 'He repositioned her too many times and snapped her vertebrae. He ruined the presentation, didn't he?'

Eleanor nodded, pleased with his assessment.

'It would have made him angry to have messed that up, wouldn't it?' responded Laurence.

'Yes, it would have. But he didn't destroy her like he did Belinda,' she coaxed.

'Because Ellis and Paget were here,' said Laurence, a little too loudly. 'When they arrived he was angry because he hadn't displayed her correctly. So he killed them and placed them in an attitude of…' He searched for the right phrase.

'Awe,' Eleanor helped him. 'They kneel in awe.'

CHAPTER SIXTEEN

Gary Le Douce stared at the man and then shook his head slowly. 'What's in it for me?' he said flatly, drawing an impressive quantity of smoke into his lungs.

'A handling fee of course,' responded the man smoothly.

Gary waited, his greed expertly disguised by practised insouciance.

'Fifty,' offered the man.

Gary snorted the last remnants of smoke out of both nostrils, turned his back on the man and began to pad across the greasy floor in the direction of his lair. He knew from years of negotiating that the final fee would be determined by the greatest desire: his for the cash or the man's for whatever illegal deal he wanted brokering. Gary could almost taste the man's hesitation as he walked, and when he heard him clear his throat, he knew he'd won. Obligingly, he turned to the man, his over-plucked eyebrows raised in an expectant feline leer.

'One hundred,' hissed the man.

'One fifty!' Gary shot back, trying not to betray his glee at having won. The man's face twitched into an expression of such contempt that even Gary felt himself shudder slightly.

'One fifty it is.' Slowly, the man looked around the dark and unhealthy interior of As You Like It, as if checking for a camera or a warm body that could oversee his next move.

Gary waited. It wouldn't be the first time he'd pushed a business deal a little too far and paid the price, but he was getting a little too old for physical violence, and the man looked no stranger to doling it out. Gary knew that to survive in his line of work one must never act like prey. So he stood his ground, hardened his expression and waited.

'The package will be collected sometime this week. I expect it to remain unopened and the recipient unacknowledged. The package' – he proffered a large folded manila envelope with 'Samuel' written in thick marker pen – 'is for Samuel.'

Gary grasped the bag and waited while the man counted out three fifty-dollar notes and held them out to him.

'I have paid well and expect a professional service,' the man said quietly.

'And I will deliver,' answered Gary, trying not to betray his discomfort.

With a final visual sweep of the room, the man turned around and walked to the entrance, closing the door quietly behind him.

With an alacrity that surprised even himself, Gary rushed forward and locked the door, fumbling with the chain lock. 'Go to hell!' he whispered quietly but with genuine feeling as the lock slid into place.

*

The man had discovered the card when he'd replenished his own supply on the noticeboard of the club several weeks ago. At first, from a purely personal point of view, he'd been a little peeved to find the card advertising 'Kidnappings Arranged'. Of course this appeared to be a commercial enterprise, whereas he would never stoop so low as to link the acquisition of financial gain with the redemptive service he offered to the deserving few. So, he'd pocketed the card. But having met Eleanor Raven and feeling so strongly that she needed more than he could offer her, he had been mulling over the possibility of it being a gift as well as an opportunity to check out the opposition. The latter was a less than lofty thought and he had made every effort to banish it from his consciousness.

He'd left his request on the cell phone's voicemail a few days ago and had been surprised to receive a response from a male who called himself Samuel and gave clear instructions as to where the money should be left. He'd been pleased to find the event priced steeply, which indicated quality in his mind. As a man who'd made a comfortable living from real-estate rentals, he viewed money as a means to establish power and status.

He walked quickly but observantly through the rain in the direction of his office building. He could have driven, but he liked to imbibe the sights and smells of the city.

Just as he turned onto Cambridge Street, he passed a florist and a strange but wonderful idea came to him. He would send Eleanor a bouquet of roses and allow her the opportunity to anticipate and thrill at the upcoming event. She had no idea that he was in possession of her name and address; this would humble her and prepare her mentally for the cleansing to come. He smiled to himself as he selected the most expensive roses and wrote out the address for the small woman behind the counter.

'It is their perfume,' she said, in an Eastern European accent.

He looked at her steadily, waiting for her explanation.

'That is why they are so expensive, sir. Most roses have to be flown in and they are selected for their shape. They all have long, thornless stems, but these are traditional roses, and while they will not look the same, they will smell like heaven itself in a day or two,' she said brightly. 'Would you care to fill in a card for your loved one?' she asked.

The man felt a wave of irritation pass at her assumption, but he was feeling genial. He selected a card from his wallet and placed it on the counter. The glossy ivory card held a single image: a yin-yang symbol. He shuddered slightly as the woman picked it up and flipped it over.

'You want to write here?' she suggested. 'Something to your lady?'

'Please deliver the card with the flowers to the address.' He paid with his visa card and turned to leave.

'You want these signed for by the lady? We deliver twice,' she added helpfully.

Ignoring her, he stepped out into the fresh, cold air.

CHAPTER SEVENTEEN

Mo was fully dressed and struggling to put on his outdoor shoes when Eleanor and Laurence arrived. 'I'm coming in,' he gasped as a lace slipped out of his swollen fingers.

'He is *not* coming in,' said Minnie firmly. 'He goes into work and he'll be the next cop on a gurney.'

'Well I'd rather die on the job than sit here gathering cobwebs!' gasped Mo, the shoelace eluding him yet again.

'That's not what those poor dead officers said! Or their partners,' Minnie replied as she kneeled down, snatched the lace and tied it for him.

'Let me have Mo for a few hours and I promise he won't leave the office. I'll have him driven back by dinnertime,' Eleanor said persuasively.

Mo smiled at his wife, stifling a belch and a grimace.

'The doctor said he was to rest!' said Minnie desperately, knowing the ground was crumbling beneath her argument.

'If I think for one minute Mo's in distress, I will personally call the medics. In fact,' she said turning to Laurence, 'Detective Whitefoot used to be a doctor and he can keep an eye on Mo.'

Both Mo and Minnie turned to stare at Laurence, who looked unhappy. 'Huh? Why'd you do that?' asked Minnie, confused.

'I… medicine wasn't the right vocation for me…' His voice trailed off as he saw Minnie's contemptuous expression.

'That we should all have such choice,' she snorted.

Laurence's cheeks reddened.

*

The atmosphere in Homicide was heavy with anger and silence as Eleanor prepared her debrief. The board that had been dedicated to the Greystein murder had been exponentially expanded to cover the entire wall, other ongoing cases having been de-prioritised and shunted off into another room.

Laurence stood back and stared hard at the narrative unfolding before him. A 'true' timeline of Lydia Greystein and the second victim had been placed next to each other. Each photograph of the murdered woman in situ and then their morgue shots indicated to even the untrained eye that this was a serial killer in action. To the left of Greystein's photographs were the more tentative connections: Belinda Myrtle and Carin Hughes. A blank card with the name 'Lee Hughes' was pinned above the photograph of Carin Hughes, with several thin red threads linking it to each of the women. Above the empty space reading 'Lee Hughes' was the colour photograph of Carin Hughes wrapped in a plastic bag.

'Haven't we got a photo of Lee yet?' asked Laurence.

'Working on it,' said Wadesky, from her station.

Laurence moved closer to her. 'No mugshots from the case? No yearbook?'

'Couldn't take one because he'd done nothing… well nothing we could prove,' said Mo, who was sitting in an armchair carried in from the chief's office. In one hand, he scanned the files he'd compiled twenty years earlier and in the other he nursed Monster's giant head, which was plonked on his lap.

'Where did this guy go to, Mo?' said Wadesky, scanning her monitor. 'It's like he stepped off the planet.'

'Could he be dead?' asked Laurence.

Wadesky shrugged and chewed her finger. 'No unclaimed, unidentified bodies appear of corresponding age. I've scanned the stats from 1992 to current day and, unusually, there are none that could be him.'

'Which means that he's alive and well hidden, or dead and well hidden,' replied Laurence. 'And you've checked the school yearbook?'

'I called his school and he disappeared before leavers' photos were taken. There's nothing official on him over the years.'

'What was your impression of him?' Laurence asked Mo.

'He was evasive but polite. Seemed very cut up about his sister being dead, but didn't get any feeling he gave a shit about Mom. He wouldn't admit to having placed his sister in a plastic bag, but who else could have done it? The garage was locked from the inside and only access was through the kitchen. But if he had, it wasn't really chargeable, not after the suffering he'd been through.'

'But the sexual abuse? Did you think it was him?'

Mo thought for a minute. 'With hindsight yes, but at the time it just didn't seem possible. We thought it was a guy, someone we hadn't met yet. Hell, we even dragged Carin's male teachers over the coals, though there was nothing doing. Maybe we could have got something out of him, but he vanished before the inquest. Gone. Didn't take a bag or money or any goddamn thing that could have helped him. He just walked.'

'That's so weird,' said Wadesky.

'What did you make of him?' coaxed Laurence.

'Christ, it was twenty years ago. I'm not sure that I could divorce myself from current events and give you an accurate picture,' brooded Mo. He was silent for a moment or two, slowly and rhythmically stroking Monster's head, as if clearing his thoughts and running through the images of the case. 'He was calm. Too calm… he said he hadn't seen the bodies of his sister and mom, but no one believed Marilyn had placed Carin in the plastic bag.'

'Why not?' asked Wadesky, still surfing possible links to Lee Hughes.

'Carin's body was the same temperature as Marilyn's, so they must have died fairly close to each other, but the lividity shows Carin was moved several hours later,' replied Mo. 'And yet, Lee couldn't have killed them because he was seen in class during the times when the deaths occurred.'

'That's a definite?'

Mo nodded. 'Something did cause him to bunk off school at lunch though. What it was, we never got to the bottom of, but he was picked up on the streets later on in the afternoon. Maybe it was some sort of premonition.' He shrugged.

'What about the sexual abuse? Could it have been him, and that may have driven Marilyn to kill herself and Carin?' said Laurence.

'Yeah, but there were no complaints from either of the two women to anyone. We asked everyone and there was shit,' replied Mo, shaking his head. 'Hey, I do remember something about Lee. He was good at art. Really good. He won some sort of state contest or something. They gave him a trophy.'

Laurence and Wadesky looked at Mo, who was straightening his back in the chair in an attempt to relieve the pain in his chest and guts, and then at each other.

Wadesky hit the keys and within less than a minute let out a stifled, 'Got him!' She spun the laptop screen round to show Laurence and Mo. The newspaper article was captioned, 'Local Greenslade High School student wins coveted state arts scholarship' and had a grainy, monochrome photograph showing an unsmiling teenager with fair hair and a slim figure holding a metallic trophy in the shape of an obelisk.

*

Eleanor cleared her throat and ran her eyes around the room. It was usual to wait several minutes for detectives to finish anecdotes, gulp final mouthfuls of coffee and saunter from a distant workstation to take up a position round the murder board. Now everyone had a pen and notebook, firearms were holstered rather than shoved to the back of desk drawers and the usual room smells of coffee, fries and doughnuts had been replaced by a sharp feral tang. Everyone wanted to get out of the office and onto the streets, but this debrief would determine which street, and who they were looking for. Eleanor was used to addressing colleagues, fending questions and motivating the masses, but this morning's debrief was very different. The usual barrier of anonymity had disappeared, and no one was sure whether tempers and professionalism could be assured with the photographs of two dead colleagues on the board.

*

Laurence's phone buzzed just as Eleanor began to explain the supposed connection between the murders of Greystein and Myrtle. Seeing it was Matt, he nodded to Eleanor and stepped quickly into the corridor.

'We've got an ID on the female victim. We had her prints on file from a DUI last year. Her name's Cassandra Willis, aged forty-nine. Autopsy's finished on her and I've emailed the documents through to you,' said Matt. 'You may wish to note that her tongue had been removed several hours before death, and the neck severance was post-mortem.'

'Jeez,' said Laurence. 'How long did she take to die?'

'She died between 9 p.m. and midnight last night. Can't make it any tighter than that. She hadn't eaten or drunk anything for at least ten hours before death. If you can narrow down her lunch period it would help. I've listed the contents on the report. We're starting on our two officers in an hour,' Matt said quietly.

'I'll talk to you later. I owe you,' said Laurence, heading towards his office.

'Not for this one, buddy,' replied Matt, breaking the call.

*

There was a silence when Laurence walked back into the room with a handful of printouts. Eleanor had run through the known information and detectives were reading through the handouts that she'd prepared earlier.

'We got anything on this guy Lee Hughes? A photo'd help,' said a stocky red-haired, red-faced man in his late forties. By his figure and repetitive style in shirts, Laurence assumed this to be Smith.

'We've got a photo now, but it was taken in the nineties,' responded Laurence, pinning the newspaper printout of Lee onto the board. 'Wadesky's onto getting the original, and when that comes through I'll get it to you.'

Smith nodded.

'We've got an ID on the victim. Cassandra Willis, aged forty-nine,' he said, putting up a mugshot with her arrest number and the date from last August. 'DUI last year for the second time. Manages a recruitment company downtown.'

Eleanor was pleased and took a moment or two to study the photograph of the woman, who was barely recognisable from her corpse.

'He'd cut her tongue out,' said Laurence.

'Who the hell are we dealing with here?' said Timms from somewhere in the back of the room.

'From what I can tell, you're dealing with an extremely organised individual with a passion for his work,' said a small, bird-like woman swathed in more wool than an alpaca.

'This is Ruby Delaware, profiler,' said Eleanor quickly. A sigh was heard from the back of the room. It was common knowledge that detectives considered the opinions of profilers little better than those of the canteen staff, and often less accurate.

'I need twenty-four hours to analyse what we have here,' said Ruby, her cheeks burning.

'Take as long as you like, darling,' came a muttered comment from the back ranks.

'We need all the help we can get!' snapped Eleanor. 'Thank you, Dr Delaware,' she said as Ruby scurried from the room clutching the handouts and jottings tightly to her chest.

'Smith, I want you to dig out Tracy Earnshaw; she knows something and I want to know what. Timms, get down to the county morgue – make sure we get everything from Dr Hounslow and follow up. Our guy used some sort of power saw – see if you can get it typed and send uniforms out to see if we can trace it. There's ballistic evidence – run it. Wadesky, you trace Lee Hughes with Mo and let's see if we can't get a timeline on him. I believe he wrapped Carin in that plastic sheet and that it was in some way symbolic for him. Give me the times he couldn't be accounted for.'

'You think it's this guy Lee Hughes? We putting our eggs in one basket on him?' said Smith.

Eleanor hesitated and glanced at the board. If she went off on a goose chase, she could lose any lead that might still be traceable, but this felt right.

'I believe it's him,' she said firmly. 'Johnson is going to retrace the case, starting from the Greystein murder and following our arrests and evidence trail. If, for one moment, he thinks we've missed something, or are heading in the wrong direction, we stop and re-evaluate, okay?'

There were mutterings of approval from the gathered detectives. Sam Johnson looked and worked with all the dispassionate rigour of a tax collector. Too bland and humourless for the majority of his colleagues, he'd gradually been withdrawn from public contact and encouraged to pursue a more academic and analytical approach to policing. A decision that relieved all concerned.

'Johnson will collate and analyse all data that comes in. He'll take the first meeting with Dr Delaware and distribute all discovery across the department. Make sure you've checked it in with him as well as me. The only way we're going to stop this killer, and bring him to justice, is by sharing information. Got that?'

Eleanor looked around the room. She'd said enough. Detectives were getting restless; they knew what was demanded of them and they would work every hour of every day to flush Lee Hughes out. At least until disappointment, despair and exhaustion took their inevitable toll.

'Okay, boss,' said Smith, grabbing his coat and heading for the door.

*

While Eleanor waited on the phone for the warrant that would allow them to access Cassandra's apartment and workplace, Laurence gave Mo a surreptitious check over. Despite the increase in stress, Mo's heart rate, though steady, was only moderately high.

'What meds are you on?' he asked Mo quietly.

Mo grinned, readjusting his position in the chair. 'Be better to ask what I'm not on.'

Laurence smiled. 'You look like shit,' he said.

Mo smiled and nodded. 'It's when I stop looking like shit everyone needs to worry.'

He paused and studied Laurence, his hand rhythmically smoothing Monster's head and neck. The dog let out deep groans of pleasure. 'You got any issues with working here?' asked Mo.

'No, not really,' answered Laurence.

Mo raised his eyebrows, inviting further discussion.

'I'm not sure that Detective Raven is ready to let go of you and recognise me as her partner yet.'

'Well who says I'm not coming back?' said Mo, sitting forward in his chair and giving Laurence a hard stare. Then he smiled. 'Just yanking your chain buddy.' He eased himself back down. 'She'll get there in her own time. You have to work hard at winning over Eleanor. She's one of the best cops I ever worked with but…' He mulled his thoughts.

'But?'

'She has an enemy,' said Mo quietly.

Eleanor walked into the room, pulling on her overcoat and juggling her phone and paperwork. She tipped her head to one side and narrowed her eyes as she saw the two men talking.

'Enemy?' asked Laurence, worried.

'Herself,' whispered Mo as he resumed his reading.

'Any danger we could go do some police work, Detective?' asked Eleanor, her eyes raised, curious to know what had passed between them.

'Yes, ma'am,' replied Laurence, standing up. 'Home by five at the latest, okay?' He pointed to Mo.

'Jeez…' muttered Mo.

'I'll take him myself,' offered Wadesky. 'Your Minnie got some home bakes?' she asked Mo.

'Yes,' snapped Mo. 'Home bakes for any jerk that comes in from the street. Not for me! I'm so goddamn hungry and calorie deprived, that dog food's looking good.'

Laurence turned to see where Mo was pointing. Someone had placed two ceramic bowls, one filled with water, and the other next to a large bag of high-protein kibble. He hadn't considered whether Monster had access to water and he'd pretty much abandoned him during the day, assuming one of the secretaries would keep an eye on him.

Wadesky smiled. 'Timms brought it in yesterday. He's taken a shine to Monster.' She returned to the screen. 'He even took him for a walk… well down to his cigar break by the trash cans.'

'Timms?' said Laurence, confused.

'Leaving,' said Eleanor as she strode out of the room.

*

Cassandra Willis lived in a modest but expensive condo, a few miles south of her workplace. Eleanor and Laurence had been granted access to the apartment by the site manager and were taking careful note of resident names from the mailboxes in the corridor. A sound of gentle but persistent knocking came from the first floor and both detectives moved silently and carefully in its direction. As they rounded the top of the stairs they saw a slim black woman with her ear pressed to a door, calling faintly, 'Miss Willis? Can you hear me? It's Aria.'

Eleanor moved slowly and silently towards Aria's back. 'Ma'am?'

Aria let out a shriek and clutched her chest. 'You scared me.' The woman took a deep breath and then studied the two detectives. Her hand moved from her chest to cover her mouth. 'What's happened to her?' she whispered.

'How well do you know Cassandra Willis?' asked Eleanor.

'I work for her. I'm her office manager – Aria Aryono. Who are you?' she asked nervously.

'I'm Detective Inspector Raven and this is Detective Whitefoot,' she replied. 'Why are you here?'

'I got a call from the people organising the conference she was attending. She was supposed to be giving a talk, but she didn't sign in. They called the hotel and she hadn't checked in there either. They wouldn't tell me if she'd been on the plane as I wasn't next of kin. I don't know where the hell she is so I came round here to check whether she got ill and just came home.'

Aria stared at Eleanor. 'Why are you here? Have you got her?' she asked cautiously.

'Got her?' replied Eleanor.

'Is she dead?'

'Have you a key to her apartment?' asked Eleanor.

Aria shook her head.

'Would you mind waiting here with Detective Whitefoot and answering a few of his questions while I take a look around?' Eleanor asked. Aria nodded glumly.

Eleanor unlocked the door and walked inside. She could hear Laurence's lowered tones as he drew information out of Aria. The apartment had a strangely detached quality to it. There were no mounted photographs of family or hints of any special interests the occupant may have had. There wasn't a trace of dust in any of the rooms, and Eleanor made a note to check on any cleaning assistance she may have hired.

There were a couple of indifferent prints on the wall and a bookcase full of manuals and textbooks, but there wasn't a single novel or any material that could have been consumed for pleasure.

The kitchen appeared to be unused. The fridge was devoid of anything edible apart from some condiments, three litres of gin and several bottles of tonic water. The freezer had a hefty selection of ready meals of a bland and limited variety.

Eleanor would call in CSI in a few minutes, but quite what they'd find mystified her. Cassandra Willis appeared to have lived her life here as if a hotel resident. There was no sign of any sexual proclivity that might have linked her to her killer; nor were there any signs of a struggle having taken place. She sighed and dialled Sue Cheung.

*

'Can't you just tell me what happened to her?' asked Aria plaintively.

Laurence paused. 'I'm afraid she was murdered.'

Aria's mouth opened into a wide O.

'Can you tell me whether Miss Willis had any enemies that you know of?' Laurence ran through the familiar and standard questions. Curiously, Aria didn't answer immediately.

'Yes.' Her shoulders slumped as if she knew what had to be revealed. 'She had poor relationships with a co-worker, Malcolm Stringer. He was the son of the previous owner, and part of the sell-off to Miss Willis was a guarantee that he would be kept on for the duration as office assistant.'

'And that was a problem for her or both of them?' asked Laurence, interested.

'Oh, both of them. He wasn't very… committed to the work, and Miss Willis was very driven. She made the company successful and wanted to get rid of Malcolm, but I don't think he was likely to find another job, and she couldn't bear to pay him for not working.'

'You think he might have killed her?'

'Oh dear Lord, no!' she answered, genuinely shocked.

'Did you like Miss Willis?'

Aria paused and thought about it. 'I admired what she did. She worked all hours and paid fair, but I could have done without all the bitching and moaning. Guess you have to let it wash over you, but sometimes I just wanted to knock their heads together.'

'So you didn't like her?' Laurence proffered.

'No, I guess not, but then that wasn't in my job description.'

Eleanor walked out of the apartment and locked the door behind her. 'Mrs Aryono, we're going to visit your workplace now; perhaps you'd like to have a coffee and a rest before you follow us?'

Aria understood what was implied. 'Of course.'

*

Petr Mensch had driven round the block twice in an attempt to find the correct building and then locate a parking space. He had several more deliveries to make that morning before he could get back home and finish his essay, which was due in tonight. He hated delivering flowers because they represented everything he loathed about this country. The decadence and the inconvenience were top of his list. Why the hell couldn't people hand the bloody things over themselves and not employ some shit-for-brains, i.e. himself, to deliver them as an excuse for forgetting an anniversary, having an affair or pretending they made up for some unloved bastard dying?

He also felt pissed off that he was indebted to his aunt who owned the shop, for paying for his college education, when it should be free and supported by the tax payer. And if he didn't get that essay in to his tutor by 6 p.m. he might be settling for a full-time career in floristry.

None of these thoughts improved his outlook on the day, so when there was no reply from Ms Raven at his insistent hammering, he was just about ready to stomp the flowers underfoot and leave them as a statement. Unfortunately, that wasn't how Petr's life worked, so he took a deep breath and knocked on an adjacent door. His luck was in. An elderly woman, clutching a small fat pug stared myopically at him.

'Can I leave these flowers with you?' he asked the woman, who continued to stare blankly at him. 'They're for your next-door neighbour, Ms Raven.'

The staring, and what could have been interpreted as incomprehension, continued.

'These roses are for your neighbour. Can you give them to her when she gets back, as we can only deliver once?'

Suddenly, the woman focussed her wayward stare on the flowers, and a small coy smile spread across her face. 'They're lovely,' she croaked. 'Lovely.'

Petr suspected that she didn't understand what was required of her, but he really needed to get back. 'Will you give these to Ms Raven when she gets back from work?' he said slowly.

'Oh yes. They are lovely,' she said, lowering the pug to the ground, who like his owner, seemed a little confused by the events unfolding.

That was good enough for Petr. He handed the bouquet of roses over to her, repositioned the card as a gesture of consideration and then left, ignoring the final comment from the elderly woman.

'You really shouldn't have.'

CHAPTER EIGHTEEN

Smith liked private gyms. He particularly liked to see the women that frequented them. These were the more ethereal types of women with tiny waists, large augmented breasts and figure-hugging Lycra sportswear. He was a member of the station gym, but the women there were colleagues, and, as such, could not be lusted after. In any case, most of the women officers he knew could deck a man with one punch and competed for bench-press tallies. He liked a less lethal and more dependent type of woman and placed the Bodyworks Gym receptionist firmly in the former category. At the sight of his badge she had rolled her eyes and scowled unpleasantly at him.

'I'm sorry, am I ruining your fabulous day?' spat Smith, glaring aggressively at her.

'I've already spoken to your colleague,' she hissed.

'Bet you were really helpful to him too.'

'Listen, I didn't know that woman who got murdered. I confirmed that she was a member of this gym and then I introduced him to her trainer,' she said.

He leaned over the desk and met her eye. 'I suspect you've heard or read that two officers were murdered last night?' Smith growled. 'The information I require may have a direct bearing on that investigation.'

'Then how can I help you, Officer?' she said slowly.

Smith's temper was simmering slightly below punch and arrest level. 'You can tell me where Tracy Earnshaw is.'

'No, I can't because she didn't show for her ten o'clock appointment,' replied the receptionist, her raised eyebrow implying there was a wealth of information in that sentence, which could be gleaned if only Smith were brighter or more palatable.

'Is that usual, her not showing up to work?' he asked with interest.

'Actually, no, she's pretty good at showing up. She only has a couple of clients; therefore her obligations are limited,' she added knowledgeably.

'How long has she been working here?'

'Not long. Couple of months at best.'

'Give me her address,' said Smith, flipping open his notebook. He detected the beginnings of a pause, so stormed in quickly with, 'And I want a photo of her too.'

With a twitch of her lip, the receptionist stabbed the request onto her touchscreen using her pen.

'I've got her address as 1117 Aldermaston Crescent, Barndale.'

'Uh-huh,' muttered Smith as he wrote it down. 'And a photograph?'

The receptionist scrolled down a couple of pages.

'Okay, we don't appear to have a copy of her driving licence or passport by the look of things.'

'That unusual?' asked Smith.

'We keep standard passport photos of all employees, so they can be transferred directly onto staff badges. There's a memo here asking for this to be supplied.'

'When's she due in next?'

'She's got an eleven-thirty tomorrow morning.'

'Well let's hope I don't have to bother you again tomorrow,' said Smith ominously, walking towards the exit.

*

'Mr Stringer? Malcolm Stringer?' asked Eleanor, appraising the man that sat in front of her. She noted his chewed fingernails and unkempt appearance; no wonder Cassandra Willis had despaired at having him as an enforced colleague. 'You seem rather unconcerned that your employer has been murdered?'

Malcolm shook his head violently and began peeling the skin away from his nail bed.

'Didn't you get on very well?'

'No, but I didn't kill her,' he said decisively.

'Do you know who did?' she asked casually.

'No!' He resumed his chewing and paring.

When she'd asked if there was anywhere private that they could go to discuss matters, Malcolm had shown them into Cassandra Willis's office. 'It's the only place you have any privacy here,' he'd complained.

'What about a staff room?' she asked.

Malcolm shook his head. 'She didn't believe in that sort of thing.'

'Are you in line to take over the management, Mr Stringer?' she coaxed.

Suddenly Malcolm was on his guard. His posture became less flaccid and his eyes narrowed.

'I'm not saying anything else until I get a lawyer,' he replied fearfully.

'You don't need a lawyer, Mr Stringer, because you haven't been charged with anything. Do you think that's likely?' she asked.

Again he shook his head.

'Who booked Miss Willis's car?' she asked innocuously.

Malcolm stared at her suspiciously, his eyes darting to Eleanor's left. 'She did it herself,' he replied quickly.

'That's rather unusual, isn't it? Surely it would be your job?' she coaxed, her voice beginning to harden as she applied pressure.

'I've never had to book a car before. My duties are mainly concerning filing.'

'You booked the car. We know you did because Mrs Aryono told us,' said Eleanor.

'What would she know?' replied Malcolm, his voice wavering.

'We asked her and she was quite clear that she had offered to do it, but you'd insisted on taking on the task yourself. Why would you insist on booking the car yourself when everyone in the office attests to the fact that you never volunteer to carry out any work outside your limited responsibilities?'

Malcolm rose slightly in his seat, his flushing with anger. But he wasn't going to be drawn. 'I didn't book the car,' he said firmly and sat down.

There was a knock at the door and Laurence entered. He nodded slightly as he took a seat next to Eleanor. A gesture she took to mean that he wanted to question Malcolm.

'Mr Stringer, I've just been to look at the CCTV footage taken around the time that Miss Willis left the building prior to her disappearance. I have to say that the coverage in this building is of an excellent quality. No fuzzy features or lack of detail,' said Laurence chattily.

Malcolm was unmoved; he stared at Laurence and selected another finger for chewing.

'Did you know there's a camera located in each elevator? And one positioned in the foyer.'

Malcolm shrugged.

'I wanted to see exactly what time Miss Willis left the building.'

Again, Laurence paused, hoping that this information would elicit some sort of response.

'She left at 4.40 p.m., with her overnight bag, but between the elevator and the airport she vanished. So we have to conclude that the driver of the car, if not responsible himself, may have information as to where she went or who she met. But here's the interesting bit…' Laurence leaned towards Malcolm, as if sharing a secret with him. 'We see you meeting Miss Willis as the elevator doors open onto the foyer. You seem agitated… am I right?'

Eleanor and Laurence watched Malcolm's face for any sign that might indicate a deeper level of involvement. But he was focussing his gaze on the door and appeared not to be listening.

'And then when the elevator doors open and Miss Willis steps out, you seem upset, so what I can only suppose was an argument took place between the two of you. Am I right?'

Again, Malcolm ignored the question, raising his eyebrows in a gesture of indifference. 'But the most fascinating part of this whole drama is when the two of you part company and you're alone in the elevator.'

Malcolm's eyebrows wrinkled together as if trying to remember exactly what had taken place.

'You start to laugh, Malcolm. Big, side-splitting hoots of laughter. The kind of belly laugh that only shakes us when something really, really funny happens.'

Laurence was moving ever closer to Malcolm, his voice slowing hypnotically. 'You knew what was going to happen to her, didn't you?'

There was a heavy silence. Malcolm's eyes narrowed and he clamped his thin lips together.

'I don't know what you're talking about,' he replied slowly.

'I think you do, Mr Stringer. I think you planned to have Miss Willis picked up and murdered, and I can prove it,' he said calmly.

'How are you going to do that when it didn't happen?' shrieked Malcolm.

'I'm going to find five thousand dollars missing from your bank account.'

The colour drained from Malcolm's flabby cheeks.

*

Aldermaston Crescent was situated in the run-down east side of the city. A mile to the west, the streets were lined with maple, ash and white cedar and attracted chickadees and nighthawks, whereas the square mile that made up the neglected estate specialised in more defensive shrubs such as buckthorn and poison ivy.

Smith knocked again on the front door of 1117. He'd been standing in the rain waiting for a response for the past three minutes and felt that if he'd stood there till the crack of doom, no one would answer.

He looked up and down the street, surprised that Tracy couldn't afford a little better. Her house was poorly maintained with an overgrown, weedy garden and filthy windows.

Smith stepped cautiously through the sodden grass and peered in through one of the windows. It was hard to see through the grime and mould, but he managed to make out a television and an armchair with a crocheted throw. Of Tracy, or any other living being, there was no sign.

'I ain't seen her for a while,' said an elderly man propped against the neighbouring picket divide. He grinned warmly at Smith, revealing very few remaining teeth.

'And you see her regularly?' asked Smith.

'Yup. I like her. She's nice to me. Fetches me stuff from the store.' He nodded sagely. 'But I ain't seen her for a while.'

'Tracy Earnshaw?' asked Smith encouragingly.

'Yup, that's her. Tracy.' He turned to go.

'Don't suppose you'd know where to contact her, would you?' asked Smith hopefully.

'Well if I did I would, 'cos I need some baccy and I'm running real low on coffee.' His voice trailed off as his attention began to wander.

Smith was irritated. He wanted to interview this woman as soon as possible, but with no access or information on her whereabouts, he decided to leave her his number and a request to contact him. Tearing a sheet out of his headed contact pad, he began to write in a large unjoined hand.

'Like I said,' repeated the old man, his attention drawn back to Smith, 'I ain't seen 'er leave for a couple of days.'

Smith stopped writing and looked at the old man. 'Let's make this clear. You haven't seen her for days, or you haven't seen her *leave* in days?'

The elderly neighbour looked thoughtful, his brow crinkling with the effort. 'I ain't seen 'er leave.'

He took a step towards the old man and spoke slowly, so he would understand the importance of what he'd just said.

'I'm going to ask you again, sir.' He held his shield in front of the man's face. 'Did you see Tracy Earnshaw leave her house and not return?' He paused to let this sink in. 'Or do you think she might still be in the property, not having left for several days.'

The elderly man looked worried, as if he'd just realised the relevance of his last comment. 'I look out of the window you see, in the mornings. But I never seen her leave.'

'Okay, sir. My name is Detective John Smith and I'm going to enter your neighbour's house, because you're fearful that something may have happened to her.'

The old man nodded mutely.

'Any access you know of before I enter through the front?' asked Smith.

The old man shook his head, frightened now.

Smith took another quick look through the front window then walked around the side of the building, testing windows and the back door, but none were open. With quick efficiency, Smith put his shoulder to the front door and, with minimum effort, cracked the door away from its architrave.

The house was dark and cold, but there was no mistaking the stench of death. Smith didn't need a handkerchief as he'd been inhaling the metallic, methanous fumes for most of his professional life. He sighed and began to move slowly and methodically through the house, his torch held at shoulder height.

He found the woman sprawled on her bed. She'd been dead for at least twenty-four hours, judging by the discolouration of the body. Smith slipped on a pair of latex gloves and touched the woman's hand. It was rigid and very cold, and the gun she still held tightly in her right hand was a Glock 45. An unusual weapon for a woman to select, he thought. But what was even more unusual was the fact that she'd shot herself in the face. Never in twenty years had Smith known a woman to have destroyed herself by using that method; generally if a gun was used, it was a bullet to the temple. As he called in support, he knew that this was no suicide, despite the fact that her hand was tightly gripping the Glock. He stared at what remained of Tracy Earnshaw's head and hoped that she'd had a penchant for easily identifiable tattoos.

*

Malcolm Stringer had been given state-appointed legal representation in the form of Miss Lana Turner, a name she had learned to appreciate with good humour, as it seldom failed to draw a second wry glance from a new acquaintance. Unlike her glamorous namesake, she was a small, dumpy, unprepossessing woman with a lesbian partner of thirty years and three adopted children – all with special needs and requiring full-time care. She had dedicated her life to the pursuit of truth, tolerance and fair play, so when she encountered Malcolm Stringer her hackles rose, and she found herself struggling to balance these principals with the miserable specimen in front of her.

'Let me run through this again, Mr Stringer, to make sure we're batting from the same ball park,' she said, trying unsuccessfully to sound sympathetic. 'You maintain that you are completely innocent of all involvement in the death of your employer Cassandra Willis.' She waited.

Malcolm nodded.

'So, you said you paid Cindy five thousand dollars for what again?' she asked, with a mixture of disbelief and outrage.

'We had "relations", and she said that she needed five thousand dollars to help pay off her debts to some mafia guy.'

'But you were happy to do this even though' – she let this sink in – 'you had known her for barely three days and aren't sure what her surname is, where she worked, or even if you'd ever see the money again?'

Malcolm shrugged. 'I trusted her. I thought we had a good future together.'

'*Had* a good future?' Lana butted in.

Malcolm paused for a couple of moments, trying to take stock of the implications of the word 'had'. 'Have,' he corrected himself nervously. 'We *have* a great future together, and that's why I don't mind sharing my wealth with her.'

'Have you spoken to Cindy at any time since arranging to hand over the money to her?' she asked.

Malcolm turned his head away and ignored her.

'Look, Mr Stringer, I suggest that you cooperate with the police and provide them with the necessary information so they can locate and question Cindy. Until that's done, they're going to make the assumption that your… generosity… is in some way linked to the death of Cassandra Willis.'

*

With a brisk knock, Eleanor walked into the interrogation room with Laurence at her heels.

'Mr Stringer, have you had sufficient time to discuss matters with your legal representative?'

Malcolm nodded and then tucked both hands neatly under his backside. A gesture not lost on Eleanor. 'You seem a little anxious, Mr Stringer. Well knowing that you have agreed to cooperate with us in this matter, I'll try to keep my questioning to the bare minimum, and hopefully we can get closure on the matter surrounding the death of Cassandra Willis.'

'What do you mean? I didn't agree anything with you!' whined Malcolm. A hand slipped from its mooring and began to wave around excitedly.

Eleanor saw Lana Turner's hand make a tamping gesture in an effort to keep him from making any detrimental comments, which was her cue to carry on niggling away until she got somewhere near to the truth.

'Malcolm, what you're about to tell us will have a direct bearing on whether you're charged with first-degree murder or manslaughter. Is that understood?' Eleanor said firmly.

Lana jotted down a couple of shorthand notes and watched Malcolm carefully before she spoke. 'As you know, my client is willing to cooperate and has accounted for the money missing from his account. He has no knowledge of the death of his employer Miss Willis and—'

'This is what we know,' Eleanor cut in. 'Cassandra Willis was collected by an unknown man at round about 4.40 p.m. on Thursday evening by a car that had been pre-booked but not from any private-hire company working legitimately out of the area. This has already been checked. The person who volunteered to take on that responsibility was you, Mr Stringer, and we have several members of the office staff who will confirm that, even overhearing Miss Willis asking you when her car was due. So, our first question is: why would you want to arrange for a car to collect her and then deny it when there's overwhelming evidence to state that you did?

'I didn't call for a car, okay? Check the phones and you'll know that I never—'

'Oh we did,' responded Eleanor, leaning closer to him and watching as his eyes saccaded in rising panic. 'You're right. We've checked your cell and the office phones to see if any outgoing calls were unaccounted for, but strangely there weren't.'

Malcolm didn't understand the implications, but they clearly weren't lost on Lana, who was shifting uncomfortably in her seat.

'All numbers were accountable.'

'So?' snapped Malcolm.

'How could someone arrange for a car to arrive at a specific time if they hadn't called or emailed anyone? We've checked everyone's mail in the office, including yours, and there was no contact regarding a pick-up. But a car did turn up at the time you were heard to say out loud to Miss Willis that it would turn up, that is at 4.40 p.m., and you have a missing five thousand dollars from your bank account. You arranged with someone *personally* that Cassandra Willis would be picked up and murdered. How do we know this? Because Cassandra Willis wasn't the first murder victim to have been killed in this manner, and for the same price.' She paused for several moments. 'I'm about to arrest you for the murder of Miss Cassandra Willis.'

Malcolm slammed both hands against the table. 'I didn't kill her! I just wanted her—'

'Mr Stringer,' said Lana, putting a restraining hand on his arm. 'I suggest you take a moment to collect your thoughts.'

'I just wanted the bitch to get a taste of her own medicine!' He looked desperately from one woman to another. 'That's all!'

Eleanor gratefully accepted the coffee that Laurence handed to her as they huddled together in the corridor outside Interview One and discussed proceedings in hushed tones.

'You've got enough to charge him with premeditated murder?' whispered Laurence.

Eleanor grimaced at the amount of sugar in the coffee. 'No, not yet, but I'm meeting Marty and the DA in five to run through what we've got. I have to get his statement signed and filed before I can join you, so while I do that, I need you to start the location procedures for Cindy. All he's given us is a physical description.' She handed him a piece of paper, which Laurence scrutinised. 'And the fact that he only met her in the coffee shop on the ground floor of his office building. If he reveals anything else, I'll call you.'

'So the implication is that the killer had a woman working with him, collecting business and organising pick-ups?' Laurence scowled. 'That seem plausible to you?'

Eleanor shrugged and frowned. 'It's not unheard of, but I've not come across that sort of relationship before.' She fell silent, thinking. Laurence seemed about to add a thought, but the expression on her face told him to give her a few minutes.

'Tracy Earnshaw,' she said quickly. 'What did she look like?'

'Tall, fit, attractive, blonde.' Laurence looked at Eleanor's brightening face and then down at the description of Cindy in his hand.

He looked up. 'You think Tracy could be Cindy?'

'Malcolm Stringer couldn't tell if a woman was wearing a wig, and the only link we have between Lydia Greystein and the kidnapper was Tracy Earnshaw.'

'But Tracy said she didn't give Lydia the phone number; that she'd already acquired it by herself the time she saw her in the gym.'

'That's what she said, but Mandy, the woman from Xxxstacy who overheard the conversation, stated that Tracy had "organised" it for Lydia. So, here we have a woman—'

'Or two women,' said Laurence.

'One or two women who are acting as middlemen for our killer. They drum up the business and link the victims up with him. Look at Cindy's description; ignore the hair because that's an easy fix. Could Tracy be Cindy?' Eleanor whispered urgently as she saw Marty Samuelson and the DA walking briskly along the corridor in her direction.

Laurence nodded. 'Yes, they could.'

Eleanor pushed the coffee back into Laurence's hand. 'Smith went to track down Tracy this morning; call him and get yourself down there. I want her in – now.'

She walked away from him, waggling her phone meaningfully.

*

Laurence watched thoughtfully as Eleanor was ushered by Samuelson into Interview Two and glanced again at the paper. He felt his heartbeat rise as he pondered the possibility that Tracy Earnshaw could be acting as a broker for the killer. First he had to check whether Tracy was alibied or could have physically managed to disguise herself as Cindy and have sufficient time to get across town to the coffee shop and meet Malcolm at the times he indicated.

He opened his phone and ran through the contacts till he found Smith. Smith answered on the fifth ring. 'Yeah?'

'Listen are you still with Tracy Earnshaw?' asked Laurence.

'Yup, lookin' at her right now,' answered Smith.

'I need to ask her a few questions,' said Laurence, striding down the corridor and heading for the car pool.

'That's gonna be difficult,' came the reply.

CHAPTER NINETEEN

Laurence tapped loudly on the door to Interview Two and heard Samuelson's exasperated tone. 'What the hell!'

Laurence opened the door and stepped in, ignoring the outraged expression on the chief's face.

'I need to speak to DI Raven, Captain,' said Laurence quickly but firmly.

'So do I and I take precedent!' barked Samuelson.

'Sir, this is of the utmost urgency,' said Laurence, feeling his throat tighten as Samuelson slammed down his pen.

Eleanor stood up and manoeuvred Laurence quickly out of the room.

'Tracy Earnshaw's dead; shot in the face and found by Smith in her home twenty minutes ago. The gun was in her hand but Smith's not buying suicide,' said Laurence quickly, once the door closed.

Eleanor stared at him in disbelief and then dialled Smith. 'It's Raven and Whitefoot, you're on speakerphone. Tell us what you've got.'

They listened in silence as he gave her the bullet points.

'You got an estimated time of death on Earnshaw?' Eleanor asked.

'Waiting on the ME. This is going to take some time as the doc's in the cutting room,' Smith said pointedly. He didn't need to add *with Ellis and Paget*.

'Who are they sending?' Laurence asked quickly.

'Crime Scene are on their way, coroner's here and Timms has just arrived.'

As if on cue, they heard Timms' voice in the background.

'Give me your best guess,' Eleanor said. 'I won't hold you to it.'

'She's in full rigor and cold as the room, so I'm guessing twenty-four plus. The neighbour hasn't seen her for a while, as he put it, so judging by the temperature and smell, between one and three days. You can narrow it down to two as she was interviewed by Whitefoot.'

'You need Whitefoot?' Eleanor asked.

The audible snort from the other end of the phone wasn't lost on Laurence.

'Okay, you and Timms process this and call it into Johnson. Find out who the gun was registered to, if she had a permit and next of kin to identify her.'

'That's gonna be a challenge for Mom,' stated Smith.

'Smith, I need you to turn the place over. You're looking for a long brunette wig, okay?'

There was a pause as Smith considered this. 'Roger that.'

'I need you to find Cindy ASAP,' said Eleanor to Laurence.

'But if she's Tracy then…' started Laurence, nursing a suspicion that Eleanor was sympathetic to Smith's desire not to have him on site.

'That was an idea not a fact, and ours to prove. Cindy is the lynchpin to finding out who the killer is, and without her I have nothing that will stick to Malcolm Stringer. If, as we believe, he paid her the five thousand to dispose of Cassandra then she knows who and where the killer is. And if Tracy Earnshaw isn't a suicide and has been murdered then Cindy might be the next on his list.'

Laurence nodded his approval. 'Where do I start?'

'Last place she was seen. The coffee shop in Stringer's building.'

*

'You've got nothing, Detective,' snapped District Attorney Ralph Heidlmann, shuffling the papers Eleanor had laid out for him. 'And that gives you forty-eight hours before you release Mr Stringer.' Heidlmann stood up and began to pack the documents into his briefcase.

'I've got three murdered civilians and two cops on the slab!' pleaded Eleanor.

'Then do the work! Malcolm Stringer may have paid to have Cassandra Willis carved up, but you've got nothing that would stand up in court. He'll walk and anything else you try to do later will fall on deaf ears. Get a confession and preferably find Cindy. Until then you cannot charge him with premeditated murder and he *will* be back on the streets in forty-eight. Are we clear?'

Eleanor nodded. Samuelson said nothing, his jaw set hard.

'Good day,' said Heidlmann as he swept out of the room.

There was silence for a moment as the two officers contemplated their next move. 'I can get him to confess,' said Eleanor.

'You need to focus and prioritise,' said Samuelson with unusual calm. 'Malcolm Stringer selected the victim, and he will serve the max for that, but he's not going anywhere. He gets released in forty-eight; he goes home to gloat. I need you to get out there and catch the bastard that's doing this, okay?'

Eleanor nodded. He was right.

'I've got to make a press statement in an hour and I want you there,' said Samuelson. Eleanor groaned.

'We make a statement and we have some control. Ignore the hacks, they print any shit and look for leaks – you know that.'

She nodded.

'Okay, what do we give them and what do we hold back?' he asked.

*

'What are we looking for?' asked Timms as he peered inside a small closet in Tracy Earnshaw's bedroom.

'Long brunette wig,' responded Smith.

Timms looked at the two polystyrene mannequin heads on the shelf above the clothing. One sported a shoulder-length blonde wig, the other a mid-length brunette. Both were obviously real human hair and looked to Timms as if they would have been costly.

'Yup, got that plus another blonde one,' stated Timms.

The closet was tidy, containing a mixture of hand-knitted sweaters and cardigans, some jeans and a couple of pairs of leather shoes with a low heel. None could be described as particularly expensive or glamorous. The shirts and tops Tracy favoured were of a functional cotton design.

Timms sighed and continued to poke around. 'Where'd you say she worked?' he asked. 'Some fancy gym on Wellesley Street?'

'Huh?' Smith was deep in conversation with the coroner, who was explaining why it was extremely unlikely that Tracy Earnshaw would be autopsied within the next forty-eight hours due to the increasing numbers of bodies being deposited at the morgue.

'Yeah, personal trainer according to Whitefoot. Why?' he answered finally.

''Cos there ain't nothing resembling gym wear here. This wardrobe ain't saying fitness guru to me,' responded Timms thoughtfully. 'I'm gonna go check her washing.'

Timms squeezed his bulk past the two crime officers, Smith and the coroner's assistant and marvelled at how so many people could have squeezed into such a small bedroom. He glanced at the body, which was still being processed.

'Something's not right here,' he muttered, to no one in particular. He'd already made a cursory search of the bedroom and spare room, finding only a mixture of underwear, pulp novels and bric-a-brac. The bathroom had yielded little in the way of information and the small neat kitchen even less.

'What are you looking for?' asked Smith.

Timms closed the washing-machine lid and turned to face Smith. 'Gym wear... Lycra. Something that tells me she worked as a personal trainer.'

'How about these?' said Smith, passing Timms a sports bag which contained a pair of top-of-the-range running shoes, two Lycra tops, one with 'Bodyworks' embroidered into the breast and a pair of tight running pants. 'That do it for ya? Found it under the bed.'

Timms scowled as he looked at the bag and its contents.

*

'There!' said Laurence, stabbing a finger at the screen.

The security officer stopped the image and ran the enhancement. 'That's her...'

He leaned closer to the screen and stared at the shadowy grey figure of a woman carrying a coffee over to the table furthest away from the CCTV. She was considerably taller than Malcolm, probably five-ten or eleven without the heels. She wore large owlish sunglasses, which obscured the greater part of her face. The long dark hair fell away from her face and formed a curtain over her shoulders. Apart from her well-toned figure, there was very little to identify her.

'Run it through a few more frames.'

The woman pulled a chair out and sat with her back to the camera. Laurence clamped his teeth with frustration as he watched her remove the sunglasses. All he could see for the next thirty minutes that the pair sat together was Malcolm Stringer's stupid face as he laughed and gesticulated wildly.

'You know what?' drawled the security operative, tapping the screen with his pen. 'I'd say she knew where the cameras were and made sure she wasn't spotted. She keeps to the edges of frame when she enters and leaves the building and never takes her sunglasses off where the camera can picture her.'

Laurence nodded in agreement. 'You can copy me the data from all of her visits?'

'Yup. Doing it now.'

Laurence had spent the last couple of hours speeding through the CCTV digital footage taken over the past week. As a matter of course, nothing older than seven days was kept on file but erased.

'You think we can enhance this any more?' asked Laurence hopefully.

'Maybe,' said the operative, unconvincingly. 'But you're dependent on the resolution. This is good, but not like the ones they use for potential high-crime areas like banks or airports.'

Laurence gratefully took the disc that the operative handed over.

'You're Homicide, right?' asked the operative.

Laurence nodded.

'She murder or been murdered?'

Laurence thought for a moment and then shrugged.

*

Eleanor took her seat next to Samuelson and stared with growing apprehension at the ever-increasing numbers of press that were squeezing themselves into the precinct's conference room. Cameramen vied with press photographers to set up their equipment along the aisles, while neatly dressed female reporters harangued technicians to move faster and secure a better position for their microphones. Eleanor had prepared a statement with the approval of her boss, who was kitted out in full regalia, including cap. Knowing that the gathered press was unlikely to settle down voluntarily, she cleared her throat and began to speak. There were several seconds of shuffling before pause buttons were flipped and a sea of red LEDs appeared along the rows of cameras.

She kept the briefing short and unemotional, sure that the media would supply that themselves – by the bucketload. She and Samuelson had spent some time discussing whether or not to reveal the 'Kidnappings Arranged' card. Not to do so would be irresponsible and may make them culpable if someone already in possession of one of the cards decided to book a sexy treat for either themselves or a loved one. But by the same token, once revealed by the press, it would make any further contacts with the killer a shoo-in for a premeditated murder charge, so it was decided that it would be their first point. There would be no mention of the name Lee Hughes, nor would the specifics of the killer's MO be described.

Eleanor ended the statement by asking the public to report any dangerous sexual encounters they may have had, all of which would be treated in complete confidence.

The second that she closed her mouth, a sea of hands and microphones shot into the air.

'Detective Inspector, why hasn't the public's attention been drawn to these murders before? Perhaps the latest victim' – a thin woman in a burgundy suit checked her notes – 'Cassandra Willis may have avoided the same fate as Lydia Greystein if she'd been notified by the press.'

'I cannot comment in detail about the specific details regarding Miss Willis's death, but I believe that not to be the case,' replied Eleanor. She watched as the reporter opened her mouth for a supplementary, but Claddis McAvoy from the *Toronto Sun* barged in angrily.

'Are you saying that your department knew that the murderer of Lydia Greystein was posting cards advertising his services and you did nothing to stop this? Despite your assurances to my colleague that the sadistic murder of Cassandra Willis was unavoidable, would it not have been if the public's and Miss Willis's attention had been alerted to these cards?'

Eleanor spoke calmly and cautiously. 'As soon as the link was made, the department and I used this knowledge to trace the cards and remove them.'

Several other hands shot up, but Claddis was on a roll. 'So you'd say categorically that after linking the murder of Lydia Greystein with the individual who left the "Kidnappings Arranged" card, you scoured the area and commandeered all of these cards, thus preventing the likelihood that any other poor soul would inadvertently arrange either their own or another's sadistic murder? Because we know that no press statement regarding this matter was made.'

Eleanor paused before responding. She'd encountered Claddis McAvoy on several occasions and his tone and increasingly smug expression were making her nervous that there was an unpleasant revelation about to be made.

'Because...' intoned Claddis, theatrically reaching inside his jacket pocket, 'this is one of those cards, picked up only this morning by myself.' He held the card aloft, adopting an expression of concerned righteousness for the photographs that he knew would make it into the evening's papers and afternoon broadcast.

Eleanor saw Marty Samuelson's jaw twitch with irritation as the proceedings descended into the usual point-scoring exercise.

'Mr McAvoy, if you've uncovered evidence relevant to this investigation, would it not have been more socially responsible to have presented this through the proper channels rather than using it to manipulate public response?' she said tersely.

Cynthia Roberts of *The Star* jumped to her feet. 'Is that an admittance from the homicide department that your evidence collecting has been shoddy at best and irresponsibly lax at worst?'

Samuelson spoke with authority and barely concealed rage. 'The sadistic murder of two women is an outrage and all of our resources and manpower have been put into capturing this man.'

'Perhaps your department has been motivated by the murder of two of its officers by the same killer,' said a figure at the back.

Both Eleanor and her boss had wanted to keep the link between the dead officers under wraps for the time being. She wasn't sure whether the reporter was merely fishing for a connection or had sourced it. She decided to play safe. 'Officers Paget and Ellis were discovered shot dead in the early hours of this morning. A link to the murder of Cassandra Willis has not been established as yet, but all avenues of investigation are being pursued. Good day.'

With that, she stood up, snatched up her prompt papers and slid through the rear door, which was being barricaded by three patrol officers. Samuelson was hot on her heels and both stared at each other as the surge and braying of the press was tamped by the door being shut quickly by one of the officers.

'Are we leaking?' snapped Samuelson as he snatched off his cap and loosened his tie.

'No more than usual,' she replied, turning and walking towards the murder room. 'Press just do what we do.'

Samuelson caught up with her. 'Where d'you think McAvoy found that card?'

'I'm not sure, but we're going to find out.'

She walked over to where Mo and Wadesky were still poring over files. 'You guys fancy a bit of gentle interrogation? Claddis McAvoy of the *Toronto Sun* discovered a card this morning that may have been left by the killer. He's here now and I'm sure is eager to get a story out of it.'

'You betcha,' said Mo, with relish. 'How'd the press go?'

'Maybe we should have been asking them what info they had, rather than the other way around!' Samuelson snapped as he stormed into his office.

*

Detective Smith hunkered down and peered back at the two rheumy eyes visible through the letter box. 'Mrs Earnshaw? Mrs Zinnia Earnshaw?' he asked solemnly.

The eyes continued to stare, blinking occasionally. Smith tried again. His back was beginning to ache. 'Are you Mrs Zinnia Earnshaw, mother of Tracy Earnshaw of 1117 Aldermaston Crescent?'

The eyes blinked twice, and then a throaty wheezing sound emanated from the box as the woman exchanged her eyes for her mouth. Smith stood up and took a pace backwards.

'Who are you?' the voice said.

'I'm Detective John Smith,' he said steadily, flipping his badge and holding it close to the letter box.

'Who?'

Smith breathed in through his nose and exhaled through his mouth, just as the therapist had taught him. 'Ma'am, would you mind opening the door as I have a serious matter that needs discussing in private.'

He saw that holding his badge next to the waist-high letter box was pointless as the woman's mouth was the only thing visible. 'Ma'am, would you look through the gap please, as I'm holding out my badge to prove who I am.'

A groan accompanied a rustle as the woman repositioned her back. 'I've done nothing you need to warn me about,' she said firmly.

'Ma'am, I have some very serious information regarding your daughter Tracy and I'd be grateful if you would allow me into your home to discuss it,' said Smith, trying to dismiss the edge that had crept into his voice.

'Tracy? She's my daughter. What's happened to her?'

'I will discuss that when you've opened the door,' said Smith, and then added a polite 'ma'am', as he realised this wasn't the best approach to informing a parent of the death of their child.

There was a rumble of chain and sliding bolt; the door opened a fraction. The woman, who couldn't have been more than five-foot-two, held the door firmly between arthritic hands and stared hopelessly at him.

'Have you a daughter called Tracy Earnshaw, ma'am?' asked Smith quietly.

She nodded silently, the edge of her lower lip disappearing under her upper dentures.

'May I step inside?' he asked.

Zinnia continued to nod silently but took no action.

Slowly and with care, Smith extended his hand and grasped hers, steering her backwards and into the nearest room. The kitchen was small and homely. Two chairs were neatly arranged around a tiny Formica-topped table, its drab and faded brown hue ameliorated by a pot of geraniums in the centre. Smith led the woman to a chair and helped her into it. Pulling a second chair towards hers, he sat down and, still holding her hand, he began the procedure of informing Tracy's mother that her daughter was dead.

Smith boiled the kettle and selected two mugs while he waited for the inevitable questions. He'd learned over the years that providing an entire package of information concerning the means, times and persons involved in a loved one's death was counterproductive to the investigative process. Grief prevented the uptake of large quantities of unpalatable facts and people usually preferred to receive these over a period of time. Generally, the time taken from the revelation of a death to the finish of the house visit lasted from between forty minutes to two hours. Smith had noted that those people who opted for a shorter visit or failed to ask the appropriate questions were usually deeply involved in the homicide/accident of the victim.

Smith watched Zinnia carefully as he handed her a cup of strong sweet tea.

'I don't understand, Mr Smith. Was she poorly?'

Smith nodded to the cup that he'd placed in her hands. On cue she took an appreciative sip.

'Is there any reason you know of that would cause Tracy to take her own life?'

Zinnia's mouth opened and then she began to shake her head rhythmically from side to side. 'Was she poorly then?'

Smith nodded at the tea again, but the woman was moving beyond the comfort that tea could offer.

'Mrs Earnshaw, Tracy wasn't ill. She was shot.'

Smith deftly caught the cup as it tipped forward and placed it carefully on the table. He'd started and had to take matters to their conclusion. 'It looks as if she shot herself, but we can't be sure at this stage.'

Zinnia stared at him with incomprehension. 'It might not have been a gun then?'

'I'm sorry, I didn't make myself clear,' said Smith, irritated with himself for being vague. 'Your daughter died as a result of a gunshot wound to the face.'

'Shot?'

'Yes, ma'am. Tracy was shot in the face.'

'By who? Who shot her?'

'Is it possible that she shot herself?'

'She hasn't got a gun!' shrieked Zinnia. 'How could she have shot herself? Did she buy one? How'd you know it was her? How could she have shot herself by accident? I really don't understand, Mr Smith. How?'

'The gun was in her hand. It looks like suicide.'

Zinnia's eyes were round as saucers and a thin trickle of saliva ran from the corner of her mouth. 'Well that's a mystery,' she said, wrapping her hands around her chest and beginning to rock herself like a wounded child. 'That's a complete mystery.'

Smith allowed Tracy's mother a good two minutes before he pressed on. 'When was the last time you saw your daughter, Mrs Earnshaw?'

'I don't really know… maybe a Christmas ago.'

'That's quite a long time, Mrs Earnshaw,' he said softly.

'Mmm… I don't like to leave the house, you see. It's safe here. I don't walk so good, and Tracy didn't like it here I don't think,' she said quietly. 'I don't think she liked me too much either. Ever since her dad died, she didn't like to be here. They were close you see, and she was our only child was Tracy. I never had no more.' She pulled a sodden handkerchief from her pocket and dried her eyes. 'Well it's done now.'

'Do you think Tracy was depressed? Is it possible that she could have killed herself?' Smith asked cautiously.

Suddenly the woman's eyes seemed clearer and more focussed. She furrowed her brow. 'You don't need to ask me that, Mr Smith, because you have forensics. I've seen those programmes on the TV. They can discover anything by studying a death. The scientists will tell you that. I didn't know her and she didn't know me.'

There was a brooding silence between them.

'When you last saw her, how did she seem?'

Zinnia smiled sadly. 'She was as she always is… disappointed.'

'With what?'

'I never knew. Life, me, the weather – there was always something disappointing her. I told her if she got a job she'd be happier.'

'A job? Didn't Tracy have a job?'

Zinnia shrugged. 'I never knew.'

'Have you a recent photograph of Tracy?'

She shook her head. 'No, she didn't like having her photo taken, and if she did she never gave me one… I've got some of her at school if that'd help.'

Smith nodded and watched as the woman stood up stiffly and made her way over to a dressing table and pulled out a drawer. She yelped as her arthritic fingers cracked and took out a brown, unmarked envelope. A smile flickered across her face as she extracted three photographs and looked at them. She passed them over to Smith, who muttered his thanks.

'Which one is your daughter?' he asked, looking at a mixed class of teenagers all dressed in bland, nondescript uniforms. The group looked indifferent to the concept of being photographed, a mixture of boredom and irritation being the most easily identified expressions.

Zinnia stretched out a finger and gently tapped the chest of a girl with mid-length brown hair, a slim, tallish frame and even features. If Smith looked away from the girl, he suspected he wouldn't be able to pick her out again. He was about to look at the second photograph when his eyes fixed on a second figure standing next to Tracy.

'Mrs Earnshaw,' he said, trying not to sound too excited. 'Which school did your daughter attend?'

'She went to Greenslade High School over on the west side. We lived there when her dad was alive.'

'And the boy standing next to her, can you remember what his name was?'

Mrs Earnshaw took the photograph from Smith and peered at the figure standing next to her daughter.

'I can.' She frowned. 'That's Lee Hughes, that is. The one whose family were killed.'

CHAPTER TWENTY

'I said I will! Now have you done anything resembling police work today, huh?' shouted Wadesky into the phone. There was a pause as she scribbled down some notes onto a jotter. 'You are shitting me!' She caught Johnson's eye and put a finger up to indicate that news was coming in. Johnson was in the middle of a reorganisation of the timeline, filling several blank spaces with photographs and data sheets. He had four coloured marker pens dangling from nylon neck holders, and a small pouch attached to his waist filled with Blu-Tack, sticky tape and drawing pins. Eleanor and Mo were the only members of the precinct who didn't snigger when they saw him in office mode.

With a look of intense concern, Johnson walked over and turned her jotter round to read the latest news. Wadesky scowled at him as she put down the phone.

'Is this coded?' he asked. 'Two full at 5 p.m.? What does that mean?'

'It means that I need to remember to put two scoops of dog food into this idiot's food bowl,' she said, pointing at Monster, who was lying on his back at Mo's feet, fast asleep. 'Apparently the information concerning our suspect was of lesser importance.'

'Go on,' said Mo, smiling.

'Guess who went to Greenslade High School?' said Wadesky.

'Tracy Earnshaw,' Johnson replied, a broad smile appearing on his face. He began to run the marker pens between his fingers, ready to attack the board.

'And better even than that. Mom has a school photo with her and Lee Hughes standing next to each other.'

'Classmates!' Johnson was excited.

'Uh-huh!' said Wadesky. 'Smith's gonna bring in the details when he's finished at the morgue. You go colour that board, Johnson. Mo and I have some press to take care of.'

Wadesky stretched her aching back and rearranged her blouse over her belly, then laughed at Mo. 'It does a girl good to see someone in worse shape, it really does. Gimme your hand.'

Mo hesitated.

'I'm pregnant not disabled!' She grabbed his hand and tugged. Gradually Mo straightened out, groaning and belching. Monster stood to attention and whimpered as Mo struggled upright.

'This is a hell of a good dog. Why doesn't Whitefoot like him?' he pondered, rubbing Monster's head, which was now buried in his crotch.

'Well my Jo always says that when a person don't like another being, be it dog or otherwise, it's because they haven't learned to like themselves,' she replied.

Mo nodded sagely.

'Johnson, how long before we're aired?' asked Wadesky.

'Major networks covering 1800 and 2200 hours,' he replied as he carefully drew a red line between the photograph of Tracy Earnshaw and that of Lee Hughes, using a straight edge.

*

The man was in the habit of taking a late afternoon coffee at his local bistro and a small plate of carpaccio, whilst he ran through the local letting papers. Having little to no interest in local or national political news, unless it affected the market, he seldom switched on his television or bought a national paper.

He was contemplating ordering a second espresso before taking a brisk walk through the park to his office for a final couple of hours of work. He nodded to the waiter and made a pinching gesture with his fingers – code for the coffee – and allowed his eyes to settle on the woman who sat at the adjacent table. She was attractive with large bovine brown eyes partially concealed by heavy dark-rimmed glasses that kept slipping down her small, well-shaped nose. Unfortunately, his study time was being interrupted as she manhandled a large newspaper, trying to find an article that took her fancy. She finally settled and pulled the newspaper higher, exposing the front page to him. He registered the shock before he had fully engaged with the meaning of the headline.

'"Kidnappings Arranged" Card Used to Lure Two Women to Sadistic Murder' screamed the type. He leaned forward to glean more information. The *Toronto Sun* had a photograph of Lydia Greystein and Cassandra Willis taken in livelier times and a reproduction of the card under the photographs.

Suddenly, the woman folded the newspaper closed and took a final sip of her coffee, preparing to leave. She caught sight of him and intuitively offered him the paper. He nodded his gratitude and immediately turned to the first page. It took him less than two minutes to digest the information and formulate some level of comprehension. The man realised that, contrary to all the signs – the daring yet honest use of the card and the promise of redemption it implied – the individual behind the scheme was a psychopath. He sighed deeply and tried to clear his mind of the disgust he felt at the sheer duplicity of mankind so he could focus on a way to stop this in its tracks.

*

Gary Le Douce was an enthusiastic reader of newspapers. His business transcended current trends both political and social, but a healthy knowledge of local activities kept him one step ahead of the game in a surprisingly competitive business. There was nothing about the murders that caused either incomprehension or outrage in him. In fact, he was frequently astonished that there wasn't more murder and mayhem around, knowing how aggressive and greedy the majority of people were. Not that he had a problem with avarice; Gary had leanings in that direction himself.

He was unsure as to what role the man he'd encountered played in the unfolding kidnapping saga, but the five thousand dollars ticked one of the boxes. Since reading about the case, Gary had been formulating something akin to a plan. If, as he suspected, the money had been deposited with him with the intention of purchasing a kidnapping/murder for some unlucky soul then either that bitch Raven would call and wrestle the money off him, or the killer would make an appearance and collect it. The latter, though somewhat unnerving, would prove to be the most lucrative for Gary. He knew that it was only a matter of time before the papers offered a substantial payment for information leading to the arrest and prosecution of the kidnapper, and when that reached an interesting-enough level, Gary would provide them with videotaped evidence that would reveal the killer.

He'd invested several years ago in some discreet video equipment, which he'd secreted behind the bar, where the lighting was good enough to pick up the features of the punters in sufficient detail to make identification pretty much certain. With the money he'd acquired since its installation, he'd maintained regular updating of technology so the system, if not state of the art, wasn't too far behind. Not that it was used regularly – that would have seen his clientele disappear faster than a rat down a sewer – no, it was backup, used strategically when Gary needed a little favour or a handy cash windfall that would keep the wolf from the door. What he hadn't taken into consideration was that the person who came to collect the money was the last person on the planet that Gary had expected.

*

Eleanor Raven flashed her badge at the security guard, placed her Glock 19 on the X-ray table and walked through the magnetic arch. Laurence followed, repeating her actions.

'You're telling me that Claddis McAvoy actually admitted to having had one of the cards made up and pretended to have found it in a phone booth?' he asked incredulously.

'And as such will be meeting the magistrates at their convenience tomorrow morning,' she replied, smiling. 'Apparently Mo walked into the room announcing that he'd been too dumb to wipe the file off his laptop. When Claddis burst out that they had no right to search his laptop without a warrant, rather than denying that there was anything to find, Mo had him. Took less than ten minutes to get a full confession and listen politely to how he was "only trying to stimulate the police force into more vigorous investigation for the good of the reading public".'

Eleanor gave a small laugh as she walked towards the storage rooms, but Laurence was quiet. He saw her easy admiration of Mo and felt a pang of irritation that, so far, he hadn't managed to get so much as a 'well done' from her.

Smith and Timms were deep in conversation and looking through a folder containing photographs and paper documentation. Both nodded to Eleanor as she walked towards them and carried on in their low tones, then Timms opened the door for Eleanor and they made their way into the cold room. Matt Gains stepped out from a small office and headed towards the huge stainless-steel door that kept the bodies at a cool two degrees Celsius and keyed in the code.

'Okay, we got the ballistics typing for Ellis and Paget, but it's going to take a minimum of a week to run through matching. I've had assurances from Bill Griffith that this will take priority,' said Timms.

'Anything unusual?' asked Eleanor.

'Well… looks like a .308 calibre rifle, but early days,' sighed Timms.

'That narrows it down then,' Eleanor replied unhappily. 'I wanted unusual, I get Costco!'

'Yeah, but… Bill took a look and said it didn't look like it had been fired from a Winchester. So watch this space!'

The detectives stopped chatting as Matt pushed a gurney in from the cold store and closed the door behind him. A black body bag complete with double-signed tags indicating first stages in the chain of evidence lay before them. Eleanor nodded that he should break the tabs.

There was very little to suggest that this had once been a human head. A small, clear plastic evidence bag had been placed next to the shoulder containing a quantity of bone and tissue that had been collected from around the bed and floor. A third of the occipital bone remained tenuously attached by tendons and skin to the spine, and hanging from that was an almost complete left temporal bone. Of the brain, there was virtually nothing left.

'How are we going to ID her?' asked Eleanor, gently moving the plastic bag around and squinting at the contents. 'I guess there's not enough to do a reconstruction?'

Matt shook his head. 'I doubt it. I've not opened the bag, but there seems to be a couple of teeth there – maybe the odontologist might be a better bet?' But neither he nor any of the detectives looked convinced.

Smith flipped open his notebook, 'Mrs Earnshaw gave me a list of distinguishing marks… okay… appendectomy scar from an op she had in third grade.'

Matt unzipped the bag to the corpse's knees, exposing stiff blood-soaked pyjamas. He carefully peeled them open to reveal a corresponding scar across the right lower abdomen.

Eleanor turned to Laurence and raised her eyebrows. He leaned over and looked carefully at the scar, nodding back.

'Agree, Matt?' she asked. He also nodded.

'Tick that box then,' said Smith. 'Um, she'd had some dental work as a kid; I'll call the records up first thing.'

'Tattoos?' asked Eleanor hopefully.

'Not as far as Mom knew. Two strawberry birthmarks on the left shoulder blade.'

The detectives all moved round to the other side of the gurney as Matt cautiously lifted her shoulder. Timms flipped on a small penlight, revealing the two birthmarks. Smith looked and compared them to the small sketch he'd made on his notebook. 'That's it! And last one, she bit her nails down to the quick apparently.'

Laurence knotted his brow. 'She had manicured hands when I saw her.'

Matt reached inside the body bag and drew out a hand, which had been bound tightly in a brown bag. 'She shoot with the right?' he asked Smith, who nodded.

'Open the left,' said Eleanor.

They watched as Matt cut open the paper bag and exposed a hand complete with perfect nails. Eleanor carefully pulled at one of the nails, which had been glued on. As the nail peeled away from the bed, it was apparent that Tracy was a committed nail-biter, there being only about a quarter of an inch of furrowed keratin left on the finger.

'We saying it's her?' asked Smith.

Eleanor frowned. 'Until we can do a DNA compare to her mother, I'd say yes.'

Matt re-zipped the bag and prepared to wheel it back into the cold store.

'When will she be autopsied?'

Matt sighed. 'Can't see it happening before the end of the week. Two days minimum. Dr Hounslow's got everyone working overtime this week, but I've got thirty bodies in storage.'

'See what you can do, Matt, okay?' Eleanor asked.

He nodded as he pushed the gurney away.

'Okaaay, what next for you two?' asked Eleanor as she fastened her coat, peering at the steady rain through the glass doors that led to the morgue car park.

'Well Smith and me are discussing the case in D'Angelo's for the next hour. Wanna join?' said Timms expansively.

'Love to,' replied Laurence.

'No, we're off to interview Miss Guthrie, ex-principal of Greenslade High,' replied Eleanor.

'We are?' Laurence couldn't hide the note of disappointment in his voice.

'Yup, you drive,' she said, handing Laurence the keys and opening the door.

*

Gary Le Douce slipped quietly away from the bar, where he'd been having a pleasant chat with a regular customer, and into his inner sanctuary. He closed the door and slipped the bolt across it, giving himself sufficient time to work out how to salvage his plan. He'd seen the man enter the club and begin to make his way through the handful of patrons and working girls in the direction of the bar. There was no doubt in Gary's mind that he'd come to check whether the money had been collected. If he said it hadn't, there was a distinct possibility that the man would want it back, in which case his elaborate plan would come to nothing. If he lied and said it had gone then it might keep the man at bay for a while, allowing the kidnapper to come and collect the money. So all Gary would have done was mess with the time frame – not a particularly bad thing in itself. Better still, the upside to this was that if the money wasn't collected, he could keep it for himself.

He looked at the surveillance feed on the small monitor. The man was staring straight at it, but how could he? It was hidden between some bottles and really couldn't be detected from the bar.

A shudder run unpleasantly along his spine. He waited for several moments, hoping that the man would realise that he wasn't there and head off, but there was nothing in his body language that indicated he was about to leave.

The knock at his door made Gary jump.

'What?' he shrieked. It couldn't be the man because he was still visible on the screen.

'Boss?' It was the voice of his bartender Brent. 'You in there?'

'What do you want? Who's looking after the bar?' snapped Gary.

'Sal is. There's a guy out there says he wants to speak to you.'

'What about?'

'I dunno. Said he wasn't leaving till he's seen ya.'

'Tell him I ain't 'ere,' said Gary, in an increasingly urgent tone.

'I did!' replied Brent defensively. 'But he wasn't buying that.'

'Why not? Weren't you convincing?' hissed Gary.

'I guess no more than usual,' was the irritated response. 'I don't like this guy.'

'Join the 'effing club!' said Gary loudly.

There was a pause before Brent started again. 'Well what you want me to do then? I could call up Len. He'll see him out.'

Len was their ageing bouncer. Gary had employed him since opening the bar in the late eighties and hadn't the heart to get rid of him – or the cash, as Len was very cheap. The guy had never taken a single night off in all the years he'd been there. Maybe it was time to think about a retirement package and get in some new blood. Gary sighed deeply.

'Tell him that—'

But Brent had anticipated this. 'He said I wasn't to bring no message back even though you "weren't" in the building. He'd only speak to you.'

Gary ground his teeth. He was cornered, but maybe he could bluff his way out.

Straightening his back and readjusting his dressing gown, Gary unlocked the door and stepped into the gloomy corridor. 'Get Len up here and tell him to watch my back. Okay?'

'Roger that, boss,' said Brent, with more chirpiness than the situation merited.

Gary followed him into the bar and beckoned the man over to a more private corner.

'The money,' said the man flatly. 'It hasn't been collected and I want it back. You can keep the handling fee.'

Gary thought quickly. 'He came in the morning after you left it. Dark-haired man, in his thirties I'd guess. So I gave him the money because that's what you'd asked me to do,' he said, with a righteous tone.

The man looked at him carefully, as if trying to peel away the many layers of deception that had woven themselves around Gary Le Douce over the half century he'd been thieving, lying and cheating those around him.

Gary held his gaze. He wasn't about to cave in over something as pathetic as whether he could hold a stare. But there was something about this man. Something that made Gary feel dirty and frail, not feelings that regularly shook him.

'The money is still here. It wasn't collected, was it?' said the man slowly.

Gary bit down on the inside of his lower lip. 'No. I've got the goddamn money,' he spat. He wasn't entirely sure what had happened to his resolve. He saw Len take up an adversarial position next to the man's right side, which should have filled him with confidence, but something told him that this man was not going to be beaten down.

Ignoring Len's frantic eyebrow communications, Gary stood up and walked quickly over to the bar, where he reached below the counter and pressed a small hidden button, which opened a drawer below the counter. Gary reached in and, without looking, withdrew the package and secured it under his robe, managing not to draw any unwanted attention from the punters who were propped along the bar in various stages of inebriation, both liquid and sexual. As he handed it over to the man, he found himself unable to look him in the eye.

Silently, the man stood up and made his way out of the building and into the night. Despite the loss of a potentially lucrative little deal, Gary felt oddly relieved. He knew the man would never come back, and for that he was extremely grateful.

*

Eleanor felt exhausted, and suspected that the throbbing sensation behind her eyes was going to have developed into a full-blown migraine before the evening was out.

'What number?' asked Laurence, peering into the rain-drenched streets as he manoeuvred the car through the evening traffic.

Eleanor looked at her notes. 'Thirty-seven Lincoln Drive. Take a left up here and it should be along the left.'

Laurence turned into the small, tree-lined drive and took tally of the numbers.

'Odd on the left… twenty-nine… thirty-three… that one,' he said quietly, pulling the car to a halt outside a small, brick-built two-storey detached. Both he and Eleanor looked at the house and saw the curtains twitch as their arrival was noted.

'Miss Louisa Guthrie, retired Principal of Greenslade High School, 1975–98,' read Eleanor from the notes Johnson had supplied.

'What are your expectations?' asked Laurence, checking his tie and teeth in the rear-view mirror.

'I'm not sure yet,' mused Eleanor. 'I'm hoping she'll remember Lee and tell us about the relationship between him and Tracy. Maybe she can provide some insight into his personality. I don't really know yet.'

She turned to look at Laurence as he prepared himself to meet Louisa Guthrie. She noted his long, delicate fingers as he ran them vigorously through his hair in an attempt to tame it and thought they seemed better designed for surgery than manhandling perps and guns. Eleanor was struck by how little attention she'd paid, not just to his appearance but who he was. She knew she didn't want him there, but only because she didn't want anyone taking Mo's place.

Who was she kidding? She didn't want him there because he didn't know who he was, and a homicide detective still grappling with those issues was a liability. But until he messed up or she managed to persuade Samuelson to team him up with Smith then she was going to have to tolerate him.

She opened the passenger door and stepped out briskly, slamming it behind her, noting the confusion on his face.

Louisa's tea was weak and flavourless, rather like the woman herself. She was quiet, with a penchant for chintz and porcelain figurines. Eleanor – and Laurence, by the look on his face – were both wondering how a woman with such little obvious personality could have been in charge of a large high school in a notoriously rough area of the city.

'Lee Hughes was an exceptionally gifted artist,' said Louisa, sipping her tea and nibbling on a small sweet biscuit. 'I even had a painting of his placed in my office,' she added with a tight smile. 'But of course I had it removed when he disappeared.'

'Why was that, Miss Guthrie?' asked Eleanor keenly.

'Well he'd turned his back on the school and therefore could not have been celebrated there,' she said with a tone bordering on religious fervour.

'What did you do with the painting?' asked Eleanor.

'I think it was burned,' said Louisa calmly.

'Do you have a photograph of the painting?' asked Laurence.

Slowly the ex-principal placed her cup and saucer on the tray. 'I rather think it's time you explained your interest in Lee Hughes. Don't you?'

'We are of the belief that he may be involved in the deaths of two women and possibly two police officers,' replied Eleanor.

Louisa raised an eyebrow and leaned forward slightly. 'And how is that possible? It was my belief that the boy was dead.'

'There is nothing to indicate that,' said Eleanor, who also moved closer.

'After the deaths of his mother and sister, Lee vanished, and to my recollection was never seen again.' By the tone of her response it seemed that Louisa Guthrie put a fair amount of score in her recollections and beliefs. She pursed her lips and raised an eyebrow as if waiting for Eleanor to present some acceptable facts to her.

Eleanor was beginning to understand why this woman had managed to maintain the headship of a difficult school.

'How au fait are you with the circumstances surrounding the deaths of Lee's mother and sister?' Eleanor asked.

'By "au fait", I take it you want to know whether my knowledge extends further than the fact that they were discovered in the garage, presumably the victims of carbon monoxide poisoning. I am also aware that Lee's younger sister Carin was wrapped in a plastic sheet of some description and that the detectives that interviewed me at the time were insistent that Lee's mother couldn't have done this. However, Lee was very definitely in school on the day and time in question and could not have been involved in the deaths.'

'You seem very sure about that, Miss Guthrie,' said Eleanor.

'I taught him English that morning and he never left my sight between second and third period. Following that he was with the Head of Art till lunchtime. He did not attend afternoon registration at 1.55 p.m., which indicated that he must have left the school during the lunch break.'

'Which ran from one till two?'

She nodded tightly. 'When his form tutor notified me of his unauthorised absence I called his home, but there was no response. I believe the police found him several hours later wandering the streets, but I'm sure you will have retained the original statements and already know that.'

Louisa closed her mouth and looked at the two detectives in a way that suggested that she did not take supplementary questions.

'You have an amazing recollection of the events, Miss Guthrie,' said Laurence, with admiration in his voice. 'You said Lee had "turned his back on the school". What did you mean by that?'

'I meant he refused the support the school offered and took himself off. That is not the way that things are done at Greenslade,' she replied, bristling with indignation. 'A problem shared is a problem halved is our thinking.'

'But you believe him to be dead. Surely he couldn't have turned his back on the school if he was no longer alive?' suggested Laurence firmly.

Eleanor glanced at him, wondering where this line of baiting was going. She suspected it would lead them quickly to the front door, none the wiser for their visit, and was just about to commandeer the questioning when Laurence spoke again.

'Miss Guthrie, I believe you're holding something back. You're toying with me, waiting for me to ask the right question, aren't you? You're not going to give me the information I need until you feel I deserve it! No wonder you were in charge of one of the most successful schools in the county. I wish I'd had you as a mentor; maybe I'd have made more of my life,' he mused, slumping back into his seat.

Eleanor gaped at him, but before she could indicate that he go and wait by the car she heard a giggle. Louisa was giggling in an unpleasant girlish manner, a hand pressed lightly against her lips.

'Don't be silly. I'm sure you were an excellent student, Detective Whitefoot. But after so many years teasing the best out of people, I'm still wedded to the old techniques.'

She sighed and rearranged her skirt, tucking it under her ample knees, then held a finger up to Laurence. 'I shall tell you exactly what I remember and endeavour to answer all your questions in the utmost detail. Fire away.'

Laurence shunted to the edge of the sofa and locked eyes with her. 'Give me your impression of Lee Hughes.'

'Well he was a quiet boy and didn't communicate easily with his fellow students. Particularly average grades apart from art. Now the piece of art I had hanging in my office was burned. I saw to that because of the relevance of its contents to the deaths.'

Laurence leaned even closer. 'Go on.'

'It was a dark painting, showing the death of Ophelia. They had been studying *Hamlet* in English, you see. But Ophelia wasn't floating in the water surrounded by the posy of herbs and flowers, as is described in the play. This Ophelia was wrapped in polythene.'

She let this sink in.

'How do you mean polythene?' asked Laurence, confused.

'The painting had a three-dimensional quality. Food wrap was used to represent the water and her shroud. It was excellent, very modern and evocative, but after learning about the death of Carin and how her body was similarly presented, it made the painting seem too macabre. So I disposed of it.'

Laurence nodded his appreciation of this dilemma. 'Was he ever in any trouble at school?'

She shook her head, and then paused and thought carefully. 'Yes, there was an incident. He was accused of inappropriate behaviour with a younger female student. But there were no disciplinary actions as the girl withdrew the accusation and moved to another school.'

'Why wasn't there any follow-up?' asked Eleanor curiously.

'The girl was a little…' Miss Guthrie sought the correct phrase, 'prone to exaggeration. So when she and her parents refused to press any charges, the matter was dropped.'

'Would you be surprised if we told you that Lee was suspected of having abused his younger sister sexually?' asked Laurence carefully.

Louisa looked at him for a moment, placing her cup and saucer on the coffee table. 'No, I would not be surprised.'

'What about his relationship with Tracy Earnshaw? Were they close?' asked Laurence.

'I recall that they were in the same class, but that's about it. Some students form close bonds in school that seem to define them as a pair. But I wouldn't have said that about either Lee or Tracy. She was a rather timid creature and lacking in any sort of academic skill.'

Laurence nodded and thought for a moment. 'Miss Guthrie, you haven't told me yet what your impressions of Lee Hughes were. You've described him as quiet and having problems with communication with fellow students, but I want to know what your real thoughts are?'

She paused, considering her response. 'I thought he was the closest example to a psychopath that Greenslade had ever seen,' she answered slowly.

*

'What are you eating?' asked Timms, sidling over to Wadesky's desk.

'This,' replied Wadesky, barely managing to make any cogent sound through the enormous mouthful of cake, 'is a gift from Minnie for taking Mo home.'

'Share!' said Timms, manoeuvring his large meaty fingers towards the slab of cake.

Wadesky snatched the staple gun that Johnson had left on the edge of her desk and slammed it on top of his hand.

'You have two seconds to take back the hand, or it stays here forever!' she spat.

'Oh maaan! I'm dying of hunger here! And you're my goddamn partner! I risk my life every goddamn day for you,' he groaned, slumping into Mo's chair.

Monster, sensing distress, began to whine and placed a comforting paw on Timms knee. 'You fed the dog though?'

'Yes, I fed the dog,' she replied, slowly placing the last piece of cake into her mouth and savouring it for Timms' benefit.

'What the hell's Whitefoot's plan? He gonna leave this puppy here for the night. Let him starve?' asked Timms, outraged. 'Like me?'

Wadesky shrugged and stood up, rubbing her lower back. 'He'll show,' she said, grabbing her bag and jacket. 'I'm going home as I've been here for fourteen hours and Jo says if I don't haul ass before nine he's coming to get me.'

'Right! Pup comes with me!' he said loudly.

'What if Whitefoot comes in and can't find him?' Wadesky asked. 'It ain't your dog.'

'He's a detective – let him work it out,' he replied.

'Hey partner,' said Wadesky, holding out a bulging paper bag. 'Got a slice for you too.'

'Awwww,' said Timms happily.

*

It was well past 10 p.m. when Laurence dropped Eleanor off at her apartment, and at least two hours after that when he realised he'd forgotten to collect Monster from the squad room. His initial instinct had been to leave the dog there, but he couldn't face the probability Monster would have trashed the room and shat on any and every available surface. So yanking on jeans and a jumper, and grabbing some necessary cleaning implements from the kitchen, he made his way back to the precinct. He took the back stairs, avoiding the mayhem that surrounded the admissions atrium and, heading past the night staff, entered the squad room.

Flicking on the main lights, he made a low whistle, but he knew Monster wasn't there. He sighed. Where the hell was he? It would be just his luck if they'd sent the bloody thing to the pound so he could be further embarrassed.

He thought maybe there was a small chance that a note had been left on his desk, so he opened the door, flicked on the light and noted with surprise and some pleasure that Mo's desk had been moved out. Maybe he was making some progress with Eleanor after all? But then he realised it had just been moved next to Wadesky's so Mo could work more comfortably there.

He picked up the phone and started to dial enquiries when his attention was drawn to the board. Johnson had pinned the school photograph of Lee and Tracy above that of the dead Tracy with her face blown away. There was something about the whole relationship between Lee and Tracy that didn't make sense. If, as everyone supposed, Tracy didn't kill herself but was murdered by Lee Hughes, then why didn't he display her as he had done every other body? The information provided by Tracy's mother indicated that the body in the house was that of her daughter, but could Tracy have been Cindy as well, and how did the relationship between Lee and her develop if there was little to indicate their friendship when they were at school?

Laurence slumped into the easy chair that had been carried in for Mo and began to think. It was well into the early hours before his ideas began to form into something plausible. As he left the squad room he sent a text to Timms: 'Thanks for taking Monster home'.

CHAPTER TWENTY-ONE

Lee Hughes had slept for over twenty-four hours and was still exhausted when he finally awoke. He stretched then leaned forward and switched on the television in the corner of his small room. He'd set the news to record overnight and was hoping that his work had been reviewed, if not generously, then at least with a sense that people had understood what he was trying to achieve and saw his potential. But twenty minutes into his viewing and he'd not managed to locate any emotional response other than repulsion and confusion. He really hadn't expected the police to be sympathetic; even he recognised that the two dead cops would be irritating and a challenge to them. But the language that was being used by the anchorman and bitch detective was very negative. Not one so called 'expert' had ventured any thoughts as to what his actions were meant to communicate.

He was finding it difficult to think under the pressure of such overwhelming stupidity and ignorance, so he closed his eyes and listened to the cacophony of voices all overlapping one another, expressing their disgust at the murders. There was no point in looking at the screen anymore because there were no images of his work. At least show the viewer and let them make their own mind up about the work – not everyone would miss the subtleties and beauty!

He breathed deeply and switched off the set. It was time to move on: take a break from his creativity for a while and wait till his beloved muse spoke again.

Carin's voice had been silent over the past few days, which he was finding slightly worrying. Without her guidance, his work was shallow and ill formed, but she'd left him before. He always put it down to her being young and temperamental. But he was strong and patient and would wait. He would always wait for her.

He looked around the room, taking account of the tools that he was loathe to dispose of and the preliminary sketches he'd made before executing the final pieces. The ones Carin hadn't approved of had been filtered out and disposed of, leaving three scenarios, including the Westex study and the second more elaborate installation in the park. He smiled: she had an excellent eye for form and detail.

He had been working on the third concept for the past few weeks but had yet to present it to Carin. He felt a little shy about it because it was very different in tone to his earlier works. He felt it captured the mischievous side of his nature; it was nothing tasteless – or rather, he hoped Carin wouldn't think that.

A few weeks ago he'd walked around an old amusement park on the edge of the city. It had been derelict for several years and, according to the bill postings, was due for demolition in the spring, when it would be cleared for a new low-cost housing development. Squeezing through a gap in the fencing, he'd discovered a magical and macabre world of rusted fairground rides. Some of the structures had already been dismantled, but several were still standing, in various stages of decay.

Of particular interest to him was the battered remains of a ghost train. It had taken several years of abuse from the local gangs, who had spray-painted every available surface in crude visuals of a sexual and territorial nature. The local hoodlums appeared to have lost interest in its kitsch value when a large section of the side wall collapsed in on itself, negating the snug and mysterious privacy it had offered.

When he looked carefully, Lee had been able to make out the images that had once advertised the terrifying experience that awaited the punter. Swirls of white symbolised the ghostly presences contained within, and skeletons and witches on broomsticks lunged towards the viewer with huge gaping maws. He had loved it. It needed some considerable restructuring if it were to act as a backdrop to one of his installations, and he'd spent a happy couple of hours wandering the site, looking for any materials that could be utilised. He'd almost yelled out loud when he discovered that the kids had torn out the old trolley seats from the ride and used them for al fresco meetings. They were heavy and filled with used condoms, needles and fast-food wrappers, but the potential was there. He could do something with this.

He'd begun developing his ideas on the walk back to his studio. In his mind he saw the ride reconstructed and fully working. Eerie piped music would startle and then amuse his audience when they entered the ride. The ticket booth would be open, and a request for donations would be painted on a board next to a bowl containing tickets. As the ride jolted uncertainly into action, the individual would pass through skeins of shredded silk that mimicked cobwebs, and then with a sudden shriek, the train would enter the installation proper. It would grind to a halt and lights would slowly rise to reveal the centrepiece: a woman so perfectly destroyed, yet terrifying and inspiring in death.

Just as his muse Carin was created for him, so he would encourage others. He was sure that Lydia and Cassandra had already begun to inspire writers, musicians and artists like himself.

The room was freezing and his skin burned as he walked around it naked. He didn't mind the discomfort at all. It had a cleansing quality and, if he was to fully understand his chosen medium, he had to be able to empathise with his subject's experience.

He absent-mindedly reached for a carton of milk, which was sitting on his desk, its contents brittle with ice crystals, and drank and chewed on the contents dispassionately.

As he began to pull together his papers and form a portable bundle, he noticed that there was still one phone left that hadn't been destroyed after its use. He knew there were four messages left in the voicemail box and that he had to delete them and destroy the phone, but he felt the hunger stir deep inside himself and wanted to recapture the moments of pride and empowerment that he'd felt over the past few weeks. He allowed himself a frisson of pleasure as he listened to the call from Tracy for the second time. The tremor in her voice had all the pathos and desperation it had possessed when she was a teenager.

'Lee? I'm not sure I can be ready by then. I will try though.' Her voice tapered off as the discomfort of making the call curtailed further comment.

The killer deleted the message and listened to the second message.

'Hey, is this for real? If it is then consider me in, man. I've got this sick bastard giving me all kinds of shit and if you could—' But he'd heard enough and disposed of that one.

He listened carefully to the final two messages and sighed. He would, under more favourable circumstances, have fulfilled the man's desires. He had even called him back and played the taped response, which explained that he should deposit five thousand dollars behind the bar of the As You Like It club and leave the woman's name and address on this number. Lee had especially liked the sound of the woman's name and rolled its rhythms around his mouth. El… ea… nor Ra… ven. It was whilst he was savouring the name that he realised he'd heard it before.

He pressed the video rewind.

Lee knew now why Carin had been silent for so long. She'd been putting her energies into creating this perfect serendipitous climax to his work. He'd suspected, or rather hoped, that she'd been planning something wonderful, but to have achieved such a coup, presenting him with the very detective that had been so contemptuous of his work…

He took a deep breath and looked around his room. There were stacks of papers that had to be kept, as they documented the planning and preparation of the installations and would be extremely important when his work was finally recognised and written about. He'd begun to separate his tools into two piles: those for destruction, which included knives, clamps, electrodes and needles, everything that could have blood residue on it, and his standard kit which contained anaesthetic drugs, hypodermic syringes, art papers and pencils and several lengths of hand-made silk rope.

His own clothing was functional and dark, consisting only of a wearable set and a spare. As for the costumes, they would all be left to be consumed by the fire that he would set before leaving. But all that had been put on hold as he worked feverishly at his final piece.

He bent over the artwork and began to visualise how he could put together such an advanced concept in such a narrow margin of time. He had to clear and prep the site and plan how he was going to secure his centrepiece, Detective Eleanor Raven, all within the next twenty-four hours. He needed to execute this before public apathy set in.

As his fingers worked the charcoal into the sheet, he felt the warmth of Carin's voice as she whispered her ideas into his head.

*

Laurence flung his car into an available slot at the morgue and tried again to call Eleanor. It was 7 a.m., a little too early for senior pathology staff to be on duty, but knowing Matt was already in, he'd have time to see whether his theory was correct.

Why the hell wasn't she picking up?

He tried once more before entering the cold room and left his third frustrated message of the morning. 'I'm in the morgue now, will call you when I've…' His voice trailed off as he entered the room.

'When you've what, Detective Whitefoot?' replied Eleanor. She was standing next to a gurney, a notebook and pen in hand. At the head of the gurney, her gloved hands on the zipper of the body bag, stood Dr Hounslow.

'Am I losing my hearing, Detective Raven?' piqued the pathologist.

'No, ma'am, I doubt that,' said Eleanor.

Laurence realised his error. 'I should have knocked, sorry.'

Hounslow raised an eyebrow and waited.

'I needed to see Tracy Earnshaw's body,' he said quickly. 'I don't believe that's who she is.'

The two women glanced at each other. 'Tracy's mother came in last night and positively identified the birthmarks on her daughter's shoulder. I'm convinced that this is the body of Tracy Earnshaw,' replied Hounslow.

'This is Tracy Earnshaw,' said Eleanor.

'No, I can prove it!' said Laurence quickly. 'Is this her body?'

The pathologist nodded.

'May I?' Laurence asked.

Eleanor nodded and he waited for the pathologist to unzip the body bag and expose the remains. Then, pulling on a pair of latex gloves, he gently opened the pyjama top to expose the naked torso.

'Tell me what you see,' said Eleanor.

'There's no muscle tone. This woman didn't work out – there's no way she taught a gym class!'

'That doesn't prove that this woman isn't Tracy Earnshaw, does it? It means that the woman you saw at the gym wasn't Tracy but someone posing as her.'

'So Tracy and Cindy could be the same woman?'

Eleanor nodded.

*

'Good detecting work,' said Eleanor, passing him a coffee and a pastry twenty minutes later in D'Angelo's. 'I was so impressed I even paid!' she added.

'You'd worked it out already though. That's why you were there, wasn't it?' he noted, shovelling in the food enthusiastically.

'I suspected as much so went to check it out. Just like you did.' She smiled and watched as his beard gathered a coating of icing sugar.

'But how are we any the wiser?' he complained.

'Every time a truth is revealed, it pushes us a little closer to capturing him. You're peeling back the deceptions he's creating. Look, we know now that he must have been living round here for some time because he had tracked down Tracy and gauged her as a suitable candidate for identity theft. You live anywhere long enough and someone knows you,' she said.

'There has to be something about her that ensured that Tracy would never try to apply for a driving licence and would be unlikely to discover what was going on. Why not just apply for the death certificate of a dead child and steal her identity – surely that would be simpler? More to the point, who's the woman who's pretended to be Tracy? If it's Cindy, then could the killer be a woman? After all, there was no penetration of Lydia or Cassandra so we don't know for sure that—'

'That would mean that Lee Hughes wasn't the killer, and Malcolm Stringer swears he had sex with Cindy, though I doubt that. So to all intents we've got a couple,' she said, finishing her coffee. 'I've got a meeting with Ruby Delaware at midday, which gives us plenty of time to go fish around Tracy Earnshaw's place. She's the closest link we've got so far.'

Eleanor stood up and noticed Susan Cheung making her way over to them with a coffee.

'Hey, guys, heard you were here so I thought I'd combine document delivery with a coffee break.' She pulled up a chair and sat next to them. 'This' – she waggled a manila envelope in front of them – 'is the pollen report from the forensic palynologist Andy Bateman. Nice guy, very thorough. Anyway, he's picked up quite a few pollen and spore samples from both victims, the majority of which are *cupressus sempervirens*, common name is the Italian cypress. Kinda unusual here. My mother always calls them cemetery trees.'

Eleanor pushed her uneaten muffin over to Susan. 'I don't suppose Andy could narrow it down to any particular area, could he?'

Susan shook her head as she chewed appreciatively. 'He said they're not exclusive to cemeteries as folks do try and grow them in ornamental gardens. However, he also found a small amount of chrysanthemum and lily spores, which says "Garden of Rest" to me.'

'Give Andy a big kiss from me,' said Eleanor.

She giggled. 'Think he'd rather have one from Captain America here. Ooh, the tox screening's there too on Lydia Greystein and Cassandra Willis. Both had hefty doses of ketamine in their system.'

'He gave them an anaesthetic,' Laurence said as he glanced down the page. 'Both women appear to have been injected with it.' He read on. 'Interestingly there was a much larger dose found in Cassandra Willis's body. Ketamine can cause instant loss of consciousness when injected intravenously. Also causes hallucinations when the patient has come to.'

'Patient?' Eleanor remarked.

'Sorry, victim,' he replied self-consciously.

'You can pick Special K up in any nightclub in the city. Any point in trying to source it?'

Eleanor shook her head. 'Not really. I'll tell Johnson to run any thefts or losses through the system, but it feels like a wild goose chase to me.'

*

'Captain America! Is that how you all see me?' asked Laurence smugly as they moved towards Eleanor's car.

'Well Timms certainly doesn't,' she replied, the phone to her ear.

'Shit!' groaned Laurence as he remembered Monster.

'Say again… Oakhurst Lawns, off the expressway. I know it. Email me her grave number and clear it with the caretaker, okay?' Eleanor spoke into her cell as she opened the door and slid into the driver's seat.

'Should I call Timms?' asked Laurence, worried.

'I think you should either get the dog rehomed or look after it properly until your girlfriend gets back from her holidays,' she said, swerving through the increasingly heavy traffic onto the parkway.

'Ex-girlfriend and—' he began, but Eleanor wasn't interested.

'Call Andy Bateman and ask him if he'll come and sample the grave site this morning. His number's on the top of the second sheet,' she said, reaching for the report on the back seat.

'What are you thinking?' asked Laurence, tapping in the number and hearing the ringing tone.

'I think that our killer may be a frequent visitor to his sister's grave, and if that's the case then someone will have seen him and might know his routine. Then we can stake it out and wait to see if he shows.'

'Andy Bateman? This is Detective Laurence Whitefoot. I've just read your report on the pollen findings from the Lydia Greystein and Cassandra Willis murders… yes, we suspect that the suspect's sister may be a possible link. She's buried in Oakhurst Lawns on the west side… yes… okay, we're going there now and I'll send you through the details… um… thanks,' said Laurence uncomfortably.

'Well?' asked Eleanor, picking up on the change in his tone.

'He's going to come up and take samples this morning. Very obliging... oh and he liked the sound of my voice, said it was very masculine.'

Eleanor laughed.

'You going to tell everyone in the department?' he asked.

'Oh dear Lord, yes!' she said, taking a sharp right onto the Gardiner Expressway.

*

'Is that guy for real?' asked Laurence as they watched the appropriately lugubrious figure of the cemetery caretaker lumber towards them. 'I swear the words Bela and Lugosi are going to slip out.'

'I guarantee they won't, Detective, as you will be listening and taking notes,' Eleanor responded firmly as she looked at the row of cypress trees interspersed between the graves.

'Mr...?' asked Eleanor, stepping forward with her hand stretched out.

'Please say Lugosi. Please!' whispered Laurence behind her.

'Semper. Arnold Semper,' he croaked, scowling at Laurence.

They all turned to stare at the immaculate grave of Carin Hughes. 'Nice and tidy that one,' remarked Semper, still scowling.

'Who has responsibility for the upkeep of the graves here? Is it you?' asked Eleanor.

'I have to make sure they don't become an eyesore, but it's the relatives that do it,' he replied, lighting a cigarette and inhaling deeply. 'I look after that one 'cos he won't touch it,' he added, pointing to an overgrown site adjacent to Carin Hughes'. 'That's the mom, but he won't go near it, so I mow it in the summer and wipe the headstone.'

Eleanor bent down and read the plain sunken headstone, which bore Marilyn's name.

'Who's the "he" you're referring to?' she asked.

Semper shrugged. 'Guess it's the brother of her. She's been dead too long for it to be a boyfriend.' He pointed to Carin's grave, which was polished and had a wreath of flagging African lilies and chrysanthemums draped around it.

'How often does he come here?' asked Eleanor.

'Regular I guess,' responded Semper.

'Give me a rough idea.'

He shrugged again. 'I dunno, maybe once a month. I ain't never spoken to him.'

Eleanor's mouth opened but Semper got in quickly. 'I dunno when he was last 'ere, but looking at the state of the headstone and flowers, maybe a week or so ago.'

'Would you recognise him?' she asked, reaching for the photograph in her bag.

Semper shrugged. 'Dunno… try me?'

She handed him the school photograph and waited as he contemplated. 'When was this taken? He don't look like that now.' He passed the photograph back to her.

'How do you mean?' she asked.

'Well he's a lad there. You got anything newer?' When she shook her head, he said, 'It's him alright but he's older. Filled out and his hair's different.'

'In what way?' butted in Laurence.

'Shorter. It's 'bout an inch all over.'

'How tall?'

'Five-ten, eleven. Shorter than you,' he said, pointing at Laurence. 'And a bit taller than you.' He pointed at Eleanor.

'How did he arrive?' Laurence asked.

Semper shrugged. 'Can't see the car park from here. Bus, bike?'

There was a pause before Eleanor nodded and handed him her card. 'I'd like you to call me if you see him here. I must advise you not to approach or communicate with him. He's an extremely dangerous man.'

Semper scowled. 'Well if he's that dangerous, how come he hasn't done me already?'

'Presumably because you've never spoken to or challenged him before,' said Eleanor. 'A scientist will be arriving this morning to take samples of the grass around the grave. I assume you have no objection?'

'Don't bother me none. No holes though,' he warned, before turning abruptly and heading back in the direction he had come from.

As soon as he was out of earshot, Eleanor pulled out her phone and spoke quickly. 'Timms? I need to get an exhumation order for Carin Hughes' body. Tell them that we've got the tox screenings on Lydia and Cassandra and they both had evidence of ketamine. I'm proposing that Lee Hughes murdered his sister and mother so will need… I know it's not going to hold water with the DA but you and Wadesky have got to find a way to get this past Heidlmann… Yes, Hughes is tending the grave. It might flush him out if we start messing with his sister's resting place… Yes… Whitefoot?' Eleanor raised one eyebrow and looked at Laurence, who was making a 'cut-off' gesture. 'Yes, he's here.'

She passed the phone to Laurence and smiled as she heard Timms yelling down the phone at him.

She was seated in the car by the time Whitefoot caught up with her. He slumped into the passenger seat and cleared his throat. 'What if Heidlmann won't agree to the exhumation?'

'It's highly unlikely that he will. But we'll set up the grave as if it's an exhumation and hope that does the same trick.'

'Won't that piss the DA off?' he added.

'I imagine it will.'

*

Lee should have been exhausted but was anything but. He knew he was putty in Carin's hands, but which artist wasn't? He smiled as he thought of Dante pining for Beatrice; his only salvation and hope had been knowing that, although dead, she would steer his pen and thoughts into creating the great poetic vision that was the *Inferno*. Carin was steering him towards his masterpiece and that was why neither cold nor hunger could deter him from his artistic frenzy.

He'd cleaned the fairground ride and managed to drag the old trolley seats from the campsite and, with the aid of a metal girder, lever them onto what remained of the tracks. He took stock for a moment and tried to evaluate what was missing. He'd replaced the missing section of wall by stapling in place a rotten hessian tarpaulin he'd found shoved underneath one of the slides. It wasn't ideal, but it did bring greater atmosphere and had the added benefit of reducing the wind that blasted through the construction, which had blown out most of the uncovered candles. There was no time for any major decoration changes as Carin had insisted that the canvas was to be collected this evening. He'd argued that point, but when Carin had started sulking and threatening to leave him on his own to tackle the project, he'd backed down. She knew best.

Although he couldn't get any real movement out of the trolley, he felt that its presence was probably sufficient to create atmosphere. There hadn't been a need to employ artificial lighting on his other two projects, as he'd had all the benefit of access to sunlight, but this wasn't possible. He needed to throw shadows, and having no source of power, he'd sunk the better half of thirty bucks into buying good quality candles, which would burn for several days, providing he'd plugged all the drafts. There would be a delicious irony to the hanging of the canvas, which would hopefully not be lost on the audience. There were at least seven heavy-duty carabiner type hooks embedded in the ceiling, presumably where papier mâché skeletons and the like were originally displayed. At first he'd been nonplussed by the graffiti sprayed on every available wall but was beginning to feel that the images had an odd urban beauty to them, so he left them where they were.

It was late afternoon when he'd finally finished the presentation. He was beginning to feel the need for some sustenance and planned to grab something from the local supermarket as he made his way back to the studio, where the initial preparation of Eleanor Raven would take place.

*

Eleanor and Laurence stared at the artist's impression of Lee Hughes. 'He's so bland!' said Laurence in disbelief. 'How the hell can we find this guy? He's wallpaper!'

'I've aged him to thirty-four or thereabouts and altered the hair and weight after receiving your call. Sorry, guys, but unless he's got some interesting facial scars, I suspect that's him,' said Lucy, the department's forensic artist. 'If you get anything else let me know and I'll adapt it as a priority. Okay?' She grabbed her coat and bag and headed for the door.

'Thanks, Lucy. Much appreciated,' said Eleanor, studying the pencil drawing of Lee Hughes.

'Anything to catch the bastard,' Lucy replied with feeling as she left.

There was a crash and then a yell was heard making its way, like a wave, along the corridor. Eleanor prepared herself for the imminent arrival of Marty Samuelson.

'Progress?' he demanded, yanking a chair from under Eleanor's table. 'Give me the progress!'

She was silent for a moment and then handed him a photocopy of the pencil sketch.

'That him?' he asked.

Eleanor nodded. 'We need to go public with it.'

Samuelson scratched his head vigorously as he thought it through. 'He's a bland bastard, and once this is out there he'll sprint. Only thing we've really got is that he doesn't know we have his ID. However, maybe someone might just connect... That's a bloody forgettable face,' he moaned. 'What do you say?' he asked Laurence.

'I think if you're going to tease him out of the woodwork with the exhumation of Carin then you might as well saturate the city with his image. If he's busy trying to hide from being recognised then he can't be planning another kidnapping. Let's put him on the wrong foot... maybe—'

Laurence was interrupted by a polite coughing. Ruby Delaware stood in the doorway, her short, stout frame enveloped in a pink poncho, which made her look alarmingly like an overgrown toddler.

'I've brought your profile and, without meaning to be rude, may I join in your discussions?'

'Please do,' replied Eleanor, gesturing towards a chair.

Ruby sat down, arranging her bags, glasses, folders of photocopies and small floral pencil case neatly on the table. Johnson looked on with barely concealed approval.

'Johnson, come and join us. Is anyone else around?' asked Eleanor.

'No, everyone's out, but Timms is due any minute.'

Neither Eleanor nor Laurence looked entirely happy about this – Eleanor because Timms' views on profilers was vociferously negative and Laurence because he'd have to face a tirade about animal neglect/abuse etc.

'Your killer is a very interesting and disturbed individual,' began Ruby, nodding to no one in particular. 'First, let me tell you that I think you're correct in your belief that Lee Hughes is a likely candidate. I know you have more circumstantial evidence that points to him now, but it was good detecting work on your part. Now, let's get to business...' Ruby flipped open the manila folder and withdrew a pile of neatly typed profile sheets and handed them round, leaving surplus sheets in a pile.

'After processing forensic, geographical and historical information about Lee Hughes, I've drawn up what I believe to be a psychologically authentic portrait. I have forwarded my profile to Quantico, but it could take weeks to get feedback from them.' She looked around the table awkwardly before clearing her throat and launching into her opinions.

'Lee Hughes was deeply, and I imagine still is, in love with his sister Carin. Having found her body alongside his mother's, he will have divided his emotion into what could be described as a hatred for all women for causing him such loss and pain and adoration of what he could consider to be the perfect but unobtainable being.'

'How'd you get to that?' asked Samuelson suspiciously.

'His attempts at preservation of the body with the plastic wrap and subsequent reproductions of the image in his later artistic works…'

'You're saying this guy considers himself to be some sort of Van Gogh?' said Samuelson.

'In his mind, yes. The women he's displaying are a homage to Carin.' She pulled out a colour photograph of the dead Carin. 'I believe he's trying to reproduce the emotional impact of discovering the body. You can see that she's beautiful in death, her lips and cheeks giving the illusion that she's merely resting. This image will have shaped his entire future.'

'Do you believe he was having a sexual relationship with both Carin and his mother?' Eleanor asked.

Ruby sighed. 'There was physical evidence from the autopsies that both women had unusual amounts of bruising between their thighs and, in Carin's case, around the breast region. However, Marilyn was diagnosed as schizophrenic and had spent some considerable portion of the children's early years in a psychiatric unit. She had medication issues and—'

'What issues?' interrupted Eleanor.

'She didn't like to take her meds and as a result became aggressive, disorientated and prone to self-harming, according to the hospital reports.' She handed several photocopied sheets to Eleanor. 'Reading between the lines I believe Marilyn's frequent absences from the family home and inadequate parenting would have forced Lee into developing an unnaturally close relationship with his younger sister.'

'What about their father?' Eleanor asked.

'Neither biological father stayed around long enough—'

'So Lee and Carin were half siblings?'

'Apparently. There's no evidence that either child received any adult supervision during Marilyn's stay in hospital. They were supposed to be looked after by a neighbour, but there's little data to suggest that was an effective strategy.'

'So we have two teenagers, effectively parentless, unsupervised and living together,' said Eleanor.

Ruby nodded. 'It would have been natural that they formed a unique bond. That it was sexual in nature would make it more unusual. There's also evidence that Carin had been hearing voices and having visions,' Ruby said pointedly.

'She was schizophrenic too?' asked Eleanor, leaning towards Ruby.

Ruby shrugged and raised her eyebrows. 'She would have been a little young for the condition to have developed fully, but her school had been worried enough by her behaviour to call in the educational psychologist, who recommended she be evaluated. But she was dead before that could happen.'

'Tell me about how he lives,' said Eleanor.

Suddenly the door flew open and Monster bounded into the squad room, barking loudly. He made a beeline for Laurence, landing both feet onto his lap and shoving his panting face into Laurence's.

'What the hell!' shouted Samuelson. 'Is this dog in training? Whose is it?' he bellowed.

'He's supposed to be Whitefoot's dog, sir, but I found him in here, starving to death last night and was forced—' said Timms angrily.

'The hell you did!' yelled Laurence, jumping to his feet and pushing the dog away.

Monster began to bark loudly. Timms whistled him over.

'Get that mutt over to the kennels at once.' Samuelson's voice was drowned out by Monster's steady barking. 'What the hell!' Samuelson yelled and lunged at the dog, who was dithering between loyalty to Laurence and his new-found master in Timms. Grabbing Monster by the collar, he stuck three fingers sharply into the dog's ribs to get its attention and pushed it into a sitting position. Monster, recognising a higher force, lapsed into silence and stared at Samuelson, making occasional whines.

'Right! Who owns this dog?' said Samuelson quietly.

'I do, sir,' replied Laurence unhappily.

'Why is Timms looking after it then?'

Timms glared angrily at Laurence.

'I forgot to collect him from the office. It's my fault and Timms was doing right by the dog,' answered Laurence quietly.

'Okay then. I've got bodies on slabs and two of them are cops. You don't look for points of contention amongst yourselves, understand?' Samuelson looked pointedly at Timms and Laurence. 'If you can't manage him, take him down to K9,' he said, stroking Monster's head. 'Now we work!'

Everyone settled down round the table; Monster crept underneath, nuzzling his head against Laurence's feet.

'Ruby, carry on please,' said Eleanor. 'You were telling us how he lives?'

'He believes himself to be an artist, and as such, he will occupy a studio of some description. Possibly an old warehouse, somewhere he won't be disturbed by landlords or other people.'

'So disused is likely?' asked Eleanor.

'I'd say so. It's unlikely that he steals his food and possible that he sells his art locally but informally, maybe in a local marketplace, but I doubt he has any contact with the public. Most likely he'll sell to a local dealer, very low-key sales. He lives frugally and will produce his artwork in the studio,' said Ruby.

'Is that where he murders the women?' asked Samuelson.

'Yes, but he won't think of it as murder. He's creating art,' she replied.

'How the hell do you know all this then?' snorted Timms.

Ruby carefully placed the crime-scene photographs of Carin, Lydia and Cassandra next to each other, and then arranged those of Paget and Ellis underneath. 'You've already linked the murder victims' appearance in death to that of his sister. We know that he was considered able artistically and has displayed his victims in a manner that not only reproduces Carin's death scene but is enhanced and celebratory. His ability to utilise the two dead officers into his—'

Timms let out a growl, his cheeks turning red. 'Utilise?' he intoned dangerously.

'I didn't mean disrespect to the two fallen officers,' said Ruby, flustered. 'I cannot let my emotions or partiality affect my analysis of the suspect's way of thinking.'

Timms set his jaw and leaned back in his seat.

Ruby paused, cleared her throat and continued nervously. 'I believe he would have been unhappy with the final appearance of Cassandra Willis due to her decapitation. I would also suggest that' – her voice dropped to slightly above a whisper – 'the two officers would have been unharmed and allowed to view Cassandra if her neck hadn't broken.' She cast a quick glance in Timms' direction and hurried on. 'But by killing the officers and making them appear as if they were kneeling in a sort of spiritual wonderment, he told us how we are to perceive his art.'

Eleanor nodded in agreement. 'Do you think he's been to an art college, and if so, where?'

'He may have enrolled but would have found it difficult to take instructions on how to paint or sculpt. I doubt he would have lasted very long, probably a matter of months, and as to where, I really can't say. He disappeared for twenty years. It's difficult to imagine how he'd manage that if he were still in the vicinity. Most likely he went to another city and lived on the periphery, possibly surviving by selling his work. He has a rich and satisfying fantasy existence and is unlikely to be inconvenienced by any physical deprivation.'

'These are all pie in the sky suppositions!' snapped Timms. 'What good is it? We need to work on facts. Detecting.'

'That's your job. Mine is to study how minds work – lots of minds, from the normal to the deranged – and by doing that, and comparing responses from thousands of subjects, we can see patterns. Your killer is insane, and every response you take for granted in a normal human being is absent from his thoughts. He feels no empathy yet is awash with feelings of love. He believes he acts for the higher good but lives in what we'd consider to be a moral vacuum. He hasn't finished killing women yet, and if there's any way that a psychological profile can help capture him then it's your duty to hear me out.' Ruby Delaware fell silent, her lips pursed with indignation.

Timms leaned towards her and spoke slowly. 'Well it depends on how much of this psychological profile has just been blasted out of your ass.'

'Timms!' bellowed Samuelson.

'Just saying is all,' Timms said with a shrug, sinking back into his seat.

'I do not "blast profiles out of my ass", Detective,' she said, gathering her possessions together and shoving them into her handbag. 'I leave that to others!' Ruby stared pointedly at Timms and left the room.

Samuelson looked as if he was about to tear a strip off Timms, but a call from the DA postponed it.

'Well handled, Timms; diplomacy in action,' said Eleanor with irritation.

She fell silent for a moment, staring at the photographs arranged on the table.

'Saturate the city with his name, details and Lucy's sketch. Someone will have seen something. He needs to know we're closing in on him. Put him on the back foot.'

She looked around the table and noted the nods of agreement. 'If Ruby's right and he's selling art then let's get out there and find dealers. Johnson?' she asked.

'No problem,' he responded.

'Timms, I want the warehouse district covering. If he's got a studio of some description then we need to find it. Catch up with Smith and get him onto it as well. Get onto Susan Cheung and find out if there's any forensic evidence that can narrow down where the women were killed.'

Timms nodded. 'Wadesky's gone to pick up Mo. She should be about fifteen.'

Eleanor smiled 'Good. They can coordinate the press coverage on Hughes. Johnson, we got any lead on the car that he used to pick up Cassandra Willis?'

'Nothing. Without the plates we're still trawling types. No company or individual has reported a car as missing. I've got guys running it now and will keep you posted. Ballistics are still processing.'

*

'How is he this good? I mean, how can a guy murder this many people in such a short amount of time and not leave a trail?' asked Laurence.

'He leaves a trail. We've just not hit the right spot yet,' said Eleanor quietly.

'Well how the hell are we going to hit it then?' he said, more aggressively than he'd meant to.

Eleanor paused. 'He's a lone predator; we're not. We work the case methodically, unemotionally and hunt him as a pack. He's left his marks out there; we have to find them and follow them. He *will* be caught.'

Laurence looked at her hard. Her lips were tightly drawn and a flush of colour on her high cheekbones was the only indication of her anger. For a brief moment he considered her beautiful. 'So where do we start?'

'With the only person who can link us with Lee Hughes,' she answered briskly, rising to her feet.

'Cindy?' Laurence said, following her out of the room.

'Carin,' Eleanor replied.

CHAPTER TWENTY-TWO

Sergeant Andy Harrison was not happy. He'd ignored the demands of his wife, doctor and therapist and returned to work the day after finding Ellis and Paget, despite alarmingly raised blood pressure and the sort of heartburn he generally only experienced at Christmas or when his daughter returned home from college. He'd taken the phone call from the outraged Mr Chen half an hour earlier and still couldn't work out whether a crime had been committed or not, and if it had, whether he gave a shit or not.

The gist of the conversation, as far as Harrison could ascertain, was that Mr Chen had returned from a month-long business trip only to discover that his brand-new black Mercedes had been stolen and then brought back in a less-than-clean state, sometime before his return last night. Mr Chen wanted an immediate investigation into this outrage and would expect detectives and crime-scene officers imminently.

Harrison felt like binning the sheet he'd written the details on, but something was troubling him. Who the hell, other than one of Mr Chen's children, would have taken a car and then taken the trouble to return it? Mr Chen had assured him that both of his teenage children were in Beijing visiting relatives.

He could do with moving his bones around, so he took the stairs up to Homicide, for no better reason than the coffee was better up there.

'Hey, buddy, pour me a cup!' yelled Timms, seeing Harrison at the coffee machine and meandering over. 'And what do we owe this honour to?' he said, thrusting out his mug.

'I get this call from some pissy guy saying his car's been stolen and then brought back and parked in his spot. Guy's pretty riled, but there's nothing missing, just half a tank of diesel.'

Timms wrinkled his forehead and frowned. 'Perps borrowing rather than stealing don't sound kosher to me. His kids?'

'No. It's a black Mercedes saloon. Brand new.'

Timms thought for a moment and then bellowed across the room, 'Johnson, we got any leads on the car that picked up Cassandra Willis?'

'Nothing yet,' he replied.

'Well we have now.' Timms turned back to Harrison. 'Fancy accompanying me on a little trip to visit the sorely abused Mr Chen?'

'Why the hell not?' replied Harrison, downing his coffee.

*

Mr Chen, despite his diminutive size, was making a great deal of noise. Timms left him with Harrison while he used his torch to peer into the car. The car had been parked, a little haphazardly, in an allocated spot in a three-level underground private car park.

Timms called Harrison over. 'Where did he leave his keys?' asked Timms, slipping on a pair of latex gloves.

'In the ignition,' sighed Harrison.

'Tell Mr Chen that invalidates his insurance and not having valid insurance is a crime in this state.'

Harrison smiled and headed back over to convey this news to Mr Chen, who let his mouth drop open in astonishment.

'Okay, Mr Chen, we're taking this matter very seriously and crime-scene officers are on their way. I'd be real grateful if you'd head up to your apartment now and wait to be contacted by one of my colleagues,' said Timms.

Still reeling from the news regarding his insurance, Chen bowed slightly and departed hurriedly.

'So leaving your keys in the ignition, that's a Chinese thing?' Timms asked Susan Cheung half an hour later as she began to process the car.

'Yeah, that's right. Every single Chinese guy this side of the yellow river leaves his keys in the car,' she replied.

'You yanking my bell?'

Susan sighed. 'Yeah, Timms. How would I know what every Chinese guy does with his keys?'

'I dunno, but you guys believe in all this year-of-the-dragon-type shit. Maybe you can tell—'

'How the hell did you become a detective?' she asked despairingly as she carefully opened the trunk to reveal a length of rope and a new set of bolt cutters.

'Charm and dedication, that's how. Shall we get this puppy down to the lab?' he asked, looking over her shoulder.

'You read my mind, Detective Timms.'

*

'Okay, this is the bottom line,' sighed Marty Samuelson after ending the call. Eleanor stood three feet away from him, her face reflecting the sigh.

'The bottom line?' she asked grimly.

'Heidlmann won't even bother putting a request for an exhumation order in front of the judge. He says it's a waste of time.'

'Does he? A waste of whose time? His?' she snapped.

'He's got a point. He says we haven't got sufficient evidence, and in five years only two exhumations have been authorised out of thirteen requests. More relevant is the fact that it could take anything up to three weeks to get a response from a judge.

After all, the dead can wait,' said Samuelson. 'You need to set another trap.'

With that he waved a hand and disappeared into his office, closing the door firmly.

'Shit,' said Laurence.

'All is not lost. Is Claddis McAvoy still in custody?' asked Eleanor.

'As far as I know,' replied Laurence.

*

Claddis McAvoy had spent most of his relatively short period of incarceration pacing and sulking. So when Eleanor and Laurence arrived with a steaming coffee and box of doughnuts, Claddis eschewed his natural suspicions and looked ready to agree to anything.

'Listen, guys, I know how pissed you are with this whole thing, but I have never been critical of this department – never. How was I to know that you were going to take things so far? I mean—'

'I've heard the DA is looking to go for a custodial sentence, Claddis. That's a bit far in my opinion, but he's mad as hell at this stunt,' said Eleanor, shaking her head in disbelief.

'W-Whaaat?' stammered Claddis, the colour draining from his face. 'You can't be serious!'

'He's looking for an example to be made, Claddis, and your antic kinda did for him,' said Laurence.

'Maybe your bosses will get you a good defence lawyer?' said Eleanor with appropriate sympathy.

Claddis looked miserable. 'Yeah… maybe.'

'You didn't run this stunt past them, did you? And now they're pissed with you for stepping outside their remit,' pointed out Eleanor.

'And for besmirching their good name,' piped in Laurence.

'Besmirching?' Claddis sniggered. 'I gotta use that word! Look, I messed up 'cos I got caught with grubby fingers. No one gives a shit about that, provided you don't get caught.'

'Well you did get caught, but we're here to offer you a way to get out and have the first interview with the lead detective when the case is closed,' offered Eleanor.

Claddis narrowed his eyes. 'Oh yeah? And what do I have to do for this?'

'A little bit more of what you're good at,' said Eleanor quietly, leaning towards him. 'We want you to create a little scenario with us that will draw our murderer out of the woodwork. We'll even give you his name.'

Claddis stopped chewing, his eyes glittering with excitement. 'Go on.'

'We're going to set up an exhumation and you're going to run it as kosher,' said Eleanor.

Claddis swallowed and flicked his eyes from one detective to the other. 'It's not a real exhumation, but you want me to write an article saying that it is? Is that right?'

'That's it.'

'You've got no authority to do this? And you want me to publish an article making out that it's real?' He shook his head in disbelief.

'That's the measure of it. We'll set up the dig and furnish you with a couple of photo opportunities.'

'I'll lose my job for that,' Claddis said flatly. 'I'll take this DA shit and smooth it over with my editor. Thanks though!' He leaned back in the chair and folded his arms.

'Okay, your call,' said Eleanor as she and Laurence got to their feet. 'But remember, you'd be directly helping in the capture of the city's most dangerous serial killer and undoing the harm to the department you caused.'

*

Eleanor opened the door and was just walking into the corridor when Claddis called out, 'I get out now. All charges dropped and an *exclusive* interview when the case is closed.'

She smiled at Laurence. 'It's a deal,' she called as she walked swiftly down the corridor and headed for the stairs.

'Great idea, but how the hell are you going to organise a mock exhumation? You can publish photos, but surely if it's going to flush him out, we're going to need to convince Hughes it's for real. A tent and police tape aren't going to cut it,' he speculated, trotting after her.

'You're right. We're going to need at least the loan of a coroner's van. We can stick Timms and Smith in a couple of white suits and then place spotters and hire a digger. But without the van we're not fooling anyone.'

Eleanor stopped on the stairs and stared at Laurence. 'You're going to call in a favour from your buddy Matt and get a van loan from the med examiner's office.'

'You're kidding… right?'

*

'Come *on*!' groaned Wadesky.

'Done!' said Johnson calmly as he finished the calculation. 'If, as we believe from Mr Chen, the tank had been filled to the brim when he left it then it should have been carrying approximately thirteen gallons of diesel. The remainder is hitting slightly under the half point on the dial, which gives us an approximate usage of seven gallons. We know that the distance from Mr Chen's apartment to the park is nine miles – that's urban cycle so it should be averaging 37.2 mpg.'

'Je-*sus*, Johnson! Just give me the figures; I don't give a shit about how you got 'em,' snapped Wadesky, a pencil hovering over a fold-out map of the city.

Johnson sighed. 'There are so many suppositions…' He caught sight of Wadesky's glare. 'At combined usage he could have covered about two hundred and fifty miles, which means that our radius starts from Mr Chen's apartment' – Johnson guided her pencil stroke from the east side and measured an arc out to several miles beyond the boundary line of the city – 'and stretches out towards the river. We know he had to cover this route.' He pointed out the park in relation to Mr Chen's apartment and reduced the radius. 'That takes us shy of the city boundaries and river. If – and this is the main if – he didn't refuel.'

Wadesky scratched her head and picked up her now-ringing phone after the second ring. 'Hey buddy…' She listened in silence, a wide smile beginning to spread across her face. 'Fantastic! Yup, will get Johnson onto it right away.'

She hung up. 'They've got Cassandra Willis's fingerprints from the door handles and leather seats and' – she looked triumphantly at Mo and Johnson – 'they've found blonde hairs from Lydia Greystein in the boot and the back seat.'

'We can triangulate. That's going to narrow it down considerably!' Johnson poured over the map and began to work out the area most likely to have been used by Hughes.

*

Eleanor sipped her coffee and watched as an unhappy-looking Laurence made his way through the traffic to join her in D'Angelo's. She'd ordered him a coffee and a selection of pastries in an attempt to take the edge off his trip to the ME's office. Looking at his expression, she suspected it wouldn't be enough.

'How'd it go?' she asked breezily as Laurence slumped into the seat opposite her. 'Will they help us?'

Laurence stared at the peace offering and pushed it away. 'Dr Hounslow's livid, and rightly so.'

'I'm sure, but will she do it?' asked Eleanor, trying to keep the impatience out of her voice.

He nodded. 'Matt persuaded her. Sue Cheung will bring the van tomorrow evening and set up the scene as if for real. There's to be no digging or displacement of the grave site under any circumstances, and I've given my word on that score,' he added firmly.

Eleanor nodded in agreement.

'Department protocol dictates that it would occur post 6 p.m., but she's adamant that the van be delivered back to the morgue before 5 a.m.' He reached for a pastry and chewed thoughtfully.

'Great work, partner,' she said.

Laurence stared at her for a moment and then smiled. 'It's all good,' he said quietly, reaching for his coffee.

*

Timms and Smith looked in disbelief at the small red circle drawn across an area of downtown covering no more than a ten-mile radius. 'You're saying Lee Hughes is holed up somewhere in there? You're sure?' asked Timms.

'Not sure, no. But if, as we suspect, he used the car to kidnap both women and transport them to an unknown place where they were tortured and killed, and then took the bodies to the Westex power station and Jubilee Park, he has to be working out of a very compact area. Things we don't know are: where he collected Lydia Greystein from and whether he refuelled the Mercedes. Neither do we know whether he has his own vehicle or not. If not, then he needs to be in biking or walking distance of Chen's apartment complex. The interesting part is that this area' – he pointed to the east section of the circle – 'is what used to be the meat-packing district, now disused and awaiting gentrification.'

'He needs a quiet place to torture the women and move them in and out without arousing suspicion, so our bet's on this area,' added Mo.

Smith scratched his head. 'We know shit about this. If Hughes refuelled then this is all bullshit. He could be coming from over the river for all we know.'

'But why pick two sites that are so close to each other? People stick to what they know. He knows this area – that's why he chose Westex and Jubilee Park. He lives there,' said Wadesky.

'Okay, we ain't exactly drowning in leads so far,' said Timms. 'Let's get down there and have a look around. How many patrolmen we got?'

'We've got four, and three after nine tonight. I've got them checking gas stations and canvassing Chen's apartment block. Mo and me are gonna take a drive around the warehouse district. If we see anything we like, we'll call it in, okay?' said Wadesky, standing up and readjusting her clothing.

'Christ, the pair of you should be on mobility scooters,' quipped Timms, appraising them.

'Go to hell, Timms,' said his partner.

Timms threw up his arms. 'Jeez, you invalids are sensitive.' He turned to Mo. 'You think this exhumation crack is gonna work on Hughes, flush him out?'

'Who knows, but it's as good an idea as we've got so far.'

*

Eleanor read the article while Laurence drove slowly around the warehouse district.

'How'd it read?' he asked.

'Good,' she said decisively, folding the paper in two. 'McAvoy's used the general information package naming Hughes as our chief suspect, but the headline advertises the exclusive. "The *Sun* learns from inside source that body of Carin Hughes to be exhumed as possible victim." Let's hope it brings him out.'

*

Laurence looked through the rain at the decaying buildings surrounded by grid fences declaring, 'Keep out. Unsafe'. 'What are we looking for?'

'Signs,' she replied.

'Like what?' he asked.

She shrugged. 'Sometimes you see something that's just not right. You can't always see it at the time. Hours, days, months later you'll be thinking of something entirely different, but your unconscious mind is still working on what it's seen, and a light goes on. So, you look.'

Laurence raised his eyebrows and carried on driving slowly through what had been the old meat-packing district. So far he'd seen nothing more enlightening than litter-strewn walkways, smashed fascias and an old, discarded amusement park.

*

'Well look at that!' said Wadesky as she pulled the car over and stopped outside a small gothic church, long since abandoned by the righteous and squeezed between two red-brick, cotton warehouses. The mournful windows and arched door gave the church an air of outrage.

Mo smiled as he read the hand-painted sign nailed to the door – 'Local Art and Crafts for Sale. Browsing Acceptable'.

'You wanna wait here?' asked Wadesky.

'The hell I do!' he said, gripping the roof bar to support his weight as he slid around in the seat and eased himself out.

'If you're gonna die, do it at home, not on my watch ,do you hear me?' she said, helping Mo to his feet.

'Copy that,' he gasped.

The church was freezing and the steady sound of dripping from the de-leaded roof added to the aura of melancholy. A small paraffin heater was fighting the odds in the middle of the aisle and two well-wrapped women were sitting around it, both crocheting at breakneck speed. They stopped chatting and turned to smile at Wadesky and Mo.

'You two look around,' one said, waving a hand expansively. 'None of the artists are here today, but if you're interested, you come and tell us and we'll help you.'

Wadesky smiled and glanced round at the tables laden with hand-knitted garments, jewellery made out of old watch parts and some attractive watercolours depicting pastoral scenes. She moved on to the next display, which had a slightly more edgy subject matter. Nudes painted in vibrant blues and oranges stared aggressively from hand-stretched canvases.

'That's my nephew's work,' came a voice from behind them. 'He went to the city university to study fine art,' she said proudly. 'I'm Jenny Evans.' She smiled and then lowered her tone. 'My friend' – she pointed to the second figure – 'says you're police?'

Wadesky smiled and whispered back, 'She's right.'

Jenny seemed pleased. 'Margie knows a thing or two. So are you here for a browse or do you want some information?'

The two women had obviously not had a single customer for several days and insisted on making Mo and Wadesky a cup of strong tea and sharing a pack of biscuits. Two plastic chairs were found and arranged around the heater.

'Fire away,' said Jenny enthusiastically. 'Me and Margie have lived here since we were girls and have learned a few things.'

'We're looking for a man in his early thirties, an artist,' Wadesky said, her tongue stumbling over the word artist.

Margie narrowed her eyes. 'What sort of artist? You don't like describing him as that, so what is he to you?'

Mo looked at her carefully. 'He's a murderer.'

Both women moved forward in the seats.

'There's a strong possibility that he sells his work to keep himself financially afloat.'

Margie laughed. 'Hell, he's outta our league then. Most we make is fifty bucks a month. Church doesn't want to sell this place till the price is higher. They let it to us for twenty bucks a month and sit on their asset till some big company wants to rebuild this area, and then they kick us out and demand a big payout and let it get knocked down. So why'd you think we'd know this murderer?'

Mo shrugged. 'His name's Lee Hughes and his paintings are likely to represent women in death. Possibly wrapped in some sort of plastic sheet or bag?'

'Who the hell'd want to buy that?' asked Jenny, horrified.

'Oh, don't be so frickin' daft, Jen. People have different tastes and weird stuff sells,' said Margie emphatically. 'That don't ring no bells with me…' She fell silent for a moment. 'That ain't true – a bell is ringing.'

'Go on,' said Jenny, excited.

'This may be nothin', but you're clutching at straws, yes?'

Mo nodded and sighed.

'Well three blocks on West Street there's a small gallery. I say gallery, but Bill, the guy who runs it does tattoos and sells a bit of jewellery and "other items".' She raised her eyebrows knowingly. 'He has some artwork for sale, most of it's porn, or comic-type stuff. But that's the type of place you might see stuff like that. Bill Gaynor's his name and the shop's called Inked.'

Mo gratefully finished off his tea and stood up. 'You've both been very helpful and that sounds like our next port of call. Thank you, ladies.'

Inked was a small oasis of colour and glamour in an otherwise industrial grey desert. A bell tinkled as they stepped through the door and entered the shop.

'What the hell is that?' said Wadesky, staring at the huge bird perched behind the counter and staring balefully at them.

'This is Morticia and she's an American crow,' said a small man proudly as he emerged from a gloomy corner. He was the most intensely tattooed individual either detective had ever seen. His face and shaved head were hidden behind a covering of green tattooed feathers, made more incongruous by a set of heavy rimmed spectacles.

'Born in 1853, she was the beloved pet of the local sheriff. He had her mounted and placed—'

'Detectives Wadesky and Morris,' cut in Wadesky quickly, fearing that Bill intended to fill in the missing years in Morticia's life in detail. 'Are you Bill Gaynor?'

Bill's expression changed to one of despair. His shoulders sagged and he let out a heavy sigh.

'We need to ask you some questions,' said Mo.

'Yeah…' Bill walked behind them and flipped the lock on the door. 'Follow me.'

'You think he's gonna cuff himself for us?' Wadesky said, giggling quietly as they walked through a bead curtain down a narrow corridor and into the tattoo parlour complete with bed, inking equipment and walls decorated with hand-drawn images of tattoos.

Bill indicated that they should pull out a chair from under a counter.

'Mr Gaynor, before you lose the will to live, let me assure you that at the current time we are not here to discuss your criminal activities, okay?' said Mo.

Bill's face twisted its way from despair, to elation, to suspicion in a matter of seconds.

'However, that's not to say that we won't be calling again.' Mo gave Bill a couple of seconds to understand the implications of the warning. 'Do you understand what I'm saying, Mr Gaynor?'

'I think so…' came the hesitant reply.

'We're looking for a man called Lee Hughes.'

Bill remained nonplussed.

'He's an artist and is likely to be producing art that may have representations of women in death. Possibly wrapped in some sort of plastic film.'

Suddenly Bill became animated. 'Yes, I know who you mean. I've got a painting here. The first one was like that, but the second one is…' He waggled a flattened palm and turned down the corners of his mouth. 'Well so-so.'

'May we see it?' asked Wadesky.

Bill climbed to his feet and headed off into the corridor, yelling back, 'Down here. It's in the back.'

Mo and Wadesky followed him down a damp corridor, through an arch and into a room, which contained at least thirty canvases, all propped against the wall. A bare, low-wattage bulb illuminated the dank space, and it was difficult to make out any subject matter.

Bill rummaged through the canvases, tutting with every inappropriate find. 'There's one here. I know I only sold the one… hang on… there!' he said triumphantly, sliding a dark frame from between several others and turning it to face Mo and Wadesky. 'Is that what you mean? The first one had a woman hanging from a tree I think. Bit "specialist" but someone liked it.'

Wadesky and Mo put latex gloves on and took the canvas carefully from Bill. It was dark, comprising three or four different shades of aquamarine. The woman's face appeared to float beneath a watery surface. Her eyes were closed, the red on her lips the only other colour used. A disembodied hand reached across the surface of the water as if trying to touch her. The subject matter, though strange, was not particularly disturbing in itself, but what did make Wadesky shudder was the expression on the dead face. It was a grimace. Authentic, brutal and unmistakable. This woman was in pain.

'Hey, what's happening?' said Bill as he watched Wadesky turn and head out of the room with the painting.

'We're confiscating this as evidence,' responded Mo.

'Evidence of what?' carped Bill.

'Evidence of your stupidity. A man that's selling drugs and illegal porn from his establishment should be thinking about how he can help his local police in the apprehension of a bigger fish,' hissed Mo.

He watched as the colour drained from Bill's face, making the green feathers even brighter.

'I'll be needing your fingerprints and anyone else's who may have come into contact with this masterpiece. Today! You'll be expected before 3 p.m. – got it?'

Bill nodded unhappily.

'When did this come into your possession?' Mo asked.

'A couple of months ago. She brought in two; the first one sold immediately,' Bill replied.

'She?' asked Mo, confused.

'Yeah, a woman. Real hot. Name was K… Kate, Ka… I can't remember what it was.'

'Cindy?' prompted Mo.

Bill shrugged. 'Maybe… nah, it's gone.'

Mo unfolded the sketch of Lee Hughes and handed it to him. 'He look familiar?'

Bill looked and shook his head. 'Not seen him before.'

'What did this woman look like?'

'Tall, blonde hair, shapely. Great legs,' mused Bill.

'Okay, I don't have to remind you that any sightings of her or contact, you should call me or anyone in Homicide.' He handed him a card and turned to leave.

'Hey, this guy. Did he murder a lot of people?' Bill asked hopefully.

Mo ignored him, waiting for the inevitable.

'Because that painting might be worth a lot of dough!'

Mo smiled at the dependability of the human spirit.

CHAPTER TWENTY-THREE

Lee Hughes was angry and confused. He stared at the artist's impression of him splashed across the front of *The Herald* and balled his fists with frustration. How was it possible that they could have worked out his identity? Could it have been Tracy? He wracked his brain, trying to see where he'd messed up, scanning the front page, but it was very vague. He knew that his face was filthy and the shopkeeper elderly so had no fear that the pencil drawing could be in any way associated with him.

He placed a carton of milk, a large bar of chocolate and the newspaper on the counter. As suspected, the old man didn't even meet his eye, just took the note and handed over the change.

Lee left the shop quickly and altered his direction. He needed to check that he could still access the car.

Feeling weak, he tore huge sections of the chocolate off and gulped it down as he walked, making his way across the disused rail line and into the lane that squeezed between the old print works and the recently renovated and refurbished cotton mill, which had been developed into three storeys of luxury flats complete with underground parking. Lee had spent several days searching for the right car to call his own. The keys had been left in the ignition, rather than on the rear wheel or inside the exhaust pipe, and the owner had left a travel itinerary in the glove compartment. He was to be away for a month and, to Lee's knowledge, there were no cameras or security personnel assigned to the car park.

He didn't need to investigate whether the car was still there having seen the unmarked police car and the scene of crime van parked outside the building. For a moment he stared with disbelief at the two officers stepping out of the car. He knew instantly that the woman was Eleanor Raven and couldn't help but let out a gasp of pleasure. She was perfect and so beautiful; instantly he wanted her.

He held his breath as she stood still and looked at the building. Her slim frame and long hair, twisted into a casual plait, framed her high cheekbones and intense eyes. A man, who he assumed was her partner, walked round from the driver's side and handed her the keys. It was prescient; again Carin was solving each irritating problem as it arose. He would use her car. She would collect him and drive them both to their combined destiny. It was simple and elegant.

As he moved quickly back across the tracks in the direction of his workshop, he realised he'd completely lost the gnawing sense of hunger he'd had before. He was going to throw away the uneaten bar, but Carin told him not to be stupid; he had to keep his strength up. Smiling, he ate the rest of it, thanking his luck that she was so sensible and tempered his impetuous nature, but wasn't that a muse's task?

*

Eleanor studied the front of the building, ignoring the cold wind that buffeted her. Laurence handed her the keys and waved to Manny as he walked towards them. 'He must live close to this building,' said Eleanor quietly, more to herself. 'This isn't a building you'd target for this sort of crime.'

'Maybe he knew the guy, Chen? Or had come in contact with him. Maybe…' Laurence considered, 'he had serviced his car and knew when he was away.'

Eleanor shook her head. 'I don't think our guy works as such. If he needs to borrow a car then it's most likely that he doesn't own or have access to one. That says very low income and isolation to me. I think it extremely likely that he lives around here.'

For a brief moment she shuddered.

Laurence smiled. 'Someone just walked over your grave?'

'Hey, Manny, what have we got?' asked Eleanor.

Manny pulled back his white hood and began to unzip his PPE suit. 'Not much I'm afraid. The car was taken in a couple of hours ago, and although it's prioritised, it's gonna take a couple more to get tyre prints, mud and pollen samples and any tissues from either victim. I'm gonna say at least twenty-four to forty-eight.'

Eleanor sighed.

'Hey, it's on the ramp. Thirty-five vehicles ain't,' said Manny, turning to leave. 'By the way,' he said, walking back to them, 'what am I up for tomorrow night? Sue Cheung says I'm to keep schtum about some secret mission in a graveyard. That right?'

Eleanor smiled. 'You could say that. I'm mocking up an exhumation on Carin Hughes.'

Manny raised his eyebrows. 'Well I'm glad the word "mock" entered the conversation as it's heading for five below tonight and I don't dig through frozen ground for anything less than a holiday bonus.'

'You're safe, buddy. No digging required,' said Laurence.

'Excellent. Well back to the fray. I'll bell you if anything turns up, okay?'

'Thanks, Manny,' said Eleanor.

'We going in?' asked Laurence, curious as to why Eleanor hadn't moved.

'There's something we're missing,' she ruminated.

'Like?' said Laurence, tightening his coat against the cold.

'Why Hughes does this.'

Laurence scowled. 'Because he likes it, presumably. Gives him power, a high. Usual psycho thrill-seeking.'

'I think that's a little oversimplified. He's creating something important. He lives frugally, the life of an artist. But why now and why here?' she mused.

'Here because this is home, and now because… opportunity?' he offered.

'Why more opportunity than at any other time? Something happened that changed the nature of his artistic vision. But what?' She looked directly at Laurence. 'All ideas gratefully received.'

'I've got one,' he said, following her into the building. 'How about a coffee?'

'That's the best you can offer?' she replied.

'Until I get a caffeine fix it surely is.'

Eleanor and Laurence had been in the building for less than a minute when her phone rang. She listened to Johnson carefully, a small smile playing across her lips. 'Okay… that's great. Text me the address and cell number. We'll head there now. Excellent work.' She ended the call.

'Johnson got a contact from a gallery owner over on Lakeside. He says he bought a piece of art from a guy who looked suspiciously like the sketch of Lee Hughes. He paid eighteen hundred bucks for it, and when he described it to Johnson, it sounded like his work. Maybe this is what we're looking for?'

*

Lee had started the fire just before sundown. He used an old oil drum that he'd dragged from the edge of the marl pit that his warehouse backed onto. The base of the drum had a gash in it and, when balanced on bricks, provided an acceptable draw in which his paperwork, clothing and used tools could be destroyed. He stared mesmerised as his sketches began to glow and blacken as the flame caught the pages.

He inhaled the acrid fumes given off by the paints and burning clothing, his eyes watering. There was so much to do in these final hours. The ghost train had to be dressed and his studio prepped for the arrival of his canvas. Every conceivable problem had been covered and alternatives put in place. He'd spent considerable effort in positioning the hook and chain that would display Eleanor Raven to the world. He couldn't risk any damage to vertebrae; a decapitation for a second time would make him look like an amateur, so he had decided on a new method of display. She would be held aloft by two large hooks that would be inserted into each shoulder blade and linked by a chain to the cross-beam. Her head would be raised by pinning it to the chain using a carabiner, which would be attached to the back of her skull. He'd studied anatomy guides, which implied that the cranial bone would be sufficiently dense to withhold the insertion of a bolt.

He sighed and left the fire to work its destruction on months of painstaking visionary planning. He would take a cold bath next and prepare himself physically for the next twenty-four hours.

*

Eleanor and Laurence stared with disbelief at Roger and Abigail Roodt's art collection. The couple were in their late fifties judging by their physical appearance but mentally still in their late teens according to their clothing. Each wore tight faded jeans and T-shirts proclaiming a belief in anarchy in Roger's case and the legendary status of Andy Warhol in his wife's. Neither wore footwear, but Abigail had compensated with large and intricate henna tattoos on both feet.

Eleanor assumed that they lacked children or pets, as the large apartment was painted white from floor to ceiling. White fur rugs enabled the Roodts to maintain their barefoot habit in a country whose average temperature hovered generally in single digits. Colour was provided by the extensive art collection, which covered every available inch of wall and floor. The Roodts' taste tended towards the macabre. A guillotine made of transparent

Perspex was surrounded by at least thirty Barbie dolls, each missing its head and dressed in red splattered bridal costume. The heads, Roger had pointed out, were neatly arranged in a sand tray.

'It's an unfinished Henry Fuseli,' stated Abigail enthusiastically as she saw Eleanor squint at a small dun-coloured canvas sporting three or four brushstrokes.

'It is?' replied Eleanor.

'Oh I knew you'd love it,' Abigail replied, clapping her hands. 'Everyone who comes to visit falls in love with it.'

'You described a painting to my colleague Detective Johnson. Could we see it?' Eleanor asked quickly.

'No, no, it's not a painting at all. It's an installation!' Abigail replied. 'It's in the guest room.'

The Roodts trotted happily through the lounge, along a narrow corridor sporting a series of lithographic prints entitled *A Day in the Bastille* and proudly opened a door to reveal the body of a naked woman, her face covered by long blonde hair, lying on a tatty, blood-stained chaise longue.

'What the hell!' spurted out Laurence.

This caused both Roodts to clap enthusiastically. 'Everyone always reacts the same way. It's so… vibrant! Don't you think?'

'I'm not sure that's how I would describe it, Mrs Roodt,' said Eleanor quietly.

'It's so very lifelike, isn't it?' thrilled Roger. 'Go on, touch it – it's the only way to believe.'

Laurence put out a hand and touched the smooth plastic skin of the mannequin.

Eleanor studied the creation while Laurence spoke.

'Why did you assume this was work of Lee Hughes, sir?'

'Oh, I can't be a hundred per cent,' he answered. 'Detective Johnson was given our name by Agathe; she thought we might be able to help.'

'The guy we met looked very similar to the image printed in the paper. He didn't give us his name, but we were shown some photographs of his recent work and chose this one.'

'Who showed you the photographs and where?' asked Laurence.

'We'd gone to the Charcoal Gallery – that's where Agathe works. It's next to the university and sells student pieces. We like it there because you have a chance to pick up cutting-edge material.'

Abigail giggled. 'At pretty rock-bottom prices.'

'So had Lee Hughes got any other pieces on display there?'

'Don't think so. He was looking at some of the pieces and we got into a conversation about the merits of some local sculptor, and then he showed us a series of Polaroids of his installations. Hell, some of them were so good they looked real!'

Eleanor and Laurence looked at one another nervously.

'Where were these photographs taken?' asked Eleanor.

'I'm not really sure,' Roger replied. 'I think a studio or maybe a warehouse.'

'How was this delivered and how did you pay for it?' asked Laurence.

'He wouldn't let us be in the apartment when he delivered. He said that the presentation was an integral part of the whole experience. So we left and when we came back it was here.'

'It was so exciting!' said Abigail.

'How did you pay?'

'Cash. A snip at eighteen hundred. He asked us to name a price and if he approved he'd sell it to us. So we had a little discussion and suggested it. He thought for a moment or two and then said, "Done." He left a message on my phone telling us to have a lunch date between eleven and two, and delivered it three days later. That was just before Christmas,' said Roger. 'My parents arrived a couple of days later and you can just imagine—'

'Have you or any of your acquaintances had any contact or seen Lee Hughes since then?' interrupted Laurence. They both shook their heads.

'You are going to receive a visit from our forensics team at some point over the next seventy-two hours. Please do not interfere with the "art" in any way. It's unlikely that it will have to be removed from your premises,' said Eleanor briskly, handing them her card.

'It won't be damaged, will it?' Roger asked nervously.

'The forensics team has a reputation for being considerate and careful. Thank you for your time,' said Eleanor.

They both sat in the car and sipped coffee. 'You think that was the trigger? Really?' asked Laurence sceptically.

Eleanor shrugged. 'I don't know, but this may have been the first time that someone really valued his work. It's notable that he didn't have a price in mind and wanted them to suggest one. Hughes wants people to give his work value. That's how people express their appreciation for something, by placing a material value on it. Though I could be overthinking this. I'll run it past Ruby tomorrow.'

Laurence yawned.

'It's late and it's been a long day. Go home and sleep,' she said gently.

Laurence looked surprised. 'Sure you don't want me come up and check the board?'

'No, Johnson says there's nothing else, and if something happens, the night crew will call us.'

Laurence opened the door and stepped out. 'Hey, you wanna eat? It's my turn?'

Surprisingly, Eleanor smiled and nodded. 'It's always going to be your turn, Whitefoot.'

'Then it's going to be cheap,' he replied, pleased that she'd accepted. 'Shit,' he groaned. 'I've got to collect the dog from K9.'

Eleanor smiled again. 'Listen I'm beat and need a bath. Catch you tomorrow.' She started the engine.

'That's a date,' said Laurence, tapping on the window before she pulled away.

'That would be contrary to department policy, Detective Whitefoot,' she replied lightly.

CHAPTER TWENTY-FOUR

Eleanor shoved her hands into her pockets and hoped that she'd left her gloves in the car. It was bitterly cold, several degrees below freezing point, and the clouds threatened snow, and lots of it. She sighed and quickened her pace. It was 6.30 a.m. and she was hoping that the three terse and uninformative messages left on her cell phone from Marty Samuelson were not a result of her plans to mock an exhumation of Carin Hughes. The likelihood of this not being the cause was slim, particularly as the *Toronto Sun* had run the story in their morning edition.

She noted unhappily that the side windows of her car were coated in a thick layer of frost that would require manual attention rather than a quick blast from the interior heater. The door handle was frozen and Eleanor was obliged to pull her jumper sleeves over her palm to protect it as she worked the handle.

With one last vigorous pull the door opened, but she didn't climb in as her attention was grabbed by a strange anomaly. Slowly she walked round to the front of the car where the windscreen had been scraped clean of frost.

As she puzzled over this, she caught the reflection of a woman in the glass. Turning swiftly, Eleanor's eyes met those of someone who could only be Cindy, and she suddenly understood how Lee Hughes had managed to evade detection for so long.

The surge of adrenaline should have given Eleanor a split second's advantage, but her hands were too cold to manipulate her weapon successfully, and as she reached behind her back to pull the gun from its holster, she felt her fingers fumble uselessly.

Cindy's fist hit her squarely in the solar plexus. The pain surged across her chest and stomach, paralysing her breathing and forcing her to double over.

Desperately trying to suck in air, Eleanor saw the fist pull back again. Knowing she couldn't take another blow, she flung herself backwards onto the bonnet of her car and, pulling back her legs, kicked out as hard as she could at the figure. One foot struck home, producing a bone crunch and a yelp of pain, and blood began to spray from Cindy's outraged face and lip.

Before Eleanor could propel herself forward and out of danger, she saw the bloodied face lunge towards her and felt a sharp needle pain in her throat, accompanied by an icy sensation and the full weight of another being lying on her.

Eleanor Raven descended into darkness.

*

Laurence had been delighted by the progress Monster had made in such a short amount of time. He'd collected him from the kennels, and although it was after office hours he'd been treated politely and with consideration by Officer Emily Hunt. Emily ran through Monster's new vocabulary of commands, which he tried himself with astonishment. Monster sat, stayed and lay down to the corresponding commands and looked extremely attentive as he waited for his treat.

Laurence was even able to bring himself to pat the creature's huge furry head as he sat obediently in the front seat on the way back to his apartment. There was hope for the dog yet, and a warm sense of satisfaction thrilled through him as he imagined Mags' face when she finally deigned to return and collect him.

Unfortunately, all these good thoughts dissipated on his return to the kennels the following morning.

'Could you repeat that; I'm not sure I understand,' said Laurence weakly.

Emily tried again, this time speaking more slowly. 'Would you like to settle up at the end of the week or on a daily basis?'

'Settle up what?' said Laurence.

'It costs $180 per day for training, food and exercise,' said Emily, with a look that he imagined she used for those hard of hearing or short on IQ.

'You are kidding me, aren't you?' said Laurence, knowing from her blank stare that this seemed improbable. 'I was told to leave him here by my boss, Chief Samuelson. He didn't mention that it was fee-paying!'

'Uh-huh. It isn't fee-paying for canines that are serving officers. Your canine isn't serving, is he, Detective?'

Laurence glanced at Monster, who was vigorously scratching an ear with his foot. He shook his head.

'If he was then he would be trained by the state for free. We offer our department's skills to fellow officers and their canine companions by popular request. This service is only offered to officers who serve our community. You cannot expect this to be a free service paid for by the state, can you?' Emily looked at Laurence with some degree of astonishment.

Laurence shook his head. 'But what am I going to do with him all day?' he blurted.

'You have two choices – either you pay for the service that we offer or you find him day care, which I suspect,' she hissed, 'costs roughly the same amount, but without the training element.'

Feeling aggrieved, Laurence snatched Monster's collar and yanked him in the direction of his car.

*

Timms was just polishing off the last piece of his breakfast pizza when Samuelson's roar shook the squad room. 'Where the hell is Raven?' he bellowed.

Timms immediately performed a pantomime of looking intently round the workspace, whilst chewing enthusiastically. 'I've not seen her, boss, but when I do…'

'What do you know about this exhumation?' shouted Samuelson, cruising towards Timms with an outstretched finger.

'Absolutely nothing,' said Timms, adopting a mystified expression.

Wadesky and Mo lumbered into the office, immediately on the alert.

'What do you know about this exhumation?' Samuelson asked the new arrivals.

Wadesky said nothing, but Mo was unfazed by anything other than Minnie and his cardiologist. 'Ellie is planning to set up a mock grave lift tonight in the hope that Hughes will be so outraged he'll come and investigate,' he said, positioning his seat.

'I told her that it had been absolutely rejected by the DA's office,' said Samuelson, throwing his arms up in despair.

'You did,' replied Mo. 'But she's not going to dig up a body. This is theatre. We borrow a van, tape it off and set up a tent. Doc Hounslow has already agreed to the loan and the only law breaker is Hughes.'

Samuelson opened his mouth, but Mo was on a roll. 'If she's right then Hughes will show. His sister's some kind of inspiration to him, according to Doc Delaware, and so far we've got shit in terms of a lead.'

Samuelson worked his jaw. 'Have you any idea how detrimental a stunt like this could be when we finally get this bastard into court?'

'The DA is paid to sort that shit out when the time comes. We've got nothing and this guy ain't gonna stop killing. You put Ellie in charge because she can think out of the box. No one else is coming up with ideas so you need to support her.'

Mo's breathing was becoming more laboured. Wadesky moved over and put her hand on his arm, encouraging him to sit.

Samuelson's face was turning carmine red. Mo had just overstepped the mark big time by confronting a superior in the presence of other officers.

'He's right, sir,' said Timms. It's a dumb-ass idea, but it's got more of a chance of getting him than us sitting on our asses waiting for him to hand himself in. Mo's right – you put Raven in charge 'cos she thinks different to us grunts.'

Samuelson was still boiling.

'She's your protégé and she needs your backing,' finished Timms on an 'in for a penny' approach.

The squad room was silent. Samuelson's reaction would decide not only the future of the case but of future careers too.

He shook his head and sighed. 'I've got her back.'

There was an audible sigh of relief from the assembled detectives.

'But where the hell is she?' bellowed Samuelson.

*

The artist spoke quietly to the canvas. He was aware that Eleanor Raven was still not fully conscious, but he knew that the ketamine should be wearing off now and he was eager to get started.

He had carried the unconscious woman from the car and fastened her to a gurney.

'Eleanor,' he whispered. 'Eleanor, it's time for you to wake up now,' he said more loudly, slapping her face.

*

'She didn't say anything last night about a meeting with someone?' asked Timms, his voice tinny through the car's speaker.

On hearing that Eleanor hadn't been seen and wasn't picking up calls, Laurence had swung his car around and was now manoeuvring against the traffic. 'No, she was due in at seven. Have you called the ME's?'

'Yeah, she ain't there. Call me when you get to her apartment, okay?' said Timms testily.

'Okay,' said Laurence, disconnecting. He tried her number again, but it skipped immediately to voicemail.

Pulling into the parking lot he knew she used, he noted that her rented bay was empty. He parked next to it and wondered if there was any point in going up to her flat, but he'd said he would.

He walked round to the passenger seat and let Monster out; it seemed like a good idea to let him pee before returning to the office.

The dog bounded out of the car, had a good sniff and then focussed his attention on a small area of tarmac.

Laurence walked towards the building whistling for Monster, but the dog stayed put, sniffing enthusiastically.

'Monster! Come here!' he yelled tightly, proffering one of the doggie treats he'd been given by Emily Hunt.

Monster put his head up briefly and then returned to sniff the ground.

Irritated and cold, Laurence took several strides towards the dog and grabbed his collar, pulling him away, only to see several large spots of blood staining the frosty tarmac. He squatted down to look at them. Alarm bells were beginning to sound.

Seeing a traffic cone nearby, he placed it over the spots and, attaching his lead to the dog, began to hurry towards Eleanor's apartment building. He dialled. 'Timms? I'm here. I've just found some blood spots on her parking bay but no car.'

Timms took a moment or so as he digested this information. 'Sure the car's not parked anywhere else?'

'Not sure, but the lot is pretty empty. I'll check when I've been upstairs.'

'Okay,' responded Timms calmly. 'I'm waiting.'

Laurence bounded up the stairs, noting that Monster didn't seem distracted by any other smells.

He approached the door, cautiously trying the handle, but it was locked. He listened and then knocked. There was no response, so he knocked louder this time, calling her name. A nearby door opened and he swung round to see a small, dishevelled woman carrying an ageing pug in her arms. She smiled vacantly at him.

'Ma'am, my name is Detective Laurence Whitefoot and I'm trying to locate my partner Eleanor Raven. She lives here.'

The woman looked at him uncomprehendingly. He moved towards her, unsure of how Monster would react to another dog. 'Have you seen Miss Raven this morning?'

'This morning?' said the woman. 'What a beautiful dog. Is he yours?' she asked.

'Yes, ma'am, he is. I need to know whether you've seen Miss Eleanor Raven today? She lives here.'

The woman looked as if she were thinking. 'No. No one's been here.' Suddenly her face lit up. 'Her flowers. I have them here for her.' She turned and walked back into her apartment. 'Look,' she called to him.

Laurence looped Monster's lead around the door handle and followed her into her rather cluttered apartment. A large bunch of roses in a crystal vase were placed on the mantelpiece. Two cards had been placed inside the plastic wrap. Laurence felt a chill run through him as he saw the yin-yang symbol.

'I thought they were for me,' said the woman sadly. 'When you see her, tell her I'm looking after them.'

Laurence discreetly slipped on a latex glove and pulled out the two cards, one supplied by the florist that delivered them, the other a blank embossed only with the logo.

He turned to the woman, who still clutched the pug, and handed her his card. 'It's very important that if she comes back, you call me. Can you do that?' he asked.

She nodded, a worried expression forming.

The Garland Shop was empty when Laurence arrived. 'I think Hughes has her,' said Laurence, his voice shaking as he spoke to Timms on his cell.

'Based on what evidence?' replied Timms tersely.

'A card came with flowers for her that were delivered to her neighbour. It had a yin-yang symbol on it,' Laurence replied, tapping a small bell to summon attention.

Timms was silent, as if thinking.

'Morning, sir, may I help you?' said a small, friendly woman as she glided in from the back of the shop carrying secateurs and several blocks of oasis.

'Are you listening to me?' spat Laurence into the phone.

The woman waited patiently.

'I'll mobilise the troops. The second you get a lead, you call me or Wadesky,' said Timms.

Laurence switched off his phone and introduced himself, explaining what he required from her. It took her moments to run through her visa receipts. 'The name of the gentleman who ordered the flowers was Mr Magnus Redman.'

*

Eleanor needed to vomit. The pain in her chest and stomach was unbearable, but she was lying on her back and couldn't move. She tried to move her head, but a strap had been wound tightly around her forehead and movement was impossible. She concentrated on tamping down the sensation, but her head was spinning, and when she opened her eyes she could see strange shadows moving in waves along her peripheral vision. Somewhere in the distance she could hear a voice. Why was she lying down? She couldn't remember why she wasn't in her own bed.

A wave of fear and nausea shook her. She was in danger and the voice she could hear was the source of that danger.

With an involuntary spasm, a fountain of red vomit sprayed her face, chest and belly. Instantly she felt better, more alert.

'Noooo!' screamed the dangerous voice. 'Don't do that!'

Eleanor closed her eyes instinctively as she saw the fist fly out and hammer down onto her chest. The second blow hit a rib and she felt it crack under the barrage. She opened her mouth and screamed.

*

'Mr Magnus Redman?'

The man stood up from his desk and nodded cautiously.

'I'm Detective Laurence Whitefoot and I believe you know my colleague Eleanor Raven?'

The man's eyes narrowed. 'What is this regarding?' he asked, stepping lightly past Laurence and discreetly closing the door to his office. 'I am acquainted with Eleanor Raven, yes.'

'What I'm about to ask you is extremely personal, but your answer may have a direct bearing on the safety of Detective Raven,' Laurence asked slowly.

'A detective?' asked Redman with a look of confusion. 'I hadn't realised…' He faltered.

'She's disappeared, Mr Redman, and I think you can help me.'

Redman paused and stroked his chin as if contemplating his next line. 'How well do you know your colleague, Detective Whitefoot?'

Laurence was beginning to feel that he knew absolutely nothing. 'I'm learning, but that may take too long. I need to ensure her safety.'

Redman nodded. 'Eleanor is a very special lady. She understands her sexual needs and satisfies them with…' He paused and withdrew a piece of paper from his desk drawer, sliding it slowly across the table. 'Deliberate caution. I responded to that and arranged, in good faith, an event that might be liberating and satisfying.'

'I don't understand what you mean,' said Laurence.

'Perhaps you will when you read this.' He nodded to the page.

Laurence picked it up and began to read. 'Caleb,' he said quietly. 'That's her safe word?'

'These are the rules that Eleanor presents to a consensual partner when she has arranged an encounter.'

Laurence felt sick. He skim-read the 'rules' and then placed the sheet on the table between them. 'Are you saying that Detective Raven arranged a sadomasochism session with you?' He heard his voice tremble.

'No, I'm saying that Eleanor Raven the private individual did. She organised a meeting in a hotel room; we had a mutually satisfying experience, but there was no penetration involved.'

Redman leaned closer to Laurence. 'You know far more than Eleanor was ever willing to tell you, and under any other circumstance I would not have betrayed her trust with another human being, but I think I understand why she needs help.'

Redman shifted his position and looked intently at Laurence. He spoke slowly and deliberately. 'I had collected a card from a club called Xxxstacy advertising a kidnapping service. Having met Eleanor I felt that this might be of interest to her so I called the number and left a message. I received an impersonal but professional message telling me to leave five thousand dollars behind the bar of another club called As You Like It. This I did, but after reading the headline in the *Sun* I realised I had made a terrible mistake and went immediately to the club and found that the money was still there. I assumed, naively I conclude by your presence here today, that this indicated that Eleanor would be safe. I am mortified that this is not the case.'

'Are you for real?' yelled Laurence to Redman's obvious surprise. 'Mortified? She could be dead, tortured and ready to be strung up in a tree as a goddamn art installation and you're mortified? These rules…' he said, waving the sheet in front of Redman's face, 'don't apply to Lee Hughes. He has his own agenda!'

Redman looked at him calmly. Laurence thrust a card onto the table. 'You think of anything that will help me find her, you call me, understand? And, Mr Redman, you can expect further contact regarding this matter.'

Redman nodded sagely, his fingertips touching as if in prayer. Laurence grabbed the sheet of rules and headed for the door.

'That is mine,' said Redman calmly.

Laurence turned to him, his voice low and dangerous. 'We're playing by my rules now.'

'Mo! I need you to meet me outside of the office,' said Laurence desperately as he swerved through the traffic.

'You found something out?' gasped Mo.

'Yeah, but I need to talk to you first. It's important.'

'Wadesky's going to the ME's; I'll catch a lift and meet you in D'Angelo's in fifteen.'

Laurence gratefully drank his coffee and wondered how and where to start.

'Spit it out, Whitefoot!' said Mo nervously.

'You told me Eleanor's worst enemy was herself.'

Mo stared at him, his jaw clamped tightly shut. 'What do you know?'

'She arranged a sadomasochistic session with some guy she'd never met before. He thought she'd like to experience a sexy kidnapping, so he called Hughes, left the money and when he realised he'd arranged a murder went and picked up his money and assumed all was okay. The jerk didn't feel it necessary to warn her of what might happen,' blurted Laurence.

Mo was silent, his brow heavily furrowed.

'What do I do? I hold back this information and we don't get her in time maybe I'll have contributed to her death. That's what the investigation will reveal. We get her and everyone in the squad knows.'

Mo wiped his brow with a handkerchief before he spoke. 'You talk to Timms about this and it goes to no one else.'

'What? The biggest goon in the squad and I trust him?'

Mo shook his head. 'You need to learn to read people – and fast. You trust him.'

Laurence looked at Mo with disbelief as he staggered to his feet.

'Drink up – we need to go,' Mo said.

'Is this some sort of joke?' hissed Timms, crunching the soda can left on Wadesky's desk with an angry fist. A spray of orange liquid hit the neat pile of papers. 'She did that! Is she sentient?'

Laurence was livid. He had doubted Mo's decision to tell Timms about Magnus Redman and now this confirmed it. He gave Mo a cold hard stare.

'Goddamn it!' yelled Timms, flinging the can at the murder board. Several carefully pinned photographs fluttered wetly to the floor. A couple of officers scowled at Timms from the edges of the room and Monster let out a yelp of disapproval from under the desk.

Timms rubbed his forehead vigorously. 'Okay, think... you got everything you can from this asshole Redman?' he asked Laurence quietly.

Laurence nodded. 'Pretty sure I did.'

'I've sent forensics down to type the blood from Raven's parking lot. Her car's on a priority find and I've sent Smith round to do a search of her apartment. This other stuff ain't material to the investigation so we ignore it, okay?' Timms looked at Laurence, who nodded.

'He won't keep her alive for long. How do we buy time?' asked Laurence.

'The only thing we have is the exhumation. The *Sun* ran it this morning, implying a 6 p.m. start. We drag it forward,' he replied.

'How will he know? If he's read the paper he'll read six, and even if we could get the story run in the evening edition, there wouldn't be a notification out till five,' said Laurence, frustrated. 'And the ME's office said that the van and equipment would only be available—'

'We set up now!' growled Timms. 'We get Susan Cheung and her buddies over to the cemetery now, and I want armed response units behind every headstone,' he added, grabbing the phone.

Laurence looked at the murder board. The photographs of Lee's victims formed an obscene montage. Under the women's bodies were the photographs of Ellis and Paget, their smiling departmental poses in full uniform a stark contrast to the bloodied remains left propped in the park. The photographs dislodged by Timms' hurled can left an empty square in the line – just sufficient room to display the ones of Eleanor Raven when they found her, he thought angrily.

CHAPTER TWENTY-FIVE

Samuelson stood in front of the murder board and looked at the anxious faces. Jaws were set and no detective was seated. He cleared his throat. 'It is our belief that Detective Eleanor Raven was abducted by Lee Hughes somewhere in the region of six thirty to seven thirty this morning. An altercation took place in the parking lot used by Raven, and blood spots were discovered by Whitefoot at 8 a.m. No evidence of a struggle was found in her apartment, and her car and keys are missing.'

Samuelson allowed a pause for expletives before starting again. 'Detectives Timms and Whitefoot will be in charge of this investigation.' He nodded to Timms, who turned to speak.

'We don't know how long Hughes keeps his victims alive, but neither Cassandra Willis nor Lydia Greystein were alive twelve hours after being kidnapped. It's nine thirty now, and that means Raven could theoretically survive till 6 p.m.'

A loud groan ran through the assembled officers.

'There's a plausible area that he may be using, and Wadesky and Johnson will assign each team a patch. We are running with the exhumation of Carin Hughes and will be bringing in a strategic response team to protect the area. You find anything – *anything*! – you call it in. The clock's ticking and we ain't letting this bastard take one of ours again. Questions?'

'How d'we know Hughes has got Raven?' asked Smith from the back of the room.

Timms met his eye. 'Trustworthy tip-off.'

Smith wrinkled his brow. 'Care to elaborate?'

Timms stared at him for a moment or two. 'No.'

No one in the room moved. Timms raised his voice. 'Raven's tough, and if anyone is going to survive, she is. Now we go and bring her home.'

*

Eleanor had been drifting in and out of consciousness for the last hour or so. Every time she felt her senses begin to close in, Lee would connect the two electrodes and send a pulse of electricity through the bottom of her feet. At some point she had received a blow to the side of her head and was finding it difficult to think clearly. A wet patch was making her hair stick to her face and neck, and she imagined that it was because her ear was bleeding. At first she'd heard a grunting sound emanating from her mouth, but now she was making a high-pitched mewling. This sound was irritating Lee and he had begun to yell obscenities at her until she quietened.

'When will this stop?' she whispered, her voice croaking.

Lee looked at her quizzically. 'When you're ready,' he answered calmly.

'Ready for what?'

'Your destiny,' he answered simply. 'Your face will tell me when it's time for your presentation.'

He leaned over her, tenderly pushing a strand of hair from her face. 'You will bring such wonder and inspiration into the world. When you've passed, you will choose your talent and raise his work to a higher level. He will become an artist because you will guide his pen, his brush, his mind.'

'Like Carin does for you?' she said with all the warmth she could muster.

He stared in disbelief at her. 'You understand? You know what Carin can do?'

'She gives you ideas about… your art,' she said carefully, her teeth chattering.

Lee tipped his head to one side and peered at her suspiciously. She could only see his face by straining her forehead against the leather strap that held her tightly to the gurney. Lee was listening and Eleanor knew this might be the only chance she would get to influence the outcome of the next couple of hours. She had to work quickly and intuitively to manipulate him into keeping her alive long enough for either a suitable escape plan to be concocted, or for Laurence and the team to work out where she was. But where the hell was she? She remembered little about the events leading to her being brought here. The room she was in was dark and extremely cold; the sort of cold that only long-empty buildings acquired. The only source of light, as far as she could tell, came from a pair of hurricane lamps.

'Tell me about my destiny,' she said, trying to keep the note of desperation out of her voice.

He paused, obviously unsure whether she was genuine or just trying to postpone the inevitable. 'You'll pass through the pain of existence and then be elevated to the status of muse,' he said, unable to keep the excitement out of his voice.

'Is that why you chose Lydia and Cassandra?'

'They were chosen for me,' he answered simply. 'Men of vision offered them up. Lydia' – he smiled – 'recognised her own destiny and arranged for own passing.'

'But Malcolm Stringer just wanted his boss tormented,' said Eleanor cautiously.

He shrugged. 'Stringer was an idiot. He didn't recognise the importance of his actions. But not many do.'

'I do,' she said slowly, unable to suppress a shudder of disgust.

Lee reached over and stroked her face with his long, delicate fingers. 'Carin was right about you. She said that you would be my greatest work yet. As did your sponsor.'

Eleanor felt an icy surge through her intestines as she processed this information. 'My… my sponsor?'

'Of course. You were selected by another.'

'Who?' Her voice cracked.

Lee smiled indulgently. 'He left me a message saying that although he hadn't known you for very long, he was sure that you would appreciate what I could give. He gave me your name and address. You were nominated by one who appreciated your potential.

' Suddenly his face hardened and he stood up.

'Who?' she heard herself scream. 'Who called you?'

Lee was puzzled. 'What does it matter now?'

'Please tell me.' She lowered her voice, but a swathe of rage was giving her the strength that she'd lost hours ago. 'Tell me!'

'A colleague? A friend? I don't know.' Lee was clearly tiring of the conversation. He turned to look at his bench, running his eye across his tool collection.

'A colleague?' Her mind was running through the possibilities. Not Timms, certainly not Mo, surely not Whitefoot? Not her partner! But he hadn't been, had he? She'd made every effort to reject him and make sure he knew that he wasn't her choice. Surely he couldn't have done this? But she didn't know anyone else, deliberately having never acquired any friends outside of the department. It didn't make sense. Why would he?

A sharp stabbing pain ran through her arm. She swivelled her eyes round to see Lee holding a huge darning needle. He raised it again and stabbed it into her shoulder, his eyes searching hers for evidence that she was ready to accept her fate, but Eleanor had never been so far away from accepting death. A flush of adrenaline sharpened her thinking and dulled the pain, providing her with clarity.

'They're going to exhume Carin!' she yelled.

Lee stood rock still. 'What do you mean?'

'Homicide is going to dig her up for a second autopsy this afternoon,' she said quickly.

'Liar!' he screamed, pulling back his fist and then hammering her chest. 'Liar!'

'I have proof!' she screamed. 'Listen to me now.' But her voice was failing.

Lee lunged backwards, his fists balled and shaking, eager to carry on the beating. Eleanor sucked in air greedily, but a clicking sound now accompanied each breath, and she suspected another rib had been broken. She groaned, unsure of whether she had the strength to take much more.

'Tell me what you know or I'll end you here and now,' he spat.

Eleanor began to dry retch; her eyes streamed. Frustrated, Lee leaned forward and undid the buckle that held her head in place. The release of the strap enabled a surge of blood to flood her scalp and face. She had to wait until the pain had subsided before she could speak.

'They believe you murdered Carin. There was no toxicology screening then, so they're going to autopsy her.'

'Noooo!' screamed Lee. He picked up a large knife from the table and held it out to her. Tears streamed down his face. 'Tell me now if you're lying. If you lie to me I will cut your skin off.'

With a sudden sweep of the blade, he sliced into Eleanor's thigh. A bloody length of skin peeled back and flapped wetly against her shivering leg. 'Do you understand me? I cannot have this happen! Prove to me they intend to do this and that it's not just your effort to buy more time.'

Eleanor was slipping into shock. Her leg felt distant, unattached and her head span.

'Headline...' She couldn't finish.

Lee shook her arm, but she was only dimly aware of it. She was beginning to lose the will to carry on. She was going to sleep and it would all stop.

Her breathing slowed and a stillness descended on her. Then there was movement around her and a stinging sensation in her arm, and suddenly her heart was beating faster – much faster – and the pain returned to her thigh and chest. Lee's voice gained volume and clarity.

'Not now! You go when this is sorted, when I say so. You've had a dose of adrenaline and that means you can hear and respond to me. What headline?'

'The *Toronto Sun*… They ran it in today's *Sun*.' She held her breath as the blood hammered against her skull.

Lee was silent for several moments as he thought matters through. 'I'm going to check this out. I don't know how long I'll be gone, but you can survive.' He looked over her carefully. 'It's cold in here and that will help you. You want to survive, don't you?'

She stared at him silently.

He shrugged. 'If you're dead when I get back, I'll bury you in the marl pit and there you will forgo immortality. We have to work together, do you understand?' He smiled at her warmly. 'This is all about you. How special and privileged you are. Be strong!' He bent over and kissed her lightly on the lips. 'You are so beautiful.'

Eleanor wanted to scream her rage and despair, but she was silent and let her face fall to a blank. Lee turned and walked away from her, and soon the only sound was Eleanor's laboured breathing, interspersed with the squeak of leather as she fought to free herself.

*

Lee was too angry to feel the cold and would have stormed out onto the street with just a T-shirt on but had sufficient composure to recognise that such an action would draw attention to himself; something Carin had frequently warned him about. So he grabbed a coat and walked rapidly in the direction of the local store. He searched through the papers and found a *Toronto Sun*, and what he read caused him to clutch at his chest. She hadn't lied; they were intending to dig his sister up and perform some obscene autopsy upon her.

He lifted his head up from the paper and saw several people were watching him curiously. Had he said anything out loud or made some sort of exclamation? He threw a dollar fifty onto the counter and left quickly. He had to stop this happening. If Carin was disturbed in any way or exposed to some grotesque indignity then she might leave him forever. The thought was unbearable. He'd lost her once, just as they had found out how much they meant to one another. He could sense her next to him, frightened and alone, just like it was in the days before she died.

Carin had sat at the table listening to the voices; the ones that told her the secrets. He'd tried to hear them too, listening in silence for hours, but he wasn't as intuitive as her. On the day of her passing, she hadn't wanted to go to school but sat at the table in her nightdress, the white one that made her look so ghostly and beautiful, not hearing him because the voices were too loud and important.

Lee had known for some considerable time that Marilyn 'did' things to Carin. Little things that she didn't like to share with him, but sometimes he heard her talking to the voices about how Marilyn thought she was a demon and needed to be punished. He had argued with Marilyn, begging her to leave them so he could look after Carin, but she would never agree with that, so he tried a different strategy. Lee told Marilyn that he had spoken with her voices and they had told him that she was to join them. If she'd just lock the garage door, turn over the engine and go to sleep, she would awake to a better world, where only the sweet voices lived. He'd made an elaborate charcoal sketch of the world beyond the garage for Marilyn. She lay in the centre of the picture surrounded by beautiful spirits, each one clad in gossamer robes and reaching out to her with gentle hands; each angel based around the image of his beloved Carin. He'd taped the picture to the fridge, hoping that it would inspire her.

For several days the sketch remained exactly where it was, untouched and ignored. Then it disappeared. He'd assumed that Marilyn had bored of the image and destroyed it, as was her wont when she became agitated.

Lee hadn't really thought about the implications of the sketch until Tracy Earnshaw drew his attention to it in his art class. He had been letting his pen and mind wander and actually started when Tracy whispered, 'Is that supposed to be your sister?' into his ear.

He had looked at the paper and was surprised to see that he'd drawn Carin as an angel, complete with wings and halo. Lying at her feet was the body of Marilyn.

'What does it mean?' bleated Tracy.

He recalled shrugging and turning his back to her, but something wasn't right. As soon as class ended for lunch he ran home. Why had he drawn that particular image?

And then clarity.

The car had run out of gas and sat almost invisibly in its shroud of poisonous blue smoke. He had opened the door to the kitchen and the back yard, and had to wait several minutes before he could comfortably enter the garage without choking. Carin's eyes were open but dull and flat, and he found it difficult to look into them as he lifted her out and laid her on the concrete floor. He didn't want her sitting next to Marilyn, but the floor was so dirty.

Flung into the corner of the garage was a discarded plastic sheet that had been left by the landlord after he'd insulated the loft.

Carefully and respectfully, Lee spread the sheet, laid his sister's body onto it and wrapped it around her. He had initially covered her face but couldn't bear that thought and tucked it under her chin. What he hadn't understood was how her lips and cheeks were so pink and healthy-looking when her body was lifeless and cold. It must have been a sign that she was in some way a higher force than other mortals, as he had always suspected.

Lee sat quietly and stared at Carin, unsure of what to do next. Perhaps if he sat very still and waited, he too would die, and then all the misery would vanish. And then she spoke to him. Carin had moved onto a higher plane she had said, and from this place she would dedicate herself to his development as an artist. He must not die there or her sacrifice would have been for nothing.

Everything, she assured him, would become clear in time.

'Hey, buddy, you okay?' said a voice next to him.

Lee turned quickly to see a small, grey man who looked at him with a false expression of concern. Perhaps he had been shouting and this was drawing attention to himself.

'Yes,' he managed to spit out and walked rapidly back in the direction of his studio. He had to act quickly.

*

Laurence wasn't handling matters particularly diplomatically. Having yelled at Susan Cheung and Manny, even he recognised that it was time for him to leave Timms and Smith to coordinate the exhumation.

'Sorry… sorry!' he said, throwing his arms up in apology.

'Look, you're not helping anyone bellowing at people who are doing their best. Go back to the squad room and help Wadesky and Mo,' said Timms quietly, grasping his elbow.

'But…' started Laurence.

'You're surplus here and need to focus on something else. This is covered, and the second anything happens, you'll be the first to ride in all guns firing, okay?' said Timms.

Laurence nodded. There were three armed response officers secreted around the cemetery. Two detectives from another precinct were dressed in workman's uniforms and were 'fixing' a broken gate, which lay detached by the entrance. A gardening company run by an ex-cop had delivered a truckload of topsoil during the night and had placed it strategically next to the tarpaulin that had been constructed around the grave. Inside the tarp were Timms and a spotter armed with binoculars and a rifle. Susan and Manny were busying themselves appropriately by moving between the ME's van and the tent. Both wore bulletproof vests and were covered by a sniper positioned on the top of the chapel roof. A local funeral home had been paid to wait in the car park.

Laurence drove slowly towards the exit, scouring the horizon for signs of Lee Hughes. So intent was he on this, he nearly managed to run over a woman with a bunch of flowers who was making her way over to a gravestone. Despite the large sunglasses, Laurence could clearly make out her swollen and cut lip, and as he waved a hand in a gesture of apology, he felt a surge of anger at the violence of men.

It took him almost three quarters of an hour to make his way through the traffic. He'd considered blue-lighting but decided that it was as good a time as ever to mull things over. He ran through the evidence they had so far. They knew who the killer was and a rough area where he was active, but so far no one had called in to report a sighting of him – well none that had panned out. Detectives were combing the areas, but so far there'd been nothing.

He felt a wave of despair. How could this have happened? What was he missing? There was something nagging him, a piece of the puzzle that he hadn't found yet.

He parked the car, and as he climbed out, his phone rang. He snatched it. 'Yeah?' He could hear Monster whining in the background.

'This dog is driving us all batshit nuts,' said Wadesky peevishly. 'How's it going out there?'

He felt a wave of disappointment when he realised there was no news. 'It's all under control. Just have to wait and see now.' Laurence walked towards the building. 'Isn't there anything?' He heard his anger rising.

'Nothing so far. That guy who owns the weird gallery called Mo. Said he remembered what the woman's name was who brought in the painting.'

Laurence stepped into the lift. 'Go on.'

'Said her name was Carin,' said Wadesky.

He froze as the missing piece slipped into place.

Laurence flung open the door to the murder room and raced in. 'You're not looking for a man!' he bellowed at Wadesky and Mo, who were working their way through piles of papers. 'Hughes is Cindy, Tracy and Carin.'

He raced over to the board and yanked off the artist's impression of Lee. 'That's what was bugging me. I couldn't see it before, because I was expecting Tracy to be who she said she was – a woman. That's why he had to destroy Tracy's face.'

Mo had heaved himself to his feet and was making tamping gestures with his hands. 'Steady on – we're not following you.'

'When I spoke to Tracy at the gym it was Lee Hughes, wearing a wig, false nails and make-up.' He started suddenly. 'Timms. We have to tell him that Hughes will come to the cemetery dressed as a woman.'

Mo began to dial.

Suddenly Laurence froze and then flung his hand into the air. 'I've seen him! In the cemetery.'

*

'What the hell! You're absolutely certain about this?' hissed Timms into the cell phone. He was doing his best to keep his voice down, but it was cold and frustrating sitting next to a grave waiting for God knows what to happen. 'Am I getting this right? We need to watch out for an attractive woman in her early thirties. Why?'

CHAPTER TWENTY-SIX

Wadesky was deep in a worried phone conversation with Timms when Laurence's cell rang. He'd been pacing the room nervously while Wadesky established whether the operation was busted or not.

'Yeah?' Laurence snapped.

'Oh, hi,' came Andy Bateman's honeyed tones. 'I have a little bit of news for you, Detective.'

'Uh-huh?' Laurence was distracted and watching Wadesky's expression, which was even more hangdog than it had been fifteen seconds ago.

'You listening there, Detective Whitefoot?'

'Sorry, yes. Carry on,' said Laurence glumly as he walked over to a spare desk and grabbed a pen.

'Well after visiting Carin Hughes' grave site I analysed two samples of an unusual mud that had obviously been dropped from a shoe tread and got some very interesting results…'

There was a pause, which Laurence picked up on. 'Yes?'

'Mmm, yes, very interesting.'

Laurence had begun to tap the pen restlessly against a jotter, wishing to God Andy would get to the point.

'Because it matched some of the mud deposited in Mr Chen's car…'

Suddenly Laurence was all ears. 'Go on.'

'Both samples contained a mixture of clay and carbonate of lime.' Andy was silent, as if this meant something to Laurence.

'Clay and carbonate of lime. What's the relevance?'

'Well in the proportions I've found it in, it indicates marl pit to me,' said Andy victoriously.

'What's a marl pit?' snapped Laurence loudly.

Suddenly Johnson was interested. He grabbed the map of the region and spread it over the desk next to Laurence.

'Well—' drawled Andy.

'Headlines only – we're on red alert here,' interrupted Laurence.

'Okay, marl pits were traditionally dug around this area, mostly the north and west side, to provide fertiliser, but nowadays they're either built on or filled in with building hardcore. This sample indicates that the marl is either still being extracted, which seems implausible, or the pit is unfilled.'

'So what am I looking for?' said Laurence testily.

'You're definitely in the right area of the city and your killer is situated in close proximity to a marl pit, judging by the percentage of minerals in the sample.'

Johnson was scanning the map and tentatively pencilling in likely spots.

'Thank you, Andy. You are a goddamn star! I owe you one.' Laurence disconnected before Andy could cash in the favour.

'Shit. If Bateman's right we've narrowed Hughes down to two possible areas, each one within the boundary of the targeted area.'

Johnson pointed out two substantial undeveloped sites approximately two miles from each other. Both sites were surrounded by empty warehouses waiting for refurbishment or levelling, both within spitting distance of Chen's parking lot.

'If it was the woman you saw, then she/he left about twenty-five minutes ago on foot. Timms is covering the area now but—' Wadesky started but Laurence butted in.

'We need to get these two areas searched now! I'm going to take this site.' He pointed to the map. 'And you get Timms to cover this one, over by the old paper works.'

Laurence grabbed one of the maps left in a pile on Wadesky's desk, a radio and checked that his Glock held a full magazine.

'This might be our last chance to get her alive,' he said to Mo and Wadesky.

Wadesky nodded, holding a phone next to her ear and a radio in the other hand.

'Make her safe,' pleaded Mo as Laurence, accompanied by Monster, raced for the door.

*

Eleanor didn't know how much time she'd have before Lee either came back, knowing the exhumation was a set-up, or she succumbed to shock and blood loss. Trying to keep her hands steady, she assessed her situation. Her head was free from restraint, but both of her hands and feet were secured by thick leather straps to the edges of what appeared to be an ancient hospital gurney. By twisting the fingers of her right hand and using a see-sawing action, she'd managed to extract her hand several inches. The last few twists had drawn blood, which was acting as a lubricant.

As she worked her hand, she peered into the darkness. Wherever she was being held, it was unpowered and damp. She couldn't estimate how large the room was, but there were no windows and no discernible wind direction.

She let out a yelp as her hand jammed tightly in the cuff, noting that there was a limited echo, which implied an unfurnished room with a high ceiling, maybe a storeroom. She thought bitterly of how many times she'd wanted a stranger to tie her up and abuse her, and how much the fantasies and controlled encounters differed from the reality of now.

She strained her neck as hard as she could and stared at her body. Her thigh was horrendous. The skin had been flayed from the muscle and was held like a tea towel by a small ribbon of skin. She took comfort in the knowledge that there was enough tissue left on her thigh to enable surgeons to reattach the skin. But what good was that if she couldn't get off the gurney? The only medical assistance she'd get was going to be from the ME's office.

Angry and frightened, Eleanor twisted her wrist violently. She felt it give and cautiously pulled it free of the strap. Enervated by the sudden hope generated by this, she leaned over and began to untie her left hand.

She had no idea how long it had taken her to free herself and climb down from the gurney – it could have been hours.

Before she could make an escape, she had to bind her leg. She had been naked since being kidnapped in the morning and there was no sign of any of her clothing, which would have enabled her to wrap it. Scanning her surroundings, she saw the bench with Lee's tools arranged on it, shuddering as she took in the knives, needles and electrodes neatly arranged. The ones that had already been used were sticky with her blood.

There was a roll of gaffer tape next to the butcher's knife. Quickly, she grabbed both and tore a long piece from the roll. Gingerly lifting the skin, she placed it back in approximate position and wrapped the gaffer tape around her leg. The pain was excruciating, and she had to bite her lip to prevent herself from screaming.

With her leg securely bound, she made a quick inventory of potential weapons. She had the long butcher's knife in her right hand and held the hurricane lamp in her left. There was a hypodermic needle next to a small ampoule of adrenaline. She filled it, emptying the trapped air and secured it to her arm with a length of gaffer tape.

It was time to leave.

*

Lee took in a deep breath and tried to calm his thoughts and refocus on his plan. His initial thoughts had been to run down to the basement storeroom and make Eleanor Raven pay for being part of this obscene desecration. But Carin's voice soothed him, echoing round his mind and soul, assuring him that her body was immaterial to her status now and that once she was exposed to the light of day, she would inspire wonder in those that looked on her. She was right; he had to rise above these emotions and focus on the task in hand.

He felt his breathing and heart rate slow.

*

Eleanor moved as quickly as she could, but she was intensely cold, and the pain from her leg and chest were slowing her down. There had to be a door in one of the walls; Lee hadn't just dematerialised.

In front of her was a small flight of steps leading up to a metal door about six feet above her head. Keeping her back to the wall and the knife outstretched, she cautiously ascended. After a couple of yanks, she opened the door fractionally and listened; hearing nothing, she stepped through it into what appeared to be a wide, rubbish-strewn corridor of some description. It was hard to get the measure of how long it was, as the only lighting was provided by a couple of grimy skylights, and the hurricane lamp was of limited use. There were lines of boot prints in the dust that appeared to be heaviest on her right, so keeping her back to the wall, she began to limp in that direction.

After about thirty paces, the corridor ended in a pair of double fire doors, the left jammed open with a brick. Cautiously she squeezed through the doorway and took stock of the space in front of her. It was a substantial disused warehouse, cluttered with rusted machinery.

Peering into the darkness, she could just about make out on the far wall a row of head-height windows approximately fifty feet away. After a quick visual sweep she made her way over, aware that her injured leg was becoming wetter and less responsive.

The glass in the windows was almost universally smashed and the latches looked like the old-fashioned casement types, but there didn't seem to be any external bars that would prevent her escape. She hesitated for a moment as she contemplated walking further and looking for a doorway, but instinct told her that this was a real opportunity and should be snatched.

An ancient filing cabinet was shy of one of the windows by just a few feet. If she could drag it closer, Eleanor would stand a good chance of reaching one and pulling herself up onto the ledge.

She hurriedly placed the knife on the floor next to the lamp and began to walk the cabinet closer to the window. Then, her hands shaking from the effort, she turned round to pick up the knife.

It took her only a fraction of a second to realise the knife was no longer where she'd placed it and that the only explanation for this was that Lee had picked it up.

Decisively, she hauled herself up onto the cabinet using her arms to compensate for the lack of strength in her leg. Both of her knees were on top of the cabinet when she felt herself grabbed and yanked backwards.

In an attempt to turn the assault to her advantage, she kicked back against the cabinet, using her weight to topple Lee and landing heavily on top of him.

Before she could respond further, she was flung back towards the wall.

Clambering to her feet, she saw Lee lunge towards the knife, which had skittered away from him as he fell. Should she run or try to disarm him? Both options saw the odds heavily stacked against her.

As he closed the gap, Eleanor knew that she wouldn't run. That Lee was going to kill her was no longer a question; her only concern now was the terms of that death. She wouldn't take a knife to the back, even though it would be quick and relatively painless, because her pride dictated that she'd go down fighting.

Neither would she give him the satisfaction of presenting her as a piece of modern art. She would fight to the end.

Lee lifted his arm and slashed wildly at Eleanor. She had been trained to cover the distance quickly in a knife attack, reducing the attacker's range; getting into his space. Spreading her weight and balance carefully, she stepped forward into his path, dodging his now ill-aimed blow by twisting to the right.

Before he had time to readjust his position and take aim again, she used her right hand to punch his temporal lobe with as much strength and speed as possible.

For a moment, Lee seemed to falter and lurch to the left.

Knowing her left leg was incapable of bearing her weight as she kicked with the right, she grabbed the edge of the cabinet to stabilise herself and kicked upwards, striking Lee squarely in the face with the bridge of her foot. His nose was still tender from the kick he'd received from Eleanor earlier that morning and the impact dropped him to the ground.

She had to act quickly before he had an opportunity to get back on his feet again.

Still holding on to the cabinet for support and balance, she lifted her foot and kicked downwards with her heel onto the back of his head. She managed to get three kicks in and hoped that he'd lose consciousness with the next, but as she raised her leg, Lee's hand grabbed her left ankle and pulled hard. Her balance askew, she fell backwards, catching the side of her head on a drawer edge as she dropped to the ground.

He lunged forward, hefting his body onto hers and grabbing her face with his hands. He held her nose and clamped her jaw shut, his eyes level with hers as he watched her die.

Digging what little nails she had into his palm, she scratched and tugged for all she was worth.

It took less than sixty seconds for the hissing in her ears to drown out Lee's screamed obscenities and the darkness of the space begin to envelop her. It wasn't as violent a death as she'd feared. The pain was draining from her body, and a calmness flooded her brain as her hypothalamus rewarded her fight with a flood of endorphins.

*

Laurence wasn't exactly sure how Monster had inveigled his way into the car and was now standing stock-still next to him and sniffing the air next to the marl pit. It was, he thought, possibly his own need not to be entirely alone when he found Eleanor's body.

The sun had set and he didn't need to look at his watch to know that 6 p.m. had long since passed.

When he stepped out of the car and attached Monster to the lead, there had been an element, however small, of hope. He'd made his way along the narrow lane next to the dismantled print works and climbed down an embankment that, according to his map, led to a couple of acres of ground where the marl pit had been left exposed and unused. But there was nothing here: no lights, no car, nothing.

He could see officers moving around the periphery of the pit and caught glimpses of patrol cars blocking the streets. A helicopter overhead filled the air with a heavy whoop and then passed on. He looked at the buildings, hoping that one of them would give some sort of indication that she was there, but despite Eleanor's assurances that he just had to provide his brain with enough information and it would compute an answer, nothing was forthcoming.

Monster was growing restless so Laurence unfastened him and let him wander.

His radio buzzed. 'Detective Whitefoot?' came a voice he didn't recognise.

'Yes.'

'Patrol Officer Banks here. Just spoken to a guy in a shop a block away from you and he's identified Hughes as having been in there earlier buying a paper. Said he was shouting at something he'd read.'

Laurence felt a small surge of hope that they were close. 'Okay, keep going. Good work.'

Laurence looked at the buildings, 'Select one,' he mumbled to himself.

He whistled for Monster, who was sniffing intently at an old oil barrel balanced on a couple of bricks. Monster looked at him momentarily and then resumed his sniffing. Laurence jogged over to the dog and looped the leash onto his collar.

For a second Laurence couldn't believe what he was looking at. Cautiously, he lifted several of the charred pieces of paper from the pile of ashes. It was hard to make out exactly what the sketches depicted. What could have been a stylised horse and a child's depiction of a white-sheeted ghost with a gaping maw were barely visible, but its meaning was clear.

'Timms?' he said as calmly as he could into the radio. 'He's here. I've found a pile of burned sketches.'

'Okay, buddy, cavalry's on its way. Back up with you in five. Location?'

'Marl pit behind the print works,' he replied quickly as he walked quickly towards the warehouse.

*

'You idiot!' Carin screamed into his ear. Lee was staring, mesmerised, at the dead face of his muse. 'You've destroyed any hopes you had of creating a masterpiece! She wasn't ready. Look at her!'

Carin was right. Her face was twisted and ugly in death. He put out a hand and tried to reposition her mouth, but the muscles were flaccid and uncooperative.

'Bring her back!' she screamed again.

'How?' Lee said despairingly.

It was as if, he thought, Eleanor had known what was about to happen. Perhaps she had been working closely with Carin and had prepared for this eventuality.

Carin's tinkling laugh broke through his grunts as he pounded on Eleanor's chest. He hadn't been entirely sure how much adrenaline had been in the hypodermic, but obviously it was enough, because within a minute of injecting it directly into her heart and commencing CPR, he felt the flutterings of a pulse.

He checked again, breathing into her lungs to help her journey back. Her pulse was settling and growing stronger, and now she was breathing on her own. Although she was still unconscious, he'd brought her back from the dead. There was still time to resurrect his plans, and her moment of liberation would be exactly when and how Carin had dictated it should be.

He sat back, exhausted and watched the change in her cheeks. From the grey pallor of death, a pink flush was spreading.

'Thank you,' he whispered to Carin. 'I should not have lost faith in you two women.'

He gently stroked Eleanor's face as he watched her eyelashes flicker.

'Eleanor?'

She let out a low groan.

'We have to go now. It's time.'

Lee knew that he had to work quickly and efficiently if he was to succeed.

Eleanor was too weak and confused to put up any form of protest as he lifted her into the back of her car, which had been parked close by in a loading area east of the entrance, and covered her with a blanket. It would only take a few minutes to drive across the wasteland and access the fairground from the south. His original plan was to keep to the roads, but he suspected from the increased helicopter activity that the police were closer to him than he'd expected.

He switched off the car's head and tail lights, knowing that Carin and Eleanor were now working together and would guide him to their destiny.

He listened to Eleanor's irregular breathing in the back. She had put herself through a great deal to get to this point and he had nothing but respect for her. He hoped he was strong enough to fulfil his small role in this unfolding drama.

*

Laurence entered the old print works through a broken window next to the west-side entrance. He shone his torch around and waited as Monster jumped through and began to move uncertainly through the darkness. He laid his hand on his neck and was surprised to feel the dog's hackles standing upright. Positioning the Glock in his right, his left hand supporting the gun and his torch, he made his way slowly through the room towards a door.

Corridors led to more rooms and more corridors. Laurence doubted he'd ever find Eleanor or Lee in such a huge and chaotic building.

Suddenly he was in a huge warehouse. It smelled of cold and damp, but there was another heavier more familiar smell – diesel fumes. A vehicle had been started in here recently.

'Timms?' he whispered into the radio.

'We're in. Where are you?' Timms responded breathlessly.

'Came in through a window on the west side and I'm in a warehouse. There's been car activity here recently.'

'Whoa. Shit…' Timms began to talk to someone else.

'What? What have you found?' asked Laurence.

'He's been here. They've found some clothes and empty food cartons… art books.'

'Eleanor?'

'No, no signs of her.'

The conversation was stopped by Monster's barking. He was running in small, agitated circles. Laurence headed over and stared at the blood drops and tyre prints. He pressed the radio. 'Timms, I've got blood and tyre prints.'

He heard Timms sigh.

Laurence was following the blood trail backwards when Timms caught up with him. 'What have you got?'

Laurence shook his head. 'If this was Raven, she was bleeding heavily, but whoever it was walked from this direction.' Monster was several feet ahead and had stopped at a metal door, sniffing intently.

'I've got you covered,' said Timms, nodding to him to open the door. Laurence felt sick as he put his hand on the cold metal and pushed it open. It was dark and bitterly cold down there. His torch illuminated a workbench and the gurney.

'No!' he gasped as he saw the bloody leather straps and the workbench covered in hammers, knives and a large commercial car battery. 'She's gone. He's killed her!' he yelled.

Timms grabbed his arm and shook him. 'Whether she was carried or made her own way out, she was bleeding. Understand?'

Laurence nodded. 'She was alive then.'

'He's got somewhere special lined up. Where?' Timms asked.

Laurence was just about to let rip with a torrent of frustrated comments when the charred images came into his mind. Something made sense. The drawings of the horse and the ghost had meaning and he knew what it was. He'd been sitting in the car with Eleanor and she'd said that he should look around and take everything in because it would make sense later on. What had he seen? He wanted to scream his frustration. What had he seen?

And then he knew.

'He's taken her to an old fairground. He's going to kill and display her there.'

*

Lee was nervous. He knew that Carin had been delighted with his efforts, but it was important that Eleanor herself approved. He'd carried her gently from the car and had propped her up in the trolley car, which he'd positioned at the beginning of the ride, next to the ticket office. He was becoming increasingly irritated by her inability to stay conscious for more than a few seconds but had decided against slapping her. That would have been rude and inappropriate now that matters had run their course and there was only the moment of display and passing left to play out.

He cleared his throat. She groaned and one eye flickered open for a second or two before she slid down further in the seat. Remembering that he didn't have too long before his public arrived, he moved things on a little.

'Eleanor?' he said loudly.

Again she shuddered and tried to come to, but her breathing levelled out again.

He reached forward and pinched her hard. She opened her eyes and looked at him with an expression of disbelief.

'Eleanor, it's time,' he said meaningfully, hoping this would energise her sufficiently.

He reached out and touched her cheek. Her eyes were wide open now and something like recognition passed across her features. This was good.

'Look,' he said, sweeping his arm in a wide arc to draw her attention to the surroundings. He felt his cheeks burn slightly as he pointed out the recently redecorated ghost train. He'd applied new brushwork to the battered images and placed the candles in clean jam jars, protecting them from the draft. The ticket office had been cleaned and a shop mannequin, outfitted in some of Cindy's old clothes, was staring blankly from the window. He'd rigged up an old CD player to a car battery, and traditional discordant piped fairground music was playing quietly on a loop.

*

Eleanor was confused but aware that she was in terrible danger. It was difficult to understand why the man was smiling and gesturing at the walls and images surrounding her. She moved cautiously, feeling a stab of pain from what she assumed were broken ribs. Her left leg felt wet and numb and her jaw and ear throbbed.

A light was slowly rising on the scene. She was Eleanor Raven and this man was Lee Hughes, and he was here to murder her.

She tried to stand up, but her feet and hands were cuffed and chained together. She tried to speak but could only form a sort of grunting sound.

At this Lee smiled indulgently at her and nodded.

Where the hell was she? She scanned the room, but the only thing she could think of was that she had found herself in some sort of cartoon ghost-train ride from her childhood.

As she tried to work out what was happening, Lee stepped behind her and began to push the trolley towards an arch, which was obscured by skeins of cotton-like gossamer.

'Don't be frightened,' he said. 'It's safe. I tried it myself last night.' He giggled coquettishly and gave the trolley one final violent thrust along the warped tracks and through the arch.

What she saw made Eleanor begin to shake uncontrollably. Her teeth chattered and her body kept shuddering. A large metal hook had been attached to the central wooden beam, and from that a length of industrial chain had been threaded through the hook and attached to a metal pulley on one end, and two meat hooks at the other. The hooks were exactly the same as those used to display Lydia Greystein and Cassandra Willis. A small table illuminated by several tea lights held a lipstick and a neatly folded transparent plastic bag.

Eleanor began to yank at the cuffs, her grunting sound developing into a monotonous scream.

*

Laurence sat in the front of the car, yelling instructions at Timms as he flung the vehicle round the tight street corners. 'Take a left there!'

Timms cursed as the car skidded and clipped the kerb. The wet streets were a reflective kaleidoscope of red and blue flashing lights as numerous cars followed in their wake.

'There,' he screamed. Monster began to bark steadily in the rear seat.

'Where's the entrance?' yelled Timms as he peered at the hedging and intermittent broken fencing that divided the roadway from the fairground.

'Stop! Let me out!'

Timms braked and let Laurence jump out and race towards the hedge. Before he could stop him, Monster had followed and they had both pushed their way through the hedge.

Timms grabbed the radio. 'Units three and four, follow Whitefoot. Find a way in!'

*

Laurence ran through the wet and overgrown grass, falling once as he slipped on an old metal frame. Barking manically, Monster raced ahead instinctively, heading for what looked like an old ghost train.

As he staggered to his feet, Laurence saw what looked like a candle flickering inside the entrance and the silhouette of a figure sitting behind the counter. Already twenty feet ahead of him, he saw Monster bound up the steps of the ride and race around looking for a way in.

*

Eleanor fought Lee with every last ounce of strength she possessed, but her body was too broken to beat him off. After lifting her from the trolley, he had pulled the plastic bag over her legs and arms, and it was now folded over just beneath her throat. His knee placed on her chest and his left hand on her forehead, he began to paint her lips with a dark red gloss.

Eleanor had pinched in her lips, but Lee had merely laughed at her, increasing the pressure on her broken rib until she succumbed and allowed him to do it.

He let go of her head and sat back, still straddling her waist, and admired her. 'You will change the face of art in this country forever.'

He sighed, and then gently pulled the plastic over her face and sealed the bag closed with transparent tape. Eleanor screamed, but the sound seemed to be trapped inside the bag with her.

She watched in horror as Lee manipulated the hook and secured it at the wall. He gave it an experimental tug to make sure that it would take her weight. Satisfied, he turned to Eleanor and smiled.

'It's time,' he said calmly.

But before he could lift her, he stopped. The sound of barking accompanied a desperate scratching sound. Lee set his jaw. This wasn't right; he needed to position her before his audience arrived.

The barking was intensifying and now human yells were accompanying the dog. Decisively, he grabbed Eleanor and lifted her to her feet. She struggled and pulled her feet up in an attempt to overbalance her killer and topple them to the ground, but Lee held her tighter, his frenzied determination giving him strength.

A battering sound could be heard from outside. Lee had placed two wooden planks across the entrance, preventing the door from being broken down before he was ready.

As suddenly as it had started, the battering and barking stopped. Lee nodded at Eleanor and reached for the hooks. He backed her towards them and then, finding an appropriate spot with his fingers, plunged one into her left shoulder then one into her right.

*

Eleanor stared into his cold, dead eyes. She'd considered pleading for her life, but there was no point. She saw that hers and those of Lydia, Cassandra and all of his other victims meant absolutely nothing to him, so she said nothing.

*

Lee grunted loudly as he twisted the hook into Eleanor's back. He looked at her shocked expression and hoped she would find some inner strength to soften her features into one more indicative of a muse.

Letting go of her, he was surprised when she didn't fall forward. The others had. None had made any more attempts to remain alive after the hook had been inserted. He shrugged and turned to the chain, which needed to be hoisted. He gave an experimental pull, noting with satisfaction that the ratchet action locked the chain off cleanly and without dipping.

Lee had just repositioned his hands and tensed his muscles as he prepared to lift the canvas higher when Monster's weight hit him. As he fought off the dog, he managed to catch sight of a man lifting his beautiful muse in his left arm and pointed a gun at him. This couldn't be happening.

Aiming a vicious kick at the dog's head, he lunged towards the man. The first bullet made little impression on him, and although he felt his right arm drop, he still kept up a forward momentum.

The next bullet turned off sight, sound and meaning for the artist.

*

Dropping his weapon, Laurence wrapped both arms tightly round Eleanor and held her rigidly in position.

'Help me! Now! In here!' Laurence screamed, his voice choking with emotion as he stared into Eleanor's dulling eyes. He couldn't let her go, couldn't try to tear the plastic, couldn't give her words of comfort; he could only hold her and pray that help would hear him.

He felt Monster barge past him, barking wildly and jumping through the hole he'd made in the tarpaulin that Lee had used to create the back wall of the ghost ride.

Suddenly there were hands and lights all around them. Exclamations of horror all interspersed with the cacophony of barking dog. Not daring to shift his eyes from hers, Laurence screamed his orders.

'Release the chain from the wall. Don't touch her!'

With one officer holding the hook carefully in position between her shoulder blades, Laurence lay Eleanor gently on the ground and tore open the plastic bag.

'Air ambulance thirty seconds to landing!' bellowed Timms from the newly opened entrance.

Eleanor opened her mouth slightly and spoke. At first it was incomprehensible to Laurence, who moved closer to her lips to catch the two syllables.

'I can't hear what you're saying, Eleanor,' he said, trying to keep the anxiety out of his voice. He placed his ear virtually on her lips, holding his breath in an effort to hear her.

She tried again. 'Ca-*leb*.'

Laurence cradled her tightly, feeling his throat tighten as he recognised the word and its meaning.

'You're safe now,' he whispered back into her ear. 'You are safe.'

CHAPTER TWENTY-SEVEN

Mo snored steadily and deeply, his feet propped up on a stool. Thoughtfully, a member of the medical team had wrapped a blanket round him and provided him with tea and biscuits.

'Don't wake him,' Eleanor whispered from the bed. 'He won't go home until I do, and I believe he's getting more visitors than me.'

Laurence smiled and pulled a chair over from the corner of the room so he could sit close to Eleanor. 'How are you doing?' he asked, picking up the clipboard from the base of the bed and skimming though her notes. He was pleased to see that the graft on her left thigh was healing well and that her fractured ribs, scapula and punctured lung were stabilised and on the mend.

'Which hat are you wearing, Whitefoot?'

Laurence smiled and replaced her notes. 'I'm here as your partner… and friend.'

She nodded and closed her eyes. 'Because I've got all the doctors I need here.'

'I need to discuss something with you,' he said quietly.

She opened her eyes and turned her head slightly to one side, meeting his gaze with something like her old strength. 'I had hoped you didn't,' she said coldly.

'You were… selected by someone for Hughes. It wasn't random.' He moved towards her, reaching for her hand with his. 'Do you understand what I'm saying?'

For a second, Laurence thought she looked afraid and he held her hand more tightly. 'But you're safe now. Mo, Timms and myself are the only ones who know, and the only ones who ever will. I give you my word.'

Eleanor stared at him. 'What are you confessing to?'

'I…' Laurence was confused. 'I had to tell Mo, who made me tell Timms. It was the only way we could get to you… if they knew.'

Eleanor snatched her hand back. 'Hughes told me that someone contacted him and arranged for him to get me. They gave him my address.'

'Yes. You didn't cover your tracks, and it made it easy for him to—'

'Him? What are you saying?' she hissed. 'He told me it was a colleague or a friend… was it you?'

Eleanor kept her eyes fixed on his.

Laurence was silent for a moment and then reached inside his jacket pocket. He handed her a folded piece of paper. Slowly, she reached for it and held it up to read. Her lips twitched as the implications became clear. 'The safe word,' she whispered.

Laurence nodded. 'He arranged it as a… I don't know why. To broaden your horizons I guess.' He turned away from her. 'His name's—'

'I don't want to know his name!' she interrupted, loudly. Mo snorted and there was a tense few moments before Eleanor and Laurence resumed their conversation.

'How did he find me?'

Laurence shook his head. 'How the hell should I know? You must have allowed him access to your purse or something when you met him at the motel.' He shifted uncomfortably in his seat, embarrassed and hurt.

Eleanor remained silent.

'You thought it was me?' he said, disbelieving. 'You meet strangers in motel rooms, allowing them to tie you up and abuse you, and you thought I had arranged to have you murdered?' He stood up, shaking his head.

'I'm sorry… I was frightened and needed to blame someone. It was stupid of me,' she said quietly. 'You saved my life, Laurence. I couldn't fight any more. I'm alive because you worked out where I was. Forgive me,' she said quietly.

Laurence stared at her for a moment and then opened the door, walking quickly out of the room. The door swung closed behind him.

*

Eleanor stared at the door and strained to hear his footsteps disappearing.

The silence was overwhelming.

'It'll be okay,' said Mo quietly. 'You'll see.'

A LETTER FROM KAREN

Dear reader,

I want to say a huge thank you for choosing to read *Cry for Mercy*. If you did enjoy it, and want to keep up to date with all my latest releases, just sign up at the following link. Your email address will never be shared and you can unsubscribe at any time.

www.bookouture.com/karen-long

I hope you loved *Cry for Mercy* and if you did I would be very grateful if you could write a review. I'd love to hear what you think, and it makes such a difference helping new readers to discover one of my books for the first time. Creating a character like Eleanor Raven makes writing extremely challenging. I need to throw situations at her, myself and the readers that force us to use our intellect and imaginations to solve. I hope you find her journeys as exciting as I found them to travel.

I love hearing from my readers – you can get in touch on Twitter or Facebook.

Thanks,
Karen Long

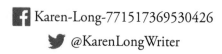

Karen-Long-771517369530426
@KarenLongWriter

ACKNOWLEDGEMENTS

I would like to thank Araminta Whitley, Peta Nightingale, Emily Gowers and Marina de Pass for their constant faith and hard work on my behalf. Likewise all of the staff at The Soho Agency and Bookouture, for their support.

I would further like to praise the extraordinary efforts made by bloggers, readers and reviewers, who make writing novels a joy. They promote, encourage and evangelise, without which few copies would be sold.

A special thanks to my family and Lou Hunter, who have never failed to read, reread and nag me when required (and sometimes when it wasn't).

Printed in Great Britain
by Amazon